WITH EACH PASSING SECOND, PETER PARKER'S SPIDER-SENSE BUZZ INCREASED IN INTENSITY.

avier was wobbly on his feet, but he didn't move or speak.

Just as Peter was about to find a place to change into his other outfit, Nariz lightly tapped Javier on the shoulder with the back of his hand. "'Sup, yo, you dissin' me now? What up with *that*?"

"Get *offa* me!"

Even as Javier said the words, he backhanded Nariz in the face. In and of itself, that would have been unremarkable, except that the blow sent Nariz twenty feet down the sidewalk, knocking over a group of seniors who were congregating.

Fourteen-year-old kids don't usually have that kind of strength, Peter thought as he realized that he wasn't going to have *time* to change clothes.

Especially when he saw that Javier's complexion had changed from its usual dark skintone to an emerald green.

There is absolutely no way this can be good.

SPIDER-MAN®

DOWN THESE MEAN STREETS

a novel by
Keith R.A. DeCandido

based on the
Marvel Comic Book

POCKET
BOOKS

LONDON • SYDNEY • NEW YORK • TORONTO

An *Original* Publication of POCKET BOOKS

 POCKET BOOKS, a division of Simon & Schuster, Ltd
Africa House, 64–78 Kingsway, London WC2B 6AH

ISBN: 1-4165-1128-8

This Pocket Books paperback edition September 2005

10 9 8 7 6 5 4 3 2 1

Cover art by Joe Jusko

Printed and bound in Great Britain by
Cox & Wyman Ltd, Reading, Berks

A CIP catalogue number for this book is available from the British Library

To Kyoshi *Paul,*
for everything he's taught me
and will continue to teach me

Historian's Note

Down These Mean Streets is consistent with the recent continuity of the Spider-Man comics published by Marvel, though one does not need to be intimately familiar with those comics in order to follow the action. However, for those who are concerned with such matters, this story takes place sometime after Mary Jane Watson decided to take up theatre work in *Amazing Spider-Man* #509 (published in August 2004).

"Down these mean streets a man must go who is not himself mean, who is neither tarnished nor afraid. . . . He is the hero, he is everything. He must be a complete man and a common man and yet an unusual man. He must be, to use a rather weathered phrase, a man of honor, by instinct, by inevitability, without thought of it, and certainly without saying it. He must be the best man in his world and a good enough man for any world."

—RAYMOND CHANDLER

SPIDER-MAN®

DOWN
THESE
MEAN
STREETS

1

Peter Parker looked at the clock on the wall, smiled, and said, "We've got a few minutes, so let's go to the next chapter: 'The Periodic Table of Elements.'"

A roomful of teenagers moaned and whined.

Peter smiled, remembering hearing similar moans in science class when he was a student here at Midtown High School and the teacher jumped ahead. Of course, Peter never indulged in those complaints himself—he was always three steps ahead of the rest of his classmates, especially in the science classes, whether it was in physics, chemistry, biology, or the general sciences that he now, years later, was himself teaching.

"Now, now," he said chidingly, "the periodic table was part of the reading you were supposed to have done by *yesterday's* class. So you all *should* have it down pat by now." He walked over to the side of the classroom, to the bulletin board situated between the room's two doors on the right-hand side from where the kids sat. "Besides, it's been up on the board all year."

"Dude, I thought it was a movie poster," Tommy Ciolfi muttered. Several of the kids around him tried, and mostly failed, to swallow a laugh.

"Well, it has been coming soon to a *classroom* near you." Peter winced even as he made the bad joke. *Why is it I'm hilarious when I'm beating up bad guys, but all the jokes I make as a teacher are lame?* "All right, who can tell me why the isotopes are in the order they're in?"

He looked around the room; only two hands, those of Marissa Blaustein and Suzyn Baptiste, went up. *Hardly surprising,* Peter thought. *They're two of the brightest kids in the class.* Marissa was pretty, popular, had perfect diction, and was on the junior-varsity cheerleading squad; Suzyn was overweight, unpopular, spoke with a Haitian accent, and was in the chess club. Both were brilliant, and they seemed to be in competition with each other academically. Marissa couldn't stand the idea of the social misfit being better than her, and Suzyn despised Marissa and everything she stood for. Peter had to admit, it made for good theatre.

However, this was a ridiculously easy question, and one that anyone who had actually *done* the homework would know. So he looked out over the class to see who besides these two really did the work.

Actually, only a few were looking at him. Most of the thirty kids were studying either their notebooks, or the window, or the floor, or the clock in the hopes that it would move faster. Peter's freshman general sciences class was scheduled for last period, and it was always difficult to hold kids' attention during the final class of the day, particularly in a required class that most of them didn't give a damn about.

Still, he was there to teach, and they were there to learn. He fixed his gaze on Javier Velasquez, the class's biggest troublemaker. Javier wasn't the only kid in the class with a rap sheet, but he was the one who took the most pride in it. "Javier?"

"What?"

Peter exhaled. "Answer the question, please." Knowing full well the kid hadn't heard it—since he hadn't paid attention to anything Peter had said all year—he threw Javier a bone and re-asked it: "What order are the isotopes on the Periodic Table in?"

He shrugged. "Alphabetical?"

One kid almost laughed, but stopped at a glare from Javier.

"L doesn't usually come before B," Peter said. "At least not in any language I'm familiar with."

"You 'familiar' with the language of kiss my ass?"

Peter grinned. "Yup. It's the language you'll be talking if you don't do your homework—or if I decide to tell the principal about the switchblade you've got stashed in your locker."

The look on Javier's face was priceless. Normally, a kid talking to a teacher like that—or, for that matter, carrying a weapon into the school—would get detention or a suspension, but Peter didn't much see the point in punishing Javier. He knew that Javier lived with the threat of getting shot or stabbed every day. Detention was going to neither scare him nor dissuade him from future infractions; suspension would just put him back on the streets for a few days, and he might decide to make it permanent, in which case, nobody won.

Peter looked around the room. "Anyone else?"

Slowly, Gregory Horowitz raised a meek hand. Gregory had the highest grades of anyone in the class, but he rarely raised his hand, despite Peter's encouragement. Seeing this as a good sign, Peter called on him.

"A—atomic mass?"

"That's right."

Indignantly, Marissa said, "No it's *not*! The book says it's atomic *weight*."

In a barely audible voice, Gregory said, "Sci—scientists prefer the term atomic mass now."

In a stage whisper, Tommy said, "Oooooh, Geekory's hangin' out with *scientists* now."

"Actually, you're both right," Peter said, overlaying Tommy. "Unfortunately, the textbook we're using is about five years old—or, to put it in simple terms, the same age that Tommy's acting—" That got a quick laugh from several kids, with the notable exceptions of Tommy and Javier. "—and since then, as Gregory said, scientists have come to prefer the more precise term 'atomic mass' to 'atomic weight.'" *Let's hear it for budget cuts,* Peter thought with a sigh. The text they were using wasn't much farther along than the one *he* had used as a fourteen-year-old.

He pointed at the upper-left-hand portion of the chart. "H is for hydrogen, which has an atomic mass of 1.00797—or just 1, for our purposes. How do you figure out the atomic mass, Marissa?"

Since Marissa had obviously done the reading, Peter figured she'd give the right answer. Without hesitating, she confidently said, "By adding the number of neutrons and electrons."

"Close. Suzyn?"

With a triumphant look at her classmate, Suzyn said, "The number of neutrons and *protons*." Marissa stared daggers at Suzyn.

"Right. It's the particles in the nucleus that make up the atomic mass. The electrons orbit the nucleus and don't figure into it."

Tommy rolled his eyes.

"Something bothering you, Tommy?"

Shifting uncomfortably in his seat at the sudden attention, Tommy said, "Uh, no, Mr. Parker, it's just—well. I mean, c'mon, who gives a damn about this crap? Atomic weight, atomic mass—it don't mean nothin'!"

Peter sighed. When he took this job, he knew it was going to be an uphill struggle. Most of these kids would rather be playing with their Xboxes or chatting with their friends online or text-messaging each other from across the room, or whatever it was that kids did these days. Peter didn't even know what kids did when *he* was that age. He had been as much an outcast as Gregory and Suzyn were: the geek, the dexter, the nerd, the one who went to a science exhibit instead of the football game or the homecoming dance.

And imagine what life would've been like if I hadn't gone to that science exhibit . . .

Looking out over the mostly apathetic faces of kids desperate to get out of school as fast as possible, he let out a long breath and walked back to the front of the class, away from the chart, and sat on the edge of his desk. "Look, I know this all seems meaningless—but look at what we're talking about here." He pointed at the chart. "This is *what everything's made of.* You, me, the desks, your books, the pavement outside, the lockers, the trees, the SUVs, the buildings, your clothes, your cell phones, your video games—this is what it's all made out of. These are the building blocks of the world. How can you not be excited by that?" Quickly holding up a hand, he said, "Don't answer that." Several chuckles followed. "I know, you don't think this is a big deal, but it really is."

He glanced at the clock. The bell would be ringing momentarily. "Any other questions?"

Ronnie Hammond raised his hand.

"Yes, Ronnie?"

"Kr stands for Krypton, right?"

Peter nodded.

"I thought that was a planet."

Before Peter could give that the answer it deserved, the bell rang. "We'll pick this up tomorrow." His words could barely be heard over the din of books and notebooks closing, desks sliding on the linoleum floor, and classmates talking to each other. Peter noted that Suzyn and Gregory weren't talking to anyone. *There but for the grace of a radioactive spider go I,* he thought wistfully. "And don't forget," he said louder, "there's a test on chapters four, five, and six on Friday!"

That was met with predictable moans and whines.

Javier was one of the last to get up. He stared at Peter the whole time, then got up and walked out, never taking his eyes off Peter.

For his part, Peter met the stare. By the time he reached the door, Javier looked royally pissed off that Peter didn't blink.

Poor kid. If only he knew . . . Peter looked like a wussy white guy from Queens, and Javier usually ate teachers like that for breakfast. But Peter had spent all of his life since he was only a little older than Javier dealing with people who would eat Javier for breakfast.

Gregory made his way out of the class slowly, not wanting to get in anyone's way for fear that someone might notice him. Peter recognized that walk oh so well. That was how he had walked all over Midtown High. It was also how he had walked into that science exhibit on that fateful day, sponsored by a company in the Pacific Northwest that was doing demonstrations at high schools across the country. He had entered slowly, shuffling his feet, not wanting to bother anybody, and therefore had been stuck at the back of the room, barely able to see the demo. When a spider had gotten into the workings and became irradiated, Peter had been the one it bit in its death throes, the radiation changing the spider bite from something potentially fatal to something won-drous. Standing at the back as he was, nobody had no-ticed Peter stumbling out of the exhibit hall, wandering aimlessly down the streets of the Forest Hills section of Queens, wondering why he felt so strange.

Now, Peter walked more confidently through the school's halls, preparing himself to head home to his wife. *No, head home to an empty apartment,* he amended. Mary Jane had rehearsal tonight. His lovely wife had a supporting part and was understudy to the female lead in a way-the-heck-off-Broadway play called *The Z-Axis.*

"Hey, Mr. Parker!"

Peter turned to see Tommy standing at his locker, wearing the same smart-aleck grin that Flash Thompson used to wear when he was about to torment young Peter Parker. Some of Tommy's friends were nearby, cleaning out their lockers and grabbing their jackets and books. "Yeah, Tommy?"

To Peter's surprise, the grin fell, and Tommy sounded serious. "That speech you gave today—I gotta say it really really really sucked." By the time he reached the last two words, the grin was back.

Putting a hand on Tommy's shoulder, Peter said, "Well, Tommy, under *normal* circumstances I'd say that you just have to tough it out until June, at which point you'll never have to take general science again."

Tommy looked confused. "Whaddaya mean 'normal circumstances'?"

Peter smiled. "Well, if you keep going the way you're

going, you're gonna have to take it *all* over again in summer school after you flunk." Removing the hand, and taking pleasure in the guffaws from Tommy's friends, Peter continued walking toward the faculty lounge.

He entered the tiny room that served as the teachers' refuge from the students. The furniture was brand-new when it was purchased shortly after World War II, the refrigerator sounded like a motorcycle with a muffler problem and only intermittently kept its contents below room temperature, and the grout in the tilework around the sink could, at this point, qualify as an alien life-form.

Just remember, Parker, you chose this job. If nothing else, it provided a more steady income than freelance photography ever had.

"How do you do it?"

Peter turned to see one of the math teachers, Elizabeth Doyle, sitting on the green sofa with the red cushions, clutching a can of diet soda for dear life.

"Do what, Liz?"

"Keep that smile on your face." She shook her head. "Damn newbies, always thinking this job's a *calling* and that it's *noble*. It's a *job*. And like every job, it sucks."

Walking over to the coffeemaker on the counter, Peter said, "Oh believe me, Liz, I've been at jobs that suck." He saw that there was about one cup left in the pot, and reached for the handle with one hand while opening the cabinet to retrieve his mug with the other. "But here at least I feel like I'm accomplishing something."

Liz looked at him like he'd grown another head. "If you say so. Don't you have Velasquez in your class?"

Peter nodded as he poured the coffee into the mug, steam twirling up from it.

She shook her head. "That's an expulsion waiting to

happen. I'm telling you, the only way he's not expelled by the end of the year is if he gets himself killed."

Whatever Peter was going to say in response was lost when he made the mistake of actually drinking the coffee. Closing his eyes and trying not to think too hard about what he was doing, he swallowed it. "I see they're still using yesterday's dishwater for the coffee."

Holding up her can, Liz said, "That's why I stick with the soda machines. Safer."

"Yah." Peter poured the rest of the coffee into the sink. *I can always grab a cup at home before going on patrol.* "Anyhow, I think it's important—"

Liz held up a hand. "I swear, Pete, you tell me you took this job to give something back to the school that taught you so much, I *will* throw up right here on this sofa."

Peering at the cushions, Peter smiled and said, "Might improve the color."

Shaking her head, Liz hauled herself up from the couch and drank down the rest of her soda. "You're a crazy man, Pete."

"I think that was part of the job description when they hired me. 'Must have been crazy since the age of eighteen.'"

Liz chuckled. "Sad, but true. You need a lift home?"

"Nah, I'll walk. Thanks, though." Peter had accepted lifts home from Liz a few times, but with MJ not being home, he wasn't in any particular rush. The walk back to the apartment would help him decompress.

"Smart man, no car in this town. Wouldn't have one myself, but *you* try gettin' to Bayside by mass transit from here."

Having spent most of his youth navigating the Queens bus lines, Peter felt Liz's pain. The only subway that came close to Bayside, the 7, didn't come through Forest Hills. She was definitely better off with a car, even the '86 Chevy junker that she drove.

After saying his good-byes to Liz, Peter went by the science office to drop off his books and check his mail. Peter had spent most of his time since high school learning to travel with what he could put in his pockets. His school-related stuff remained in the science office—he didn't have anything to grade tonight, and he'd prepare for tomorrow's lessons in the morning—and everything else he needed fit in either his pants or jacket. It was a bit nippy out on this spring day, but Peter was wearing a skintight outfit underneath his button-down shirt, jacket, and slacks, so he figured he'd be warm enough.

Bidding farewell to his fellow science teachers—several of whom made their usual disparaging remarks about Peter's leaving all his work at the office—he headed toward the exit, allowing the teenagers dashing through the halls to get to their parents' cars or the bus stop or just *out* to zip past him. Among the many gifts the dying spider had conferred upon him was a sixth sense that he referred to as his "spider-sense," which allowed him to avoid danger. In practical terms it meant that, in a hallway full of high school kids desperate to be outside, not one of them crashed or bumped into Peter.

The biggest buzz from that extra sense came just as Peter was approaching the metal door at the end of the hall and was about to push the horizontal bar in to release it. Stopping his forward motion and moving to the side gracefully—and so quickly that he doubted anyone would even notice—Peter avoided being rear-ended by Javier. For his part, Javier stumbled forward unsteadily, not even acknowledging Peter's presence.

I was expecting another dirty look from him at the very least.

Resolving to live with the disappointment, Peter followed Javier to the sidewalk. During the one hour after school let out, this side street was closed to vehicular traffic except for the city buses that Midtown High commissioned to serve as shuttles to various neighborhoods. They were lined up one in front of the other on the curb, kids milling toward the front doors, faculty proctors making a valiant (and futile) attempt to keep the students in some semblance of single file. Peter shuddered, knowing that he would catch this duty in two weeks and dreading it.

Then he whirled back toward Javier—mainly because the spider-sense buzz Peter got off the kid hadn't died down.

In fact, it was intensifying.

"Yo, Javier, 'sup with you, man?" asked one of his friends. Peter didn't know the kid's given name, but had seen him before hanging out with Javier, who called him Nariz. Given the enormous schnozz on the kid, the nickname—the Spanish word for "nose"—fit.

Nariz held up his hand, expecting Javier to clasp it in return, but Javier was just standing unsteadily in the middle of the sidewalk. "You gonna leave me hangin', yo?"

With each passing second, Peter's spider-sense buzz increased in intensity. Javier was wobbly on his feet, but he didn't move or speak.

Just as Peter was about to find a place to change into his other outfit, Nariz lightly tapped Javier on the shoulder with the back of his hand. " 'Sup, yo, you dissin' me now? What up with *that?*"

"Get *offa* me!"

Even as Javier said the words, he backhanded Nariz in the face. In and of itself, that would have been unremarkable, except that the blow sent Nariz twenty feet down the sidewalk, knocking over a group of seniors who were congregating.

Fourteen-year-old kids don't usually have that kind of strength, Peter thought as he realized that he wasn't going to have *time* to change clothes.

Especially when he saw that Javier's complexion had changed from its usual dark skin tone to an emerald green.

There is absolutely no way this can be good. Super strength and green skin was a combination that generally meant enhancement by gamma radiation—the most spectacular example being the Hulk. *How does a street kid from Queens get gamma-irradiated?* Peter asked himself, but saved it for later. *Maybe he got bitten by a radioactive wombat—worry about that when he isn't about to tear up the street and the students.*

One of the security guards at this door was a retired cop named Pat "Lefty" Lefkowitz, who'd been keeping an eye on things at Midtown High since before Peter's student days. Upon seeing Javier clock someone, he waddled over toward the kid, hand on the butt of his .38 revolver. Peter, hoping to keep this civil and knowing full well he probably couldn't, also moved toward Javier. *If nothing else, maybe I can keep Lefty's gun in its holster.*

" 'Ey, Velasquez, wha'd I tell you about—"

Javier turned around and snarled. His face was getting greener by the second, and Peter noticed that he was also growing, his new physique straining against his clothes.

"Sweet Jesus!" Lefty cried, and unholstered his revolver.

Before he could fire a shot, Javier was on the retired

cop, punching him in his huge belly, sending Lefty sprawling against the metal door, wheezing. Peter swore he heard the sound of bones cracking.

Kids and faculty alike started screaming, but Peter tried not to pay attention to any of it. Grabbing Javier's arm, he whirled the kid around into one of the metal doors, hoping that his own super strength would give the push enough force to render the kid at least insensate for a few minutes until one of the other guards showed up with a pair of handcuffs.

Unfortunately, being smashed into a metal door served only to make Javier angry. "Kill you!" he cried as he jumped at Peter, who could only let Javier knock him to the ground, using his abilities to roll with the attack enough so that it only hurt a little when they collided with the pavement.

"Get offa him, Velasquez!"

Peter recognized the voice of the other security guard assigned to this door, an ex-jock with delusions of competence named Brian Klein, but Brian's words concerned Peter a lot less than Javier's face. He was as green as the Hulk now, and based on the way he'd slammed into Peter's rib cage, he was starting to get near the Hulk's strength class, too.

Before Peter could kick Javier off him—and later come up with a feeble explanation for how a skinny white science teacher could toss a superstrong kid around—Javier suddenly screamed as if he was in pain, rearing his head back and shouting at the clear sky.

Then the kid collapsed right on top of Peter.

Deciding discretion was the better part of keeping his secrets safe, Peter played the helpless teacher and whimpered, "Uh, help?"

Javier, now a dead weight on Peter's chest, started twitching. A moment later, the weight was gone, as Brian had rolled him off. Clambering to his feet, Peter looked down to see the green hue fading from Javier's epidermis, even as the kid was convulsing.

From the ground, Lefty said, "I called 911." Peter turned to see Lefty still on the ground, but holding a cell phone. He clambered to his feet, wincing in a manner Peter recognized as that of a man with cracked ribs.

"Good call, old-timer," Brian said.

Lefty snapped, "Don't call me old-timer, you little punk." Lefty, Peter knew, had never had much use for Brian. "You okay, Pete?"

Peter nodded. "Just a little winded."

Brian stared at Peter. "That was a brave thing you did, Parker—throwing him into the door like that."

"Brave, hell, that was just stupid." Lefty was now clambering slowly to his feet. "Leave the security to the guards next time, Pete."

"Yeah, like you flat on your ass?" Brian asked with a sneer.

Javier's convulsing started getting worse. Peter also noticed he was sweating.

"Ambulance should be here in a minute," Lefty said, ignoring Brian. "Figures that Velasquez is usin' as well as dealin'. We—"

"I *kick* his ass!"

Peter whirled around to see that Nariz was back on his feet.

"Where the hell is he, I gonna kick—"

Even as he spoke, Peter had moved to intercept him faster than Brian or Lefty could have. "Easy, Javier's already down."

"Get out the *way,* teacher-man, I gonna—"

Peter forcibly stopped Nariz, putting his right hand on the boy's left shoulder and his left hand on the kid's right biceps.

Giving Peter a menacing look that probably would've scared most science teachers, Nariz—who was bleeding from his outsized hooter—said, "You *best* be lettin' go'a me, teacher-man."

"Javier's not going anywhere, Nariz. Take a look." He gestured with his head to the ground, where Javier was still twitching, without actually taking his eye off Nariz.

Nariz looked down at Javier. "*Damn.*" He looked at Lefty. "Wha'd you do to him?"

"He didn't do anything," Peter said quickly before Lefty or Brian responded in kind. "He just collapsed. Is he on anything that would do that?"

Nariz just stared at Peter. "You got two seconds to be lettin' go'a me 'fore I get up in yo' *face.*"

Peter let go just as he heard sirens growing closer.

Turning his back on Peter, Nariz walked away. "This ain't over."

The ambulance pulled in behind one of the buses. Only then did Peter notice the crowd that had gathered, barely being held in check by a couple of faculty members and the other security guards, who'd come to check out the ruckus.

One of the English teachers, a small woman named Constance Dobson, looked at Peter and shook her head. "The guard was right about what you did, y'know."

Not sure which guard she meant, Peter asked, "About being brave or about being stupid?"

"Both."

Unable to help it, Peter laughed. "Yeah, maybe. Still, if I hadn't done anything—"

"Lefty or Brian woulda taken care of it. Leave that to the pros, Parker."

"I'll remember that," Peter lied. He'd stood by and done nothing when he had the power to help once. It was a mistake he would never make again.

The EMTs started working on Javier, and based on their chatter, they were assuming he was coming down off a shot of ecstasy. Peter frowned. *That doesn't track—he was straight in class. He had to have taken it after the bell rang. But you don't burn through an X high that quick.*

But then, an X high didn't turn you green and give you superstrength.

Nariz was right, Peter thought as he brushed off the paramedic who approached, assuring her that he was fine. *This isn't over.*

2

An old saying had it that familiarity bred contempt, which explained why Eileen Velasquez hated Parkway Hospital so much. She'd certainly spent enough time here, and she'd come to despise the place.

It all started when she was pregnant with her first child, Orlando. The pregnancy was deemed high-risk by the doctors, and she spent the four months leading up to his birth checked into the OB/GYN ward on twenty-four-hour bed rest. She hadn't wanted another child after that, and she had talked her husband, Carlos, into letting her get one of those fancy birth control implants. Unfortunately, something about the implant didn't work right, and she became pregnant with Javier. That pregnancy went fine, though the labor took twenty-three hours, and she spent all twenty-three back here again. Somehow, Carlos talked her into a third child, which became four when her doctor told her she had twins: Jorge and Manuel.

Then Orlando got into that accident with his bike, necessitating an emergency-room trip. Then Javier got into a fight at school, the first of many. Then they found out that Manuel had a bone disease, one not shared by Jorge. That meant lots more trips to and from not only Parkway

Hospital, but also Mount Sinai in Manhattan, to visit the specialist.

And then there was the accident.

Eileen worked at Dilmore, Ward, and Greenberger, Attorneys-at-Law, as a receptionist. It was there that she got the phone call from Mr. Harrington, the principal of Midtown High, saying there was an "incident." Usually that was code for "Javier got into a fight," which it turned out was true again as far as it went—but that Javier had been high on something was a new twist.

She knew Javier had been dealing. She didn't know he was also taking.

Mr. Ward, the managing partner, was completely okay with letting her go early, so she hopped on the V train and made the oh-so-familiar walk from the 71st Street station to the Parkway Hospital emergency room. The whiff of antiseptic mixed with sweat that characterized the hospital's E.R. filled her with an overwhelming feeling of disgust.

She had hoped never to come back here again.

Walking past the waiting area, with its cracked and dirty plastic chairs, she proceeded to the long, high desk, behind which sat a harried-looking white man in his twenties wearing light blue scrubs, though he didn't seem to be a doctor or nurse. He didn't have the casual arrogance that every doctor Eileen had ever met carried, nor the seen-it-all look that most nurses had. The desk was at Eileen's neck level, and the receptionist was seated, so she had to peer down at him.

The young man was on the phone. "Excuse me," Eileen said.

Holding up a finger, the receptionist said, "No, Fred, we need them down here *now*. Yeah, I know they're backed up, but we got a serious situation here. It's sixty degrees out, Fred, we really don't need the AC on full blast. Look, I—"

"Excuse me," Eileen said a bit more forcefully. "I need to see my son."

Again, the receptionist held up a finger, this time mouthing the words *just a second.*

"Fred, I've got Doc Shannon crawling up my butt, and he ain't gonna leave there until this gets fixed. Can you *please* just send somebody. I don't even care if they fix it, just have someone *show up,* okay? Thank you." He hung up the phone and looked up at Eileen. "Sorry 'bout that, it's crazy here. Now who—"

"My son—Javier Velasquez."

Even as the receptionist started typing something onto his keyboard, the phone next to him rang again. He picked it up. "E.R. Yeah. Yeah. Yeah. No. No, she's not on right now. No, she's not due back until tomorrow. Yeah. Yeah. Yeah. I really don't know that, you'll have to ask her. *Really,* ma'am, you have to ask her. Yeah. Sorry. Bye." The receptionist let out a long breath. "Sorry 'bout that. What's your husband's name again?"

Through clenched teeth, Eileen said, "It's my son, Javier Velasquez."

"Could you spell that, please?" Before she could, the phone rang again. He picked it up. "Hang on. E.R."

Eileen was two steps shy of reaching down and yanking the phone out of the floor jack it was plugged into when a voice from behind her said, "Excuse me, are you Javier's mother?"

She turned to see another white man in his twenties, but this one had darker hair and a kinder face than the harried receptionist. He was dressed in a sports jacket, button-down shirt, and slacks. Nothing fancy—nothing like her coworkers at Dilmore Ward—and obviously not a doctor or a detective. *A teacher, maybe?*

"Yes, I'm Eileen Velasquez."

"Hi, I'm Peter Parker—I'm Javier's science teacher." *I was right.* "Were you the one—?" She hesitated.

"I, uh—I was the one who subdued your son. Kind of." He smiled. "Actually, he pretty much subdued himself and I happened to be standing closest. It was right after school was over, so I figured I'd come down, make sure he was okay."

"I—I just got here, I—" She shook her head. "That was really nice of you, Mr. Parker, thank you."

"Call me Peter, and, uh, don't thank me yet—there's a detective from the 112th Precinct here, and he's probably gonna want to talk to you. Not to mention the doctor. I've already spoken with both of them."

"Did they tell you anything about Javier?" To her own ears, Eileen sounded like a woman desperate for news— which she supposed she was, even though a big part of her didn't want to know the answer.

"Nothing I didn't already know. Looks like he took a hit of ecstasy, apparently, and then just went nuts—he hit one of the other kids and one of the guards, then jumped me before he collapsed into a pile of goo. Not literally," he added quickly, though Eileen had assumed he was speaking figuratively.

Though with the way the world is today, it wouldn't be the craziest thing I ever heard of.

Parker then said, "Ms. Velasquez—I know Javier's had some problems, but I've never known him to take drugs before. Deal, yes, but—"

"I don't know, Mr. Parker. Truth is—I don't know my

son anymore. Javier's my second oldest—his older brother went off to college, and he's got two younger brothers, but—" She took a deep breath. "One of them, Manuel, died a couple years ago, along with my husband."

"I'm sorry." Parker sounded like he meant it, which Eileen appreciated. "And as I said, it's Peter."

Eileen didn't think it appropriate to refer to one of her son's teachers by his first name. "I wasn't really there for Javier much, especially after Manuel and Carlos died. I've got my hands full raising him and Jorge, and with the lawsuit—" She cut herself off. Parker didn't need to know about that.

" 'Scuse me, Parker?"

Parker turned around, and Eileen followed his gaze. The speaker was a heavyset black man in a dark suit, a shoulder holster bulging from under his pinstriped jacket, a gold-colored badge attached to his belt. *This must be the detective Mr. Parker was talking about.*

"Hi, Detective—uh, Detective Pierce, this is Eileen Velasquez, Javier's mother."

Pierce's eyes widened. "Oh yeah? Good, I need to talk to you, ma'am." The detective removed a pad of paper from his inner jacket pocket and started flipping through it to a blank page, the paper making crinkling noises.

"I need to know what happened to my son."

"The doctors are taking care of him, ma'am, but he'll be okay. Now I need to ask you—"

"I have to see my son," Eileen snapped.

Parker said quickly, "Would it hurt to let her see Javier, Detective?"

Pierce looked all put-upon, but Eileen didn't care. Finally, he said, "Yeah, okay. Follow me."

The detective led them down one of the corridors to a room with four beds in it. Back here, the antiseptic smell was still strong, but the sweat was gone. She supposed out of the way of the craziness of the reception area, that was to be expected.

Eileen didn't pay attention to the other three beds, focusing solely on the one closest to the door, where Javier lay sleeping.

That's the most peaceful I've ever seen him.

"What's wrong with his skin? I've never seen him look so pale," she said after a second.

"Actually," Parker said, "that's an improvement. At his highest, he was green."

"Green?" This was the first Eileen was hearing about this. "Why was he green?"

"Excuse me." At the new voice, Eileen turned to see a young Asian woman standing in the doorway alongside a tall black man in a nurse's uniform. "You people aren't supposed to be—" Then she noticed Pierce. "Oh, it's you. The kid's not waking up for a while yet, Detective, there's no need—"

"Dr. Lee, this is Javier's mother."

"Oh. I'm sorry, Ms. Velasquez, nobody told me you were here."

"That's okay. Can you tell me what happened to my son? Mr. Parker here said it was ecstasy."

"Not quite," Lee said. "It's a new variant that's been hitting the streets—laced with gamma radiation, which is why they turn green when they get high. It's called 'Triple X' on the street. He's lucky, though."

Eileen couldn't imagine how that could be. "What do you mean?"

"Your son's the fourth case I've seen in the last week.

He's not showing any signs of radiation poisoning—which puts him one up on the other three. That means he's probably only taken it once or twice."

Pierce put a hand on Eileen's shoulder. It took all of her willpower not to shove it off violently. "Thanks, Doctor—let me know when he wakes up, okay? Ms. Velasquez, if you'll come with me, I've got to ask you those questions now." The detective led her out of the room.

As they went, she heard the doctor say something quietly to the nurse. The nurse responded in a loud, deep voice: "Will do, Doctor."

Once in the hallway, Eileen did shake off the detective's hand. "I don't need you to push me, Detective, I can walk on my own."

"I'm sorry, ma'am, but I need—"

"I know what you need. So ask your questions, so I can be with my son."

She provided him with some basic information—address, full name, her job, phone numbers where she could be reached, and so on—and then he asked about their family situation.

"It's just me, Javier, and Jorge now. My oldest, Orlando, is at college in Florida. He doesn't come home anymore. Jorge's nine."

"Anybody else? Husband?"

"My husband and Jorge's brother, Manuel—they died two years ago."

"Were their deaths drug-related?"

Eileen snapped again. "What, you see Latino family, you figure drugs right off?"

"Take it easy, Ms. Velasquez." That was Parker—Eileen hadn't even heard him come out of Javier's room. "And Detective, go light on her, willya?"

"This ain't your business, Parker."

"Javier's my student—that makes him my responsibility."

Pierce rolled his eyes. "What a load of crap. Look, unless you can tell me something new about Javier that you didn't tell me before—"

"I told you everything I know."

"Fine, then shut the hell up. Ms. Velasquez, I'm trying to find out what happened to your son. Yeah, okay, maybe I jumped the gun with what I asked, but when you do what I do—"

Eileen didn't care to hear the man's rationalization. "My husband and son died in a car accident. Manuel had a bone disease, and we had to see a specialist in Manhattan. Carlos was driving him home after visiting that doctor, and a piece of concrete hit the car. It came from one of those super hero battles."

Eileen had spent a long time in the emergency room after the car was totaled, hoping that Carlos and Manuel would awaken from their comas, knowing that they'd both probably be crippled for life even if they did survive. Three days after the accident, Manuel died; Carlos's older, stronger body gave out another four days after that.

Life had been a succession of nightmares since then. Jorge became sullen and uncommunicative without his twin brother. Javier's descent into criminality got worse, to the point of his being arrested more than once, though nothing that resulted in any kind of jail time. Orlando had gone off to college in Florida and refused to ever come home.

Her subsequent wrongful-death lawsuit against the Avengers, who had been fighting a group that called themselves the Wrecking Crew at the time Carlos and

Manuel happened along, had been going on for some years now. Despite the lengthy interval, Eileen kept at it.

Maybe if I hadn't kept at it so hard . . .

She shook her head. "So it didn't have anything to do with Javier—unless you think the Avengers gave him this Triple X stuff."

"Yeah, well, it wouldn't surprise me," Pierce muttered.

"What does that mean?" Parker asked.

"Nothin'. Look, I'm sorry, Ms. Velasquez, but I just need—"

"You got everything you need," Eileen said, turning her back on the detective and heading toward the waiting area.

To her relief, Pierce didn't follow. However, Parker did. Walking alongside her back to the front of the emergency room, he said, "The guy was just trying to do his job."

"What'll he do, Mr. Parker? Find out who did this to my son? He doesn't need to do that, I know who—it was me. I haven't been there for my son, and this is what happens."

"It's not your fault," Parker said in a gentle voice. "With what happened—"

She shook her head. "You don't understand."

And he wasn't about to—the fact was, Eileen had never wanted Javier, and she had treated him that way ever since he was born. She resented him: the baby that wasn't supposed to happen. Sure, it was easy now to blame it on the accident, to say that Carlos and Manuel's deaths made her neglect her son. *But what was my excuse the ten years before that?*

Instead of telling this to Parker, she just asked him, "Javier'll be expelled for this, right?"

The teacher hesitated. "That *is* the school policy," he finally said. "But let me talk to the principal. Maybe I can . . ."

He didn't say what he would do. In truth, Eileen knew that there wasn't anything he *could* do. But at least he was trying. "Thank you, Mr. Parker. Really. I know Javier isn't the best student in the school."

"Actually, he's not that bad."

She gave him a look. "I know what he's like. I know he's a problem in class, and I *do* see his report card."

Parker smiled ruefully. "Yeah. But still, he deserves a chance. They all do."

Eileen let out a breath. "I don't know if I can believe that anymore, I really don't."

"I have to." He grinned. "Part of the job description." He reached into his pocket and pulled out his wallet, retrieving his business card. "This has my number at the school." He removed a pen from his jacket pocket and wrote a number with a 917 area code, which meant it was probably a cell phone. Sure enough: "I'm writing my cell number on it, too. If you or Javier need anything, just call."

She took the card, stared at it a second, then looked at this young man who was doing all this for her and her son. "You teach science, you said?"

Parker nodded. "Javier's last-period general science class, yeah."

Looking down, she saw a wedding band on the teacher's left ring finger. "You got a wife to go home to, and you're taking time out of your day to talk to me and make sure my son's okay. My son, who I know got a D in your class last term, and who'll probably be expelled."

"Yeah," Parker said with a shrug.

"Why are you doing this?"

Another shrug. "Like I said before, he's my student, so he's my responsibility."

She snorted. "What's the *real* reason?"

A pause. "I lost my parents when I was really young, so I was raised by my aunt and uncle. I learned a lot from both of them, and one thing that Uncle Ben always taught me was that I should always take my responsibilities seriously."

Smiling, Eileen said, "Sounds like your uncle's a good man."

"He was. He, uh, he died a while back. Got shot by a burglar."

Eileen shook her head. "Makes you wonder why anybody lives in this city."

"I guess."

She looked at the kind young man. "Thank you again, Mr. Parker. I'm going to go sit and wait for my son to wake up. You get back home to that wife of yours. She's probably worried sick about you."

Grinning, Parker said, "Actually, my wife's an actor, and she's got rehearsal tonight, so right now she's mostly worried about hitting her marks. So I can stick around if you want."

"No, I—I think I'd like to be alone for a bit, if that's okay."

Parker nodded. "Okay. Call if you change your mind."

"I will," she said, though she had no intention of bothering him anymore. He'd already done far more than his fair share for her son.

"Dr. Lee! The patient's crashing!"

Eileen looked up sharply. *I know that voice.* It was the

deep voice of the male nurse who was with Dr. Lee, checking on Javier.

Oh God, no.

She ran down the hall, Parker following behind. As soon as she got to the door, the nurse—who was fairly large—blocked her way. "Ms. Velasquez, you can't come in here."

"My son's in there, you have to let me in!"

Behind the nurse, the doctor said, "CI—get me epi, *stat!*" Eileen had no idea what that meant.

Perhaps noticing her confusion, the nurse softened and said, "CI is a cardiac infarction, ma'am—your son's having a heart attack. The doctor's gonna help him, but you have to wait outside."

Parker put a hand on her shoulder, one she found far more comforting than the detective's. "Ms. Velasquez, the nurse is right. Let them do their jobs," he said in a quiet voice.

Nodding, she let Parker lead her back toward the waiting room. The teacher was talking as they walked. "I read somewhere that Henry Pym of the Avengers, when he was Giant-Man, had heart problems relating to changing size all the time. The same thing might've happened to Javier because he changed size."

Eileen nodded absently. *My son is dying, and there's nothing I can do.*

She swore that if Javier lived through this, she would make their lives different—make them better. She'd lost Carlos and Manuel and Orlando already, and she was damned if she'd lose any more.

3

"All right, but I think you're crazy."

Mary Jane Watson stared at Valerie McManus. Mary Jane's line was a cue for the blond-haired woman standing across from her on the cramped stage. Between them was Lou Colvin, the third actor in this scene.

For her part, Valerie just stared blankly back at her. In the silence that followed, Mary Jane could hear the whispers of the tech crew and the costuming people as they dashed about doing their appointed tasks to get *The Z-Axis* ready for its forthcoming opening.

Then Valerie blinked. "Oh God, my line's next, isn't it? I'm sorry, I just totally blanked. I'm *so* sorry. I'll get it right this time, honest."

Somehow, Mary Jane managed not to scream—which was more than could be said for Dmitri Voyskunsky, the play's director and writer. "Valerie, my darling girl—you are aware, are you not, that we are opening in *one week*?"

"I'm sorry, Dmitri," Valerie said. "I'll try to—"

"No! No no no *no*!" The Russian got up from his seat at front-row center in the tiny fifty-seat theatre and started pacing in front of the stage. "We are off book now. My play, it opens in one week, and I do not wish to hear about not knowing the lines. The time for 'try' is past. The time is now for not 'try.' Time is now for 'succeed.' Okay?"

Lou whispered, "Thank you, Yoda." Valerie giggled.

Dmitri stopped pacing and stared at Valerie—an effect diluted by the sunglasses that the playwright always wore, along with a battered old Brooklyn Dodgers cap. With all that, and his full beard, only the presence of his nose made it possible to be sure he actually had a face. "Oh, this is funny, you think? My play is going to open with leading lady who stares at the back of the wall with mouth hanging open, and you are laughing?"

"Sorry, Dmitri," Valerie said, "I was—I was thinking of something else, honest. I wasn't laughing at you. Really, I wasn't, okay? Can we take it again?"

"Okay." Dmitri retook his seat and adjusted his cap. "From Jane Mary's line."

Having long since abandoned any hope of getting Dmitri to stop mangling her name—she was half-convinced that he did it on purpose to annoy her anyhow—Mary Jane simply turned to Valerie and said once again, "All right, but I think you're crazy."

"You *want* me to think that, don't you?"

Valerie must have noticed the look Mary Jane was now giving her, because she then said, "Oh no, that's not the line, is it?"

"No!" Dmitri said. "That is line from *next act*. Okay?"

Mary Jane was about to say something, when Valerie started waving her arms back and forth. "I got it this time, really, I got it. Honest. I got the line down pat this time, you watch. Let me try again."

"Hang on a sec," said Heidi. She was congregated around the soundboard with several other members of the tech crew. "These levels are wrong. Give me two seconds."

"I will give you five seconds, but no more!" Dmitri said.

Mary Jane knew *that* was a lost cause. Heidi had been complaining about the wonky sound system from the get-go.

They were standing on the second floor of Village Playhouse Central, a small theatre on MacDougal Street in the heart of Manhattan's famous Greenwich Village neighborhood. Downstairs was the lobby and box office, as well as the VPC offices. Within an hour or two, people would start milling about on the first floor to see tonight's performance of *Up the Creek Without a Fiddle,* a show by a different playwright. It would be running for one more week, at which point *The Z-Axis* would debut. *Up the Creek* had a minimal set—just a leather couch and a wooden rocking chair—which had been moved upstage and out of the way so Dmitri could run *The Z-Axis* without his actors tripping over the other play's set.

Although the place seated only fifty, most of the shows didn't sell out. Mary Jane was playing the supporting role of Irina, and she was also Valerie's understudy for the lead female role of Olga.

If she keeps up like this, I'll get that lead. In truth, Mary Jane was starting to truly worry about Valerie. She'd blown lines before, but she usually just cursed and got it right. She didn't babble a mile a minute the way she had been doing today.

Ever since she and Peter Parker had ended their thankfully brief separation and she moved back to New York, Mary Jane had been doing more theatre work, mainly in the hopes of improving her acting chops. As good as she was at modeling, she found acting to be much more fulfilling—and to offer more long-term possibilities once she got too old to represent products targeted to women or to stand next to products targeted to men. However, her acting experience to date consisted of a wretched soap opera and low-rent action movies, so she had recently decided to take advantage of the city's tremendous theatrical opportunities.

Despite the playwright's abrasive manner, she had found *The Z-Axis* to be a challenging piece—her smaller part of Irina was actually a stronger one than Valerie's lead. Olga was too reactive for Mary Jane's tastes; she just let things happen to her and didn't really appear to grow. Irina was more proactive, and actually went through changes as the play went on. It was a role that, despite the comparative paucity of dialogue, required nuance.

She looked closely at her costar, and noticed beads of sweat forming on Valerie's face. The lights weren't all that bright, and it wasn't all that hot in the room.

"Okay," Heidi said half a minute after Dmitri gave her five seconds, "we're ready to go."

Before Mary Jane could say anything, Valerie looked up and said, "All right, but I think you're crazy."

Dmitri uttered a stream of words in Russian, none of which Mary Jane knew, though she suspected that their equivalents in English were mostly spelled with four letters. Then Linnea, the costuming director, walked over to him, holding three swatches in her hand. Mary Jane figured that they were about to get into yet another fight over the color of the dress that Olga was supposed to wear in the opening scene. *That'll distract Dmitri for a few seconds at least.*

"You okay, Val?" she asked.

"Yeah, yeah, I'm fine. Really, I'm fine. Honest, let's do this and do it right."

Dmitri waved his hand in front of Linnea's face and

yelled at Valerie. "Do it *right*? Oh, this is your brilliant plan now, to do it *right*?"

"I got it, Dmitri, really, I just . . ." Valerie put her head down and trailed off. "I'm fine, really, I—oh, shit."

Mary Jane moved closer, and saw that Valerie was starting to look a little green. "Dmitri, I think she's sick."

"*She* is sick?" Dmitri got up and started pacing again, ignoring the daggers that Linnea was staring at him. "No, it is *I* who am sick! We are opening in a *week,* and . . ."

Ignoring Dmitri's rant, Mary Jane put her hand on Valerie's shoulder. The other woman's head was down, her blond hair covering her face. "Val, you okay? Val?"

Lou had also moved closer. "Yo, Valerie, c'mon, get with the—"

Then Valerie raised her head.

The face Mary Jane saw was mostly recognizable as belonging to Valerie McManus. It had her hazel eyes, her prominent cheekbones, her button nose. There were, however, two major differences. One, her mouth was twisted into a snarl, revealing sharp, pointed teeth.

And two, her skin was now emerald green.

"Val?" Mary Jane said in a small voice.

Then Valerie let loose with a scream that Mary Jane felt in her spine. As she screamed, she struck out at Mary Jane and Lou. Crying out in pain as Valerie's fist collided with her stomach, Mary Jane stumbled backward, falling off the stage—which, thankfully, was less than a foot higher than the floor—and landing awkwardly on her shoulder, wrenching it.

She looked up at the stage to see that Lou had been knocked back to the wings at stage right, where he'd stumbled into two of the tech crew who'd been adjusting one of the lights.

As for Valerie, she was now green all over. What appeared to be bat wings had ripped through the back of her costume.

Several people behind Mary Jane screamed, including Linnea, who dropped her swatches on the floor next to Mary Jane.

Valerie started flapping her new wings and slowly rose toward the rafters. Then, with a burst of speed, she went through the rafters and to the ceiling beyond it. With a resounding crunch of shattered concrete, she then flew *through* the ceiling.

Several chunks of debris and insulation and plaster fell down onto the stage, which was now occupied only by the couch and rocker from the other play and Lou, who shouted several expletives when a piece of concrete landed on his leg.

"Lou!" Mary Jane awkwardly got to her feet and, holding her wrenched shoulder, hopped onto the stage. Right behind her was the stage manager, Anne Grace, who joined her and the tech guys as they crowded around the injured actor.

"Oh my God!" That was from the audience: Michael— the high-strung guy playing Sasha—whose eyes had gone wide. Next to him, his boyfriend, Joseph, was just staring with his mouth open, drool hanging off his lip-ring.

As for Lou, he was bleeding profusely from the leg. Mary Jane shook her head. "Looks like you broke a bone there, Lou."

One of the lighting guys looked at her with surprise. "You can tell *that* just by looking?"

Mary Jane had spent a significant chunk of her adult life being very close to a full-time super hero, including a fair amount of time recently being married to him. The sad reality was that she knew a broken leg when she saw one. However, she couldn't very well say that out loud.

"OhmyGodohmyGodohmyGodohmyGodohmyGodohmyGod!"

Mary Jane looked over to see Heidi screaming and waving her arms. Some of the other tech crew were trying to hold her still. One of the tech guys was hiding under the soundboard asking if it was safe to come out.

Jumping down off the stage, still holding her shoulder, Mary Jane went to her purse, took out her cell phone, and turned it on.

"Who you call, Jane Mary?" Dmitri was staring at Mary Jane. He had removed his glasses and was cleaning plaster dust off them with his shirt.

"An ambulance—Lou's hurt, and everybody's freaking out."

"No, there is no need. We can bring him to St. Vincent's, okay? Do not need to bring ambulance. Ambulance bring police, police close theatre, no show tonight, then Alfredo angry. Alfredo angry, maybe he decide *The Z-Axis* no good."

Before Mary Jane could say anything, Anne stepped down from the stage. "Dmitri, shut up. There's a big hole in the ceiling, Heidi's having a nutty, Lou's leg is broken, and I'm about two steps away from a heart attack. The theatre is gonna be *closed.*"

Dmitri was too smart a director to argue with his stage manager, and so he said nothing. As soon as she got a signal, Mary Jane dialed 911.

Waiting for an answer, she wondered what happened to Valerie to cause that kind of transformation. Unfortunately, being married to a super hero meant she had some pretty reliable theories on *that* score as well.

• • •

The ambulance and the police arrived almost simultaneously, the former from the very same St. Vincent's Hospital that Dmitri wanted to take Lou to—*And what were we supposed to do,* Mary Jane wondered, *call him a cab?*—and the latter from the 6th Precinct. The EMT who checked her over was a fan, as it turned out, with fond memories of Mary Jane's brief role on the soap opera *Secret Hospital,* and not only pronounced Mary Jane fine, but even gave her a small packet of painkillers. They had also managed to calm Heidi down, get both Linnea and Joseph to come out of their stupors, and help Anne when she started hyperventilating.

As for the cops, what surprised Mary Jane was that once they learned what happened to Valerie, one of them immediately contacted their dispatcher and asked for someone whose name she didn't get from "the Two-Four." She also heard the word "task force." Mary Jane's knowledge of police procedure was limited to second-hand information from Peter and watching *Law & Order,* but she knew that that meant the 24th Precinct, which, if she remembered correctly, was uptown. Certainly nowhere near here. *Which means that Valerie isn't the first person to turn all green and super powered, and the NYPD already have a task force dealing with it. Wonderful.*

After the EMT finished with Mary Jane—the ambulance had long since taken Lou to St. Vincent's—a uniformed cop walked up to her. He was about Mary Jane's age, with short black hair that had been moussed within an inch of its life, sideburns that were tailored to the height of fashion, and no discernible neck. His nameplate read SPINELLI.

She gave him her best smile, and asked, "What can I do for you, Officer Spinelli?"

He returned the smile and said, "Just gotta ask a few questions, Ms.—?"

"Mary Jane Watson." She provided her personal information first, and then described what happened to Valerie in as much detail as she could.

When she was done, and had answered a few follow-up questions, Spinelli said, "If you don't mind my sayin', Ms. Watson, you're takin' this a lot better'n—well, anybody else."

She shrugged. "It's New York."

"Yeah."

After asking one or two more questions, Spinelli said, "It's gonna be a little while more. But if you want, we can take you home when we're done. Or, uh, anywhere else you, uh, you wanna go." He smiled widely at that.

Oh God. "I'm sure my husband'll be very glad to know that I'm getting a police escort all the way back to Forest Hills."

The smile fell. "Well, just let me or Officer Pérez know. 'Scuse me." He beat a hasty retreat.

Just as he did, two people walked into the theatre area from the door at the rear: a tall, pale, lanky man in a beige trench coat over a brown suit, and a short, stocky, freckled redhead wearing a green pantsuit. Both had badges on their belts. *I'm betting these are our task force detectives.*

Spinelli and the other officer—Pérez, presumably—talked with them for a few moments, then Spinelli pointed at Mary Jane.

"*Ex*cuse me! I wasn't done *talk*ing to you two!" A short, skinny man with jet-black hair cut close to his scalp, a small goatee, and wearing an NYU sweatshirt came in behind the two detectives. This was Alfredo Garber, the owner and operator of VPC, and one of the more excitable people Mary Jane had ever met. "I simply *can*not have this! It's out*rage*ous!"

The male detective spoke in too low a volume for Mary Jane to hear, but whatever he said didn't placate Alfredo in the least.

"I have a *show* tonight! Do you know *noth*ing of the theatre? The show *must* go on!"

After a moment, the male detective left it to his partner, who didn't seem pleased at being left to deal with Alfredo by herself. She continued to talk to the theatre owner, leading him back out the door and downstairs to the lobby, where Alfredo could continue to shout.

The detective made a beeline for Mary Jane. "Hello, Ms. Watkins, I'm Detective Shapiro."

"It's Watson, actually."

"Of course," Shapiro said, sounding wholly uninterested in the subject. "Officer Spinelli tells me you saw the whole thing."

Mary Jane nodded. "Valerie was having trouble holding on to her lines, and then she turned green and grew wings, and flew through the ceiling." *Just another day in the big city.*

Shapiro remained expressionless. "I take it that Ms. McManus has never shown any indication of having super powers before?"

She shook her head.

"Does Ms. McManus take drugs?"

That question threw Mary Jane for a loop. From what she knew, both from the news and from Peter, super powers usually came about because of industrial accidents or exposure to radiation or genetic mutation.

"It's a simple yes-or-no question, Ms. Watson," Shapiro said after Mary Jane didn't answer for a moment.

"She's an actor, Detective. She—" Mary Jane hesitated.

"Do you do drugs, Ms. Watson?"

"I don't see that that's any of your business."

He shrugged. "You're an actor, Ms. Watson."

She sighed. "We've been to a couple of parties together. She wasn't always one hundred percent straight. Beyond that, I'm not really prepared to say without an attorney present."

Shapiro rolled his eyes. "Cool down, Ms. Watson, I'm just trying to paint a picture here."

"I'd rather my friend wasn't framed, if that's okay." She sighed again. "Look, there were drugs at the parties. There was coke, there was X, there was booze, there were cigarettes. For my part, I've only done the booze and the cigarettes, and I haven't smoked in a while now—well, okay, I've snuck one here and there, but don't tell my husband." She hit Shapiro with the same smile she used on Spinelli.

Shapiro did not return the smile. He just made notes and then said, "So she took ecstasy?"

"Probably. I wasn't really keeping track."

"Did she look like she was on something this afternoon?"

Mary Jane chose her words carefully. "She was having trouble with her lines. She was a little sweaty. It's possible she was high. It's also possible she had a fever or half a dozen other things." She pursed her lips. "Detective, is anyone out *looking* for Valerie?"

Shapiro nodded. "We've got an APB out, Code: Blue's looking for them, and we've alerted the Avengers and the

Fantastic Four, since they tend to pick up on this kinda thing." Code: Blue, Mary Jane knew, was a special NYPD unit that dealt with paranormal activity.

The detective then asked, "Do you know if Ms. Mc-Manus associated with any known super heroes? Spider-Man, Daredevil, anybody like that?"

Shaking her head, Mary Jane said, "Not that I know of. And she would've mentioned it. She met Hugh Jackman at a party once and has yet to stop talking about it, so if she knew a super hero, she'd have said. You should probably talk to her boyfriend."

For the first time, Shapiro looked something other than bored. "She has a boyfriend?"

Mary Jane nodded. "Greg Halprin. They live in an apartment on Avenue C around 10th. I'm not sure of the exact address—Anne, the stage manager, she probably has it. She's the one breathing into a bag over there."

After writing that down, Shapiro closed his notebook and got up. "Thank you, Ms. Watson. You're free to go." He reached into the pocket of his trench coat and fished out a business card. "If you have any other information about Ms. McManus you'd like to share, please call me. And I may be calling you again as well."

Mary Jane reached up and took the proffered card. Sure enough, Detective Jeroen Shapiro worked at the 24th Precinct, located on West 100th Street.

Alfredo came back in, the redhead behind him. "Ex-*cuse* me, but this *wo*man is telling me that we can't have our *show* tonight!"

"This room's a crime scene, Mr. Garber. Until I release it, it stays as is."

"But the *show*—"

"Your show is canceled, Mr. Garber. Live with it." Shapiro then went to talk to one of the uniforms.

Alfredo stormed over to Dmitri. "Can you be*lieve* this?"

"The police, they are the same everywhere," Dmitri said in a more subdued voice than Mary Jane had ever heard him use.

"Oh, people are going to hear about *this,* let me tell *you!* I *know* people, and they will most *def*initely hear of *this.* That Detective Shapiro is walking a *beat* by Friday! You *watch!*"

Mary Jane got up and joined the two men, as did another actor, Regina Wright, a willowy blonde who had a lead role in the play currently running at VPC and who was serving as Mary Jane's understudy for *The Z-Axis.* "Uh, Alfredo?" Regina said. "There's, like, a *hole* in the ceiling? We're supposed to perform here tonight, *how,* exactly?"

Alfredo rolled his eyes. "You've *nev*er heard of open-air theatre?"

Regina sighed. "Whatever."

"Dmitri," Mary Jane said, "if it's okay, I'd like to go home."

"Your shoulder, it is okay?" Dmitri asked.

Nodding, Mary Jane said, "Yeah, the paramedic gave me some pills. I'll be fine."

"Okay. You need to be your best—Olga."

Mary Jane sighed. She had been expecting this. "Dmitri, I—"

"You are understudy." He looked at the blonde. "Regina, you will play Irina and Jane Mary, you will play Olga."

"But Valerie—"

Dmitri adjusted the bill of his Dodgers cap. "I cannot

have Olga with wings and green skin. The green skin, that perhaps Svetlana could work with in makeup, but wings? No good."

Mary Jane sighed. *The show must go on.* However, unlike Alfredo, she couldn't bring herself to actually utter the cliché aloud.

Regina snorted. "As *if* we're gonna even get to rehearse with Detective Sipowicz over there on the case."

Sounding confused, Dmitri said, "His name I thought is Shapiro."

"*NYPD Blue?*" Regina said with an incredulous look. "Hello, television?"

It was Dmitri's turn to snort. "I do not watch television. It is for fools."

"Whatever."

"I'm gonna get going," Mary Jane said.

"Night-night, MJ," Regina said. "You sure you're okay?"

Mary Jane nodded. "Yeah, I'm fine." She'd been terrorized by super villains in her time. By comparison, this was a walk in the park, wrenched shoulder notwithstanding. Right now, what she wanted more than anything was to be home with her husband.

However, she couldn't bear the notion of taking up Officer Spinelli's offer of going home in a blue-and-white police car. She passed by the uniformed cop as she headed to the exit. She also heard the redhead talking to Shapiro. "Look, I'm willing to finish up the interviews, but I don't think Garcia's gonna sign off on more OT without more of a case than we got. The shift ended at four, so—"

"Fine," Shapiro said, "then we'll go home after this. But let's finish the interviews."

Whatever the redhead said in response was lost to Mary Jane as she went downstairs. She grabbed her denim jacket and awkwardly put it on, trying to take it easy on her bad shoulder, then headed out the door to MacDougal Street.

The sun was starting to set, and was behind most of the buildings, leaving MacDougal pretty well shaded. A slight breeze tousled Mary Jane's red hair, and was blowing a plastic bag in circles on the street, causing a rattling sound. A man yelling profanities into a cell phone crossed in front of Mary Jane as she stepped down the stoop that led to VPC's front door.

She decided to take a cab home. It would be a bit pricey to go out to Queens from here, but after the day she'd had it was worth it to not have to deal with the subway.

Predictably, the first three cabs she saw were occupied, but the fourth pulled right in front of VPC and disgorged a passenger who was, Mary Jane suspected, about to be disappointed with regards to tonight's performance.

As she clambered into the cab and gave the driver her address, she thought, *Can't wait to tell Peter about my day. For once, mine is likely to be more exciting than his. . . .*

Spider-Man stood on the roof of an apartment building, staring out at his city.

His current perch was right on the Long Island Expressway, not far from Parkway Hospital, where Peter Parker had changed into his red-and-blue uniform, complete with full face mask and gloves, and made his way here. He needed a few minutes to himself, and one of the advantages his super powers gave him was a wide range of options for places to go and quietly think.

It wasn't completely quiet, of course. It was now well into rush hour, so cars heading out to Long Island were backed up on the LIE, horns beeping, engines revving up and slowing down in the bumper-to-bumper traffic. Someone in one of the top-floor apartments had the window open and was watching the local news at a loud volume while frying something on the stove, the anchor's words competing with the sizzle of the pan. *Smells like chicken* . . .

But for now, Spider-Man was focused less on sounds and smells than he was on sights. He was perched on the cornice of the west-facing wall of the thirty-five-story building, staring down the ribbon of the LIE to the Midtown Tunnel, and beyond it to the Manhattan skyline, the slowly setting sun bathing the skyscrapers in a lovely yellow-and-orange glow.

When he was a kid growing up in Forest Hills, Manhattan was the mecca, the holy grail, the light at the end of the Midtown Tunnel. Young Peter Parker loved taking trips to Times Square and Rockefeller Center and Chinatown and Central Park and especially the American Museum of Natural History (his science geek cred was established early in life).

Now, though, he looked out on the skyline and mostly was reminded of conflicts. Each landmark prompted a memory of a fight against one of the dozens—maybe hundreds at this point—of costumed loonies he'd faced over the years. Even the campus of his alma mater, Empire State University, had as many super villain clashes associated with it as it did academic memories.

And now I've got students Hulking out.

"What're you, nuts?"

Spider-Man turned around to see a large black woman exiting the rooftop access door. She was waving her arms back and forth as she walked toward him, the metal door slamming shut behind her.

"Get the hell down from there, you crazy?"

"I'm, uh—I'm not crazy, ma'am, I'm just—"

"Shyeah, right, not crazy. Standin' there in some whacked-out costume on the edge of the roof. You jump, we get cops all up in here, and I ain't havin' that. Hell, that ain't even a decent Spider-Man costume. Don't look *nothin'* like the real thing."

Smiling under his mask, Spider-Man said, "Really?"

"Yeah, really. I seen Spider-Man up-close-like, and his costume looks *much* nicer than that thing you wearin'. Now get yourself *down* from there, 'fore you hurt yourself."

"Nah." Spider-Man turned his back on the woman. "Think I'll just jump."

With that, he leapt off the roof. With a double tap of his palm, a line of webbing shot out from the web-shooters in his wrists and snagged another building across the way.

As he swung around in the general direction of home, his only regret was that he couldn't see the look on the woman's face. *I love this town. . . .*

The wind whipped against Spider-Man's mask as his body sliced through the air in an arc. When that arc reached its apogee, he shot out another web, letting go of the first one. The new web struck a billboard advertising an upcoming movie, and Spider-Man hit a new arc.

This is the only way to travel.

He wouldn't admit it out loud—not even always to himself—but this was the part of being Spider-Man that

Peter Parker loved most. When he first started, web-swinging had been difficult—constantly having to figure out angles of trajectory, where to leap, which parts of buildings to have the webbing adhere to, etc.—but soon enough, all of that became second nature. He didn't even think about that sort of thing anymore. Mary Jane once called it "Zen and the Art of Web-Swinging."

Now, he just enjoyed himself. The freedom of movement; the magnificent view of the city from that high up, with the people and cars looking like toys; the sound of the wind shifting (one of the first tricks he learned was to discern wind changes by listening); and so much more.

When he swung among the buildings of his hometown, he could lose himself in the joy of it all.

As he approached the apartment he and Mary Jane shared, though, those troubles came back to the fore. Dr. Lee said that Javier wasn't her first case with this so-called Triple X drug.

He planned to stop only for a moment and check in with his wife, who he knew should be coming home from rehearsal soon, but then he saw the yellow cab on the street below discharging a familiar red-haired figure. *What's she doing taking a cab home?* Peter was making a steady, if small, salary at Midtown High, and Mary Jane was still doing modeling work in addition to the acting, plus they both got occasional checks from past work—residuals from old acting parts of hers, royalties from reprints of his photographs—so they weren't in danger of starving anytime soon. But they generally weren't shelling out for cab rides from Manhattan without a good reason, either.

Coming in through the window as soon as his spider-sense died down enough to assure him that no one would see Spider-Man going into Peter Parker and Mary Jane Watson's apartment, he removed his mask and went to greet his wife.

As she opened the front door, Peter put his hands on his hips and said, "I spend all day working my *fingers* to the bone beating up bad guys, and is dinner waiting for me? No-o-o-o-o-o-o."

Mary Jane looked up in surprise, apparently not expecting Peter to be home, then gave him a wry smile. "Tiger, if that's what you were expecting, you *definitely* married the wrong woman."

"Well, I know *that's* not true, 'cause I have it on good authority that I married very much the *right* woman."

Peter looked at his wife and, for about the eight thousandth time, marveled at his luck that this woman had chosen to spend the rest of her life with him. Mary Jane was tall, with a huge mane of red hair framing her gorgeous face, knowing smile, and magnificent green eyes. She had been pretty much destined for a modeling career from high school, and she had excelled at it.

The day he met her was still seared on his consciousness. His aunt and Mary Jane's aunt, who had been best friends and neighbors for years, had been trying to set them up for months, but they kept missing each other. Peter had been convinced that Anna Watson's niece was some dull, uninteresting, unattractive woman. So when Peter—who at that point had had at least a few possibilities of relationships with other girls, among them fellow ESU student Gwen Stacy—finally met the gorgeous Mary Jane, he was totally floored.

"Face it, Tiger," she had said then, "you just hit the jackpot."

It wasn't until years later that they finally settled down

to get married. For one thing, there was Gwen, and the rough period he went through after she was killed, and then Mary Jane had disappeared from his life for a while. In retrospect, however, their being together was inevitable. Mary Jane had known that Peter was Spider-Man long before he ever thought to tell her, and she had come to love him even more because of it. Though their marriage had had some rocky roads—from a pregnancy gone wrong to a miserable separation—they had come out of it stronger than ever. Having the woman he loved to come home to had made his life mission as Spider-Man in many ways more important—it gave him something concrete to fight for.

Now, he walked up to her and was about to give her a hug, when he noticed the way she was favoring her right arm. "What'd you do to your shoulder?"

"Oh, thereby hangs a tale. Brew me some coffee, and I'll tell you all about it."

Soon, they were sitting on the couch, each holding a steaming mug of coffee. Peter had handed his wife the mug with the dictionary definition of the word coffee written on it; for himself, he'd taken the one with the tiger engraved on it that Mary Jane had given him for his birthday last year, in honor of her longtime pet name for him. Peter waited to sip, for the moment enjoying the warmth and the smell of the drink. He neither smoked nor drank, nor purposely took any illicit drugs—super powers and impaired mental function were a dangerous mix—but Peter would never have been able to survive all these years without coffee.

Mary Jane then told Peter a story that floored him—not so much for the actual events, which, sadly, were pretty ordinary happenings in New York City these days, but for their similarity to those of Peter's day. By the time she was done, he'd set the mug down unsipped-from.

After she finished talking about Valerie, Peter told her about Javier.

"That can't be a coincidence," she said.

"I'm thinking not, no." Peter finally drank some of his now-lukewarm coffee.

Mary Jane shook her head. "I have to admit I fibbed a bit to the detective. The fact is, every time I've seen Valerie at a party, she's been high on *something*—her and her boyfriend both. Thing is—it's only been at parties. When she's on the job, she's *never* stoned."

"Yeah, well, I didn't know Javier ever sampled the product he was dealing, either." Peter sighed. "I'm thinking this Triple X is some *seriously* good stuff."

"Well, if it turns you into a—what's the buzzword?" Mary Jane asked with a smile. "Paranormal? That's a pretty good incentive to take it right there."

Putting his mug back down on the coffee table, Peter said, "Just what this town needs: a drug that doesn't just get you high, but puts you in a position to damage more property than the Hulk and the Avengers combined—*and* will probably kill you."

"People don't usually die from X, Tiger."

Grimly, Peter said, "This stuff is laced with gamma radiation. Yeah, it gives you powers, but Dr. Lee at the hospital said that she's seen cases where the user has radiation poisoning. And Javier suffered a heart attack, probably because of the size changes. Who knows what other problems might crop up?"

"Oy."

Peter nodded. "'Oy' is right." He stood up. "The cops

already seem to have a bead on this. I should head over there, see if they'll share info."

Mary Jane fixed her husband with a dubious expression. "You think that's likely?"

Letting out a breath, Peter said, "I dunno, MJ, but it's worth asking." In his career Spider-Man had been both hunted and helped by the police. It was always a crapshoot as to how any given member of the NYPD would respond to his presence.

"Well, I wouldn't bother tonight. When I left they were talking about how they were going off-shift and their supervisor wouldn't sign off on overtime for them. So they're probably not there until tomorrow."

Peter shook his head. "Figures. Well, I should still do my nightly patrol. Don't want the criminals thinking Spidey's taken a night off."

Mary Jane stood up and put her good arm on Peter's shoulder. "Go get 'em, Tiger. Me, I'm gonna take a hot bath."

"Good plan." His wife was far less accustomed to the bumps and bruises that were part and parcel of Spider-Man's daily existence. The hot bath would do her good.

He gave her a deep, heartfelt kiss, then put his mask back on and, once his spider-sense gave the all-clear, leapt back out into the evening air.

4

Hector Diaz threw his books into his locker with a little more force than was probably necessary. He got the
usual from Mom this morning—like it was any of *her*
business what he was doin' with his life. Not like she
gave a damn before; he didn't know why she was up
in his face now. It was like as soon as he hit high
school, suddenly it was time for her to start bein' a
mom after not giving a damn for fourteen years. Hell
with that.

Biggie came up to him when he closed the locker.
Hector didn't even know what Biggie's real name was—
didn't matter none, since he was bigger than any other
damn person in the schoool, even the seniors and the
teachers, and he was a sophomore. Any other name
wouldn'ta meant nothin'.

"Yo, Hector, what up." Biggie offered his massive
hand. Hector took it, his own full hand smaller than Biggie's palm. "Listen, I got the good stuff, yo."

Hector winced. "Naw, man, I can't be doin' that. My
Moms is all up in my face."

"The hell's that got to do with nothin'? I'm talkin'
quality product here, you feel me?"

"Yeah, man, but I can't be doin' that. Not right now."

Biggie shook his head, which looked pretty crazy since Biggie didn't have much by way of a neck. "That's messed up, yo. Look, this be the high you been waitin' all your *life* for. You can't be passin' this up."

Hector thought this sounded like a big pile of crap. "This the same stuff Javier be takin'?"

"Man, why you want to be bringin' that up?" Biggie let out a big breath. "Look, Javier ain't right in the head."

"All's I know is, Javier went crazy, then went to the hospital."

Biggie shook his head again. "Look, this ain't stepped-on, a'ight? Now Javier be buggin', but you ain't Javier, yo. He think he all that, but he ain't. You can take this."

Hector closed his locker. "Nah, man, I can't. My Moms, she's all up in my face right now. I get high, she'll be tossin' my ass to the *street,* yo."

"A'ight, I get what you sayin'. But you change your mind, you know where I be?"

Biggie was part of Ray-Ray's crew, and that meant the Robinsfield Houses in Long Island City. "Same bat-time, same bat-channel?"

"Most def."

Hector nodded. *Still at them Houses, then.* Biggie held up his hand. Again, Hector returned the handshake.

Not that Hector planned to take Biggie up on that offer. He might go down there to score some blow or some weed, if he could figure out a way to get it by his mom, but Triple X? No way. No matter what Biggie said, Javier wasn't no fool, he was hardcore, and if that was sending his narrow ass to the hospital, Hector was stayin' the hell away from it. He got high 'cause it was nice and 'cause it beat the hell out of sitting at home watching his mom drink herself to death the way she been doing since Dad walked out on them.

But when high started to mean hospital, Hector wasn't playing.

Martha Diaz came up to her locker, which was right next to Hector's, since the lockers were assigned alphabetically. Martha and Hector weren't related, of course—there were a total of ten Diazes at Midtown, and the only ones who were family were Martha and her older sister Wilma—but they'd been tight since grammar school.

"Hey, girl, you hear from Javier?" Hector knew that Martha's best friend was Javier's cousin, Rosanna.

Martha opened her locker door. "He still in the hospital. Last I heard, he ain't even waked up yet."

"Damn. That's messed up." Hector shook his head. "You figure they gonna expel his ass?"

Shrugging, Martha gathered up her books for the day. "School policy."

"Yeah. He been arrested?"

Frowning, Martha said, "I don't think so. Rosanna didn't say nothin' 'bout that."

"That don't make no sense. He hit Nariz and that fat guard, and Mr. Parker."

"Yeah, but I'm feeling a *lot* better now."

Hector turned around to see Mr. Parker. Both he and Martha immediately straightened up. Teachers hated when kids had bad posture, Hector learned that much in the first grade.

Mr. Parker shook his head. "Why do kids always do that?" He smiled. "Look, as long as you do your homework, I don't care if you look like the Hunchback of Notre Dame. Just stand the way you always do."

"The whoback of what?" Hector asked. Like most teachers, Mr. Parker didn't make no sense most of the time.

"Never mind. Look, I'm sorry, but I heard you two talking, and I think I know why Javier hasn't been arrested."

"Oh yeah?" Hector didn't see how a science teacher would know about that.

"I was talking to the doctor at the hospital."

That confused Hector at first, but if Mr. Parker was one of the ones who got hit when Javier went all crazy, then he woulda been at the hospital, too.

Mr. Parker went on: "She said there's a concern that Javier might get radiation poisoning from the Triple X."

"Triple X? What's that?" Hector asked, hoping he sounded cool.

"Calm down, Hector, I'm not wearing a wire. Right now, the main thing I'm worried about is this drug. If Javier *does* get radiation poisoning, then he's gonna be in the hospital for a long time—which is probably why they didn't arrest him."

Hector exchanged a quick look with Martha, who looked as confused as he felt. "What's that got to do with it?"

"If Javier's arrested while he's checked into Parkway, the NYPD then becomes responsible for his hospital bills. They're not gonna pay for that, and besides, it's not like he's going anywhere. If he's released, they'll probably read him his rights on the way out the door."

"That's messed up." Hector slammed his locker door shut. "Them cops are *totally* messed up." Then he looked again at Mr. Parker. "How you be knowin' all this about policin'?"

Mr. Parker grinned. "I wasn't always a teacher, Hector." Then he got all serious again. "Look, I need to ask you if either of you know where Javier got the Triple X."

Hector gave the teacher a nasty look. "Thought you said you weren't wearin' a wire, yo."

"I'm not. I'm just worried. Nariz and Mr. Lefkowitz and I were lucky that we weren't hurt too badly. The next person who gets in the way of a Triple X junkie may not be so lucky."

"Javier ain't no junkie," Martha said.

"Sorry, I didn't mean to say he was," Mr. Parker said. Hector was surprised to realize that it sounded like the teacher actually meant it.

Still, Hector wasn't buying Mr. Parker's act. He figured that the cops set him on the kids 'cause maybe the kids would talk to him. And for a teacher, Mr. Parker was okay. He made stupid jokes a lot, but he also talked to the students like they was people instead of pets like most teachers did.

But what got Hector going was what Mr. Parker said about why Javier wasn't arrested.

"What'll happen if Javier got radiating poison?"

"*Radiation* poison—and if he does have it, his cells will break down, his hair will fall out, he may get cancer. No matter what, he's pretty likely to die."

"I thought radiation give you super powers or whatever."

"It can. It can also kill you. Sometimes it does both. And who knows, Javier may be fine. But what about the next kid?"

Hector thought about what would happen if his hair all fell out and he got all sick. Then he looked up at Mr. Parker. "Look, I ain't sayin' nothin' here, a'ight, but—

well, if you wasn't so white, I'd say you might want to check out Long Island City."

"I won't blend in, huh?"

"*Hell,* no." He turned around. "Look, I gotta be gettin' to class."

"Me too," Martha muttered.

Both Diazes packed up their books and went to their homeroom, leaving Mr. Parker behind.

As soon as they were out of earshot, Martha got all up in Hector's face. "What you be *tellin'* him that for?"

"Look, it's one thing gettin' high, but hair fallin' out? Dyin' of cancer? No way. Old folks die of cancer. I ain't seein' nobody goin' like that."

"He a *teacher,* Hector. He just tell the cops, you watch. 'Sides, what the hell *you* care about all this? You ain't takin' it, right?"

"Hell no!" Hector wondered why he *did* tell the teacher. If Javier got all dead, it wasn't nothing to him.

He thought about it all the rest of the day.

The cacophony of the *Daily Bugle* City Room assaulted Peter Parker's senses: the sight of interns dashing back and forth, running errands for the reporters; the sound of reporters talking on their phones and typing on keyboards with rapid-fire clacks; and, of course, the lingering smell of publisher J. Jonah Jameson's cigars.

There are times when I've really missed this place.

Peter came here straight from school, the route from Forest Hills to the East Side's *Daily Bugle* Building so ingrained in his mind he barely even had to pay attention. This was the first of two Manhattan stops he needed to make this afternoon, especially after what he'd heard from Hector, and after Mary Jane's voice mail informing him that no one had seen Valerie since she flew through VPC's roof.

He navigated unerringly among the desks that were all butted against each other, his spider-sense allowing him to avoid collisions with interns rushing to run errands and reporters rushing to chase stories and editors rushing to berate reporters. He caught sight of several former colleagues and gave them each a polite wave.

Walking over to Betty Brant's desk, he saw her talking on the phone and typing on the keyboard of a small laptop that sat amidst the papers and Post-it notes on her desk.

Betty had dropped out of high school to work as Jameson's assistant at the *Bugle* when her mother became too sick to continue in that job. She was also Peter Parker's first crush—mostly by virtue of being the first woman who ever gave Peter a second look, or even a first one. Sadly, their relationship never really went anywhere romantically.

She had also been through more than any six people should. Her brother had been killed by Dr. Octopus; her husband, Ned Leeds, was brainwashed by the Hobgoblin and then killed by an assassin known as the Foreigner; and she herself was taken in briefly by a cult.

Somehow, though, she'd come out the other side of all those traumas stronger than ever. No longer a glorified secretary, she was now an investigative reporter, and a good one. She brought down both the Hobgoblin and the Foreigner with her mightier-than-a-sword pen, had reported stories from as far away as Latveria, and had won a couple of awards to show for it.

Every time he looked at her, he remembered something she'd said to him shortly after Peter started taking photos for the *Bugle*. Jonah had been engaged in one of his usual rants, with Peter as the subject. Betty—who, up to that point, was just the person Peter got his pay vouchers from, but not much else—sidled up to him and whispered the words that became imprinted on his brain: "Don't feel too bad, Peter. I may only be JJ's secretary, but *I* think you're *wonderful*."

Nobody had ever called him *wonderful* in quite that tone of voice before, and certainly not while wearing lilac perfume. Peter long suspected that the only reason why he had the courage to even talk to the likes of Gwen and Mary Jane was because Betty had expressed interest in him back then.

She smiled at Peter as he approached and mouthed the words *hang on* while she listened and typed. "Yeah, Marty. Yeah. Yeah. Okay. Great, thanks for the tip. Yes, you'll get credit. *Yes,* that means your name in the paper. I'll even spell it right. Okay, thanks, Marty. Bye."

Hanging up the phone, she immediately stood and wrapped her arms around Peter. "Long time no see, Petey!"

Returning the hug, Peter said, "Too long, Betts. How goes the reporter's life?"

"Busy as always. I'm actually working on a pretty big story right now. How's that corruption of the youth of America coming?"

Laughing, Peter said, "Slowly but surely. Actually, the youth that I'm corrupting is why I'm here. I had one of my kids Hulk out after school, and the E.R. doc said he was on a new drug called Triple X. It's a gamma-hyped ecstasy. One of MJ's fellow thespians is taking it, too— she knocked a hole in the ceiling of the theatre last night. I was wondering if anybody was covering this for the *Bugle* or not."

Betty grinned. "Trying to bring us a scoop?"

Returning the grin, Peter said, "Nah, my days in the fourth estate are behind me."

"Really?" Betty gave him a dubious look.

"Yes, really."

Shaking her head, Betty said, "I don't buy it. You'll be back to taking pictures eventually. It's in your blood. You forget, I knew you when you *started* as a shooter."

Peter shrugged. "Maybe someday, but today isn't that day. Right now, I'm just looking to find out more about this. I get the feeling this kid isn't the only one at Midtown High trying it out, and I'm worried."

Sitting back down at her desk and offering her guest chair to Peter, Betty picked up a pen off her desk and started tapping her cheek with it. After Peter sat in the guest chair, she said, "Actually—*that's* the story I'm working on." She pointed at the phone. "Marty there is a nurse at St. Luke's uptown. They've gotten a few cases up there—in fact, the first one was in a housing project up on Amsterdam in the 90s."

That explains a lot, Peter thought. The 24th Precinct was located on West 100th Street, so if they'd caught the first case of Triple X, it made sense that the task force would have been formed there.

"Do you know who's dumping this crap on the street?"

Betty snorted. "I wish. If I had the supplier, I'd have the story of a lifetime—and a way to get at the creep. Whoever it is, they're making a mint. From what I've been able to find out, the dealers slinging this stuff are raking in three times their usual take. They can probably carry some heavy weight if they keep this up. Unfortunately, all I know is that it's been showing up more

and more and people really like it. And who can blame
them, really? I mean, it not only gives you the same high
you get from X—"

"Actually, I think the high is stronger," Peter said. "My
kid got toasted really fast yesterday, and MJ's friend was
willing to get high while working, which she never did
before."

Nodding, Betty said, "Yeah, that makes sense. Either
way, though, you've got the high *and* the super powers.
Every day, you hear about the latest super hero fight.
They're all over the place, especially in this town, and—
our publisher's preferences notwithstanding—they're
mostly glamorized." She chuckled. "You know that,
since he was revived, Captain America's been on the
cover of *Time* and *Newsweek* more than the sitting pres-
ident?"

"Doesn't surprise me." Peter tried not to sound bitter,
but he himself rarely got that kind of publicity. The
Avengers and the Fantastic Four were major celebrities,
true, and other heroes tended to get lavish news coverage
right alongside the actors and the sports stars. Spider-
Man, though, had never had that kind of luck.

"So if you're the type of person who fits the profile for
taking drugs—down on your luck, crappy home life, not
much hope of improvement—" Betty hesitated.

Peter felt a pang of sympathy—Betty could very well
be describing her own life before she got it together.

She shook it off. "You're that type of person, and you
see the super heroes getting all the ink and news coverage, and you think, *I wanna be that*. Triple X gives you
that chance. Not surprising that it's the hottest new
drug."

"Yeah, right up until it kills you from radiation poisoning."

Betty nodded. "But that doesn't really make it any different from any other drug. They all kill you in the end, it's just a question of how." She leaned forward. "Anyhow, that's all I've really got so far. I don't know how it'll help your student or Mary Jane's friend, though."

Grinning, Peter said, "Well, like I keep telling my kids, knowledge is power. Thanks, Betts."

"Parker! What the hell're *you* doing here?"

Peter looked up to see the ever-scowling face of J. Jonah Jameson, framed by his flattop haircut and highlighted by his trademark Charlie Chaplin mustache. Wearing his usual white shirt and suit pants—rumpled from a day of ranting and raving—with his omnipresent cigar between the first two fingers of his right hand, the lanky Jonah stood over Betty's desk.

"Just dropping by for a visit, Jonah."

"This is the City Room, Parker, not a Starbucks. Last time I checked, you didn't work here anymore, and that makes you a trespasser in my newspaper office."

"Actually," Betty said before Peter could respond, "Peter's a source on my Triple X story. He was just telling me about two more cases."

"Really?" Jonah's eyes lit up. He popped the cigar in his mouth, puffed, and blew out a cloud of acrid smoke. "Don't suppose you have pictures?"

"'Fraid not, Jonah. I'm just an ordinary citizen talking to a reporter."

"Bah! You were never 'ordinary,' Parker, that much I'll swear to. Well, all right, Brant, keep this ingrate around—let him sit there and pretend that I never brought him up from nothing and made a celebrity of him, only to have him turn his back on me. But when he's done, he's gone, got it?"

"Absolutely, Jonah."

"Hmph." Jonah took another puff. "You used to call me 'Mr. Jameson.'"

Betty smiled sweetly. "I used to be your secretary. All the other reporters call you Jonah."

"Yeah, that was my first mistake." Something caught his eye. "Snow! What the hell are you doing here? Why aren't you out covering that damn press conference?"

Jonah stalked off to yell at Charley Snow. Once he was out of earshot, both Betty and Peter burst out laughing.

"Sorry about that, Peter."

Waving her off, Peter said, "Don't worry about it. Honestly, it was kind of refreshing."

Looking at him like he was crazy, Betty said, "You're kidding."

"No. It's kinda nice. It brings stability to my world to know that, no matter what else might happen, Jonah's still a cantankerous old coot."

Again, Betty laughed. "That's for sure. Look, I'd better type up these notes I got from Marty—hey, since I already told Jonah you were a source, can you give me specifics on your kid? Or Mary Jane's friend?"

Peter hesitated. He didn't want to make Eileen Velasquez's life any more difficult. "I'd rather not give a name."

"I'll be vague—a high school student in Queens and a theatrical actress in Manhattan?"

"That's fine," Peter said with a nod. "The kid turned into a mini-Hulk, and the actress turned into a green harpy."

Betty typed all that into her computer. "Great. I may call you later, run the text by you?"

"Thanks, Betts, I appreciate that."

"And if I learn anything that can help your student or Mary Jane's friend, I'll try to pass it on."

Putting a hand on Betty's hand, he said in a quiet voice, "Thanks again."

"Hey—always willing to help out a friend, Petey. And you've always been one of the best."

5

"And then she asks me why the DNA tests ain't done yet."

Jack Larsen, the desk sergeant at the 24th Precinct, was only half-listening to Detective Christopher Carter. Most of his energy was focused on filing the day's run-sheets. Inspector Garcia was on a paperwork kick ever since he got reamed at the last ComStat meeting for the Two-Four's crappy paperwork, so of course the inspector was taking it out on Larsen.

But the desk sergeant was always willing to let Carter go off on one of his rants, mainly because Larsen knew that the short, bald, pudgy detective had worn down the patience of the other occupants of the precinct house. It didn't bother Larsen any, and it kept Carter out of the other detectives' hair. Usually, Larsen was able to use this service as currency to actually get the damn run-sheets in on time. It mostly worked—he'd gotten everyone's but O'Leary's today, and O'Leary was working on hers right now.

"So I tell her, I says, 'Look, lady, we only got the soda can yesterday. It'll be *weeks* before we get the results.' And she just looks at me, and she says, 'But on *CSI* they do DNA tests in a couple of hours!' Can you believe that crap?"

Having caught the interrogative, Larsen quickly said, "Yeah, it's nuts." Then he went back to searching for Detective Wheeler's run-sheet. *It was here a minute ago.*

"I dunno what's worse, TV or the damn costumes." Carter shook his head. "Nah, it's the TV. Costumes at least sometimes help out, y'know? But TV don't do nothin' but spread misinformation to an already sad and pathetic general populace."

Larsen took Carter's brief pause for breath as an opportunity to make an incoherent grunt, thus creating the illusion of paying attention. Right now, he was running his hands through what was left of his red hair and getting seriously concerned about Wheeler's run-sheet. The detective had brought it by, talked for a few minutes about his latest conquest—a student at the Fashion Institute of Technology with what Wheeler called the hottest lips he'd ever kissed on a woman—and then gone to check on something for the Triple X Task Force.

"*CSI*'s the worst. Like anybody'd let some crime scene geek near a suspect. Or give 'em a weapon. Hey, can you imagine *Gardner* with a nine in his pants?"

"No, I can't." In that, Larsen was honest. Steve Gardner, the head of the Crime Scene Unit, wouldn't know what to do with a nine-millimeter pistol that he wasn't bagging for evidence.

" 'Course it ain't all bad. Wish the job was like *NYPD Blue,* where you can yell at suspects for half an hour without them lawyering up. I swear, I never saw nobody ask for a lawyer on that damn show. You know what the only show that got it right was? *Barney Miller.*"

"Oh yeah?" Larsen asked as he riffled through the existing run-sheets for the fifth time, on the ever-less-likely theory that Wheeler's got mixed in with someone else's.

If that didn't work, he was going to bang his head against the ugly white-and-bright-green walls that made the whole precinct house feel like a 1950s public school.

"Yeah. On *Barney Miller,* they spent all their time fillin' out paperwork and dealing with whack-jobs in the squadrooms. Sounds like my day-to-day, lemme tell ya. We won't even talk about—"

"Carter, would you mind explaining what in the seven levels of *hell* your posterior—not to mention the rest of your rather sad-looking self—is doing out here?"

Larsen turned to see the sergeant in charge of the day-shift detectives, Bill Green, in the entryway to the squad-room, his tiny hands resting on his ample hips. The sergeant was affectionately known to his detectives as "The Jolly Green Giant," generally simplified to "Joll." He weighed about three hundred and fifty pounds, which he proudly proclaimed was "all fat—especially what's be-tween my ears." Joll was shaped like one of those clowns that you punched that bounced back up, complete with thick middle and ovoid head—covered with a thick patch of brown hair that the balding Larsen was jealous of, es-pecially since Joll was older than Larsen by five years.

Carter rolled his eyes. "Just givin' the sarge here my run-sheets, Joll. I—"

"What you were doing, *Detective,* was wasting the good sergeant's time with your tiresome diatribes on the tele-visual medium's portrayal of our noble calling. This is in direct opposition to what you should be doing, which is being by the phones, seeing as how you're up."

Carter straightened. "We got a call?"

Green nodded and removed a Post-it from his shirt pocket. "Break-in at 98th and CPW. You're taking Barron with you."

Wincing as he took the proffered Post-it, Carter asked, "Does it have to be Barron?"

Putting his hand over his heart, Green asked, "What's this? Can it be that you have a problem with the good Detective Barron? Is it possible that there is strife in the heretofore calm and friendly ranks of the Two-Four's detective squad?"

"It's just—" Carter sighed. "She insists on driving."

"So?"

"You ever been a passenger with her?"

Green shrugged. "It's rush hour—how fast can she go?"

"She'll find a way," Carter said gravely. "I gotta go to my desk, get my Dramamine."

Kelly Barron then came bursting out from behind Green, holding up a set of car keys and heading to the front door. "C'mon, Carter, let's go. I got us a car."

Rolling his eyes, Carter followed her. "I'm driving."

"I got the car."

"Like hell you do, I ain't taken my Dramamine."

"Don't be such a wuss."

Larsen watched them leave, unable to hold back a chuckle. Green turned to him, grinned, and said, "It's always so touching whenever the kids leave home for the first time, isn't it?" Growing serious, he asked, "How're we with the run-sheets?"

"Almost perfect."

Green looked pensive. "I like the word 'perfect.' It has a certain ring to it. Flows off the tongue almost effortlessly. That is, when it's by itself." Fixing Larsen with a hard look, he added, "It's when it has that modifier that it loses some of its innate charm. The word 'almost' ruins the effect—to the point where it is likely to make our wise and beneficent precinct commander unhappy. And when Inspector Garcia is unhappy, he tends to kick downward—at his sergeants. Meaning thee and me, my good friend. So what is this 'almost' crap?"

Sighing, Larsen said, "I can't find Wheeler's run-sheet. He dropped it off, talked for half an hour about that FIT student he bagged—"

"The one with the lips?"

"That's the one," Larsen said with a nod. "Now I can't find it. I looked everywhere."

"Well, it's not up here."

The voice scared Larsen out of about ten years of life, mainly because it came from above him. He jumped back, his hand automatically going to his weapon.

Looking up, he saw a strangely contorted figure with no face hanging from the cheap tile-work that passed for a ceiling.

After a second, he realized that the figure was human, and wearing a blue-and-red bodysuit, down to the mask. After another second, he realized that it was Spider-Man. He was hanging by one of his web-lines, upside down, knees bent and feet together, both over his head, which was now looking down at Larsen.

"How the hell'd you get in here?" Larsen asked.

"Ah, c'mon, Sergeant, you can't expect me to give away all my trade secrets. They'll make me turn in my hero union card." If he squinted, Larsen could see a jaw moving under the mask, but it was still creepy. The eyes in the mask were opaque and didn't blink, and Larsen could only make out the shape of a nose—and no mouth. That was the creepiest part.

"You guys have a union?" Larsen managed to ask.

"I wish. It'd save me a bundle on dry cleaning."

Green asked, "Would you mind explaining your presence in our precinct house, kind sir?"

"'Kind sir'? I like that. I'm trying to find some information about Triple X. Word on the street is that the task force is here, so I figured I'd just drop in."

Larsen wondered if the pun was deliberate. Probably, he thought.

"Most of the task force is out with their ears to the proverbial ground right now. However, you're in luck— one Detective Una O'Leary is still present and accounted for. She's finishing up her run-sheet." Green said that last with a look at Larsen. Larsen swallowed. Then Green smiled up at Spider-Man. "She's a bit late with it."

"That's the nice thing about my end of this business— no paperwork."

Green gazed at Spider-Man for a couple of seconds. "Maybe, but I don't think I'd be able to pull off wearing the spandex." For emphasis, he patted his ample belly with his hands, then he pointed to the door to the squadroom. "Go through there, and then head upstairs. O'Leary's the redhead."

"Much obliged, uh—?"

"Sergeant Bill Green, at your service. And what do I call you?"

"Spider-Man's fine—or Spidey. I also answer to 'Hey you.'"

"Fine, Mr. Hey You, just head through there."

Larsen heard a chuckle from Spider-Man. "Everyone's a comedian. Thanks, Sergeant!"

With that, he swung around and leapt over to the squad room door in a manner that just was not natural. Somehow he jumped without having anything to push off, and twisted his body around to land hands and feet first over the door. Then he skittered through the doorway. It made Larsen nauseous just to watch it.

He turned to Green. "You're just gonna let that creep run loose in the squadroom? In the precinct?"

Green fixed Larsen with a gaze. "You remember Jean DeWolff?"

"Oh yeah. She was good police," Larsen said. DeWolff was a captain downtown, till she got herself shot by a fellow cop who had gone nuts and begun to call himself by one of those crazy costume names, Sin-Swallower or something like that. Larsen had liked DeWolff; her father was a cop, too, and she was carrying on the tradition, like a real police. "What about her?"

Pointing at the door through which Spider-Man had just gone, Green said, "That's the gentleman that caught the bastard who killed her. And he was right there from the very beginning of the investigation, trying to avenge her, working with us. Far as I'm concerned, that man's welcome in my house."

Larsen wasn't entirely sure he agreed—but that was mainly because he was still feeling the burrito he had for lunch crawling back up his throat from watching Spider-Man twist and turn and jump. "Yeah, okay, whatever. But if Garcia asks what he's doing here, I was in the bathroom when he came in."

"Why don't you go to the restroom now, Jack—see if Wheeler's run-sheet's in the urinal?"

Letting out a long breath, Larsen said, "I'll find it, Joll, I'll find it."

"See that you do, Sergeant, because if the inspector does get in a kicking mood, I'm gonna make sure that, despite my own gluteus maximus providing a much more inviting target, the only behind his foot finds is yours. Am I perfectly clear in my meaning?"

Nodding, Larsen said, "Yeah, like a glass, Joll."

Una O'Leary hated doing run-sheets.

No, it was more fundamental than that. She hated doing paperwork of any kind. For some reason, when she became a cop she thought that she'd spend all her time chasing bad guys and grilling suspects, and doing all the fun stuff you saw on television. She'd be like the Invisible Woman or the She-Hulk or the Wasp—her role models, really, women who made a difference in the world. Yeah, they had super powers, but O'Leary figured she could make up for it with her training at the police academy.

However, as Carter was happy to carry on about at a loud volume, life wasn't like it was on television, especially if you were a cop. Instead, you had lots and lots of paperwork.

And it got worse when she made detective. She was only a third-grade, and she had tons of the stuff, three times what she had as a uniform, and it would only get worse as she moved up to second- and first-grade.

Assuming I live that long. Assuming Joll doesn't string me up by my short hairs for not getting the run-sheets done. One advantage she had was that she had learned how to touch-type at a young age. Her mother had insisted, as it meant she'd have "a skill you can *use*" when she got older, never imagining for a minute that her little girl would become a police officer. O'Leary had been on the job seven years, and her mother was still trying to wrap her mind around the idea.

In any case, she was up to a hundred-and-fifty words a

minute—which also meant that she was the one who usually got stuck typing up reports and such. But it was worth it not to have to suffer the agony of watching Wheeler hunt and peck with his right index finger. He wouldn't even use his left; drove her crazy.

Right now, the clacking of her keyboard was the only sound in the detectives' squad room. Carter and Barron were out on a call, Johannsen and Ursitti both were on vacation, McAvennie had called in sick, and the rest of this shift's detectives were, like O'Leary, on the Triple X Task Force, and were all following up leads. That left O'Leary alone with her run-sheet.

The squad room took up most of the tiny second floor of the Two-Four. The upper story was really the attic, but a few years ago it was converted to offices for the detectives during a rare instance when the city pro-vided *more* money for the cops instead of less. However, with the pipes running along the already-low ceiling, that left them without much head clearance—really only a problem for Fry, who was six-eight.

"Wow, that's some fast typing."

O'Leary looked up, but didn't see anyone standing by her desk, and she hadn't heard anyone come in.

"Up here."

"Ohmigod. You're Spider-Man," she said as she looked up, but before her conscious mind entirely regis-tered that the hero in question was hanging from one of the pipes.

"Your friendly neighborhood," the hero said jauntily. "I bumped into Sergeant Green outside—he said you were the person to talk to about Triple X."

I don't believe this. Spider-Man's coming to me *for advice. This is so cool!*

Then she came to her senses. *This has to be a joke.*
"Wheeler put you up to this, right? He's still pissed at me
'cause of what happened at the pizzeria. C'mon, who's
that under the mask?"

"Uh, Detective, I'm hanging upside down from a pipe."
Then, suddenly, the costumed figure did a triple forward
flip, landing squarely on his feet in front of her desk. Then
he did a backflip, landing perfectly on O'Leary's guest chair.

Okay, so maybe this really is him.

"So," she said without missing a beat, "you want to
know about Triple X."

"Yup. I've been coming across it lately, and—well, it's
not good. People getting super powers while in a drug-
induced haze isn't exactly a recipe for keeping the peace."

"That would be a big no." She opened one of the
drawers in her desk and pulled out one of the dozens of
files they had on this case. "This is one we pulled yesterday—woman rehearsing a play in the Village, turns into a
harpy and flies through the ceiling."

"Boy, even these off-Broadway plays are getting special effects budgets these days."

O'Leary couldn't help but chuckle. "Yeah. From what
we can tell, the woman's already a druggie—an actor taking drugs; what're the odds, right?—and she graduated to
Triple X."

"'Graduated'?"

Nodding, O'Leary said, "This isn't a beginner's drug.
This is the stuff they go to when they're tired of their
regular high. Every case we got so far has a history."

"And it started around here?"

Again, O'Leary nodded. "Down on Amsterdam in the
90s. Some kid turned all green and got a big head. Started
throwing things with his mind."

It was Spider-Man's turn to nod. "Telekinesis."

"Whatever. All I know is that the kid wrecked the lobby of his apartment building and one of the parking lots across the street from it before he came back down. Docs found weird stuff in his blood—like X, but not really. We only know the name Triple X from some of our CIs."

Spider-Man paused. She wondered if his face changed under the mask, but she couldn't really see it. *God, I love that disguise.* Finally, he said, "Cardiac infarctions?"

"Confidential informants. It's all any of them are talking about." She leaned back in her chair. "The biggest problem is that we don't have a sample of the drug itself. Every victim we've found has swallowed all of what they got." She looked at Spider-Man, who was impossible to read, just sitting there in his full face mask and being enigmatic. "This help you?"

"A little."

"Good. Can you give me anything back?"

Spider-Man seemed to consider it for a second. "I know that this stuff might be coming out of Long Island City."

That surprised O'Leary—she really hadn't expected a positive answer to her question. "Why didn't you say that before?" She riffled through the papers on her desk trying to find a pen, then remembered she'd stuck one in her hair to hold it up. She removed the pen, causing her red tresses to fall sloppily onto her shoulders. "LIC, huh? That means it might be one of the crews in the Bridgeview Houses or the boys at the Robinsfield Houses." She wrote down both names on a Post-it. "Or somebody we don't know."

"I'd lean toward that, honestly," Spider-Man said.

"This stuff has some serious science behind it. Irradiating a drug—especially with just the right amount of gamma radiation to do what this stuff is doing—is not something that just anybody can do."

O'Leary nodded. "Again, no sample, no luck."

"Tell you what—if I find myself facing off against a crazed horde of green druggies, I'll try to get at their stash and send it to you guys."

That surprised O'Leary. "Really?"

"You sound surprised."

And he sounded amused. "Well, you guys aren't known for being all cooperative." She leaned forward, having wanted to have this conversation for *years*. "And you really *should*. God, if we could share information with you guys more often, we could do the job so much better. You guys have access to stuff we can't get near. And people will talk to a super hero who won't come near a cop. Besides, you guys have anonymity, which I think is great, really. Yours is the best—the way that mask covers everything, and the way you stand all hunched over like someone folded your spine in half. How's anyone supposed to ID you? You white, black, Hispanic, Asian, what? Can't tell height, can't tell facial hair, can't tell hair or eye color. Best we can do is weight, and your build looks slightly above average, but that's about it. And I'm babbling again, I'm really sorry—it's just that I've always wanted to meet one of you guys and talk about this stuff."

"That's—that's all right," Spider-Man said slowly. "Look, we'll get a chance to talk again, I promise. Right now, I want to head out and see what else I can find. And I'd definitely check out those places in Queens."

O'Leary snorted. "Yeah, like I can use the word of a

guy in a mask as PC for a search." Inspector Garcia would have her head if he knew she was even talking to a "costume," as he, and several others in the department, called them. If he found out Spider-Man was her probable cause, he'd go ballistic. "Still, I can talk to the One-Oh-Eight, tell them to keep an eye out."

"Great. I'll do likewise." Spider-Man jumped to the floor from his squatting position on the chair.

He didn't move from that position the entire time, and now he doesn't even look like he cramped up. How does he do that?

She threw some papers and Post-it notes around, finally finding her card-holder. "Here's my card—stay in touch, okay? I think if we work together, we got a much better chance of beating this thing."

"I hope you're right, Detective. Thanks!"

After putting the card in a compartment in his belt, he jumped up to the ceiling pipe, crawled along it to the window, opened it, and then leapt out. O'Leary heard the *thwip* of his web-shooters.

She got up, walked past Wheeler, Ursitti, and Petrocelli's desks, and closed the window behind him—it was too chilly to let the late-afternoon air in. Besides, O'Leary liked it warm in here, even if the pipes overdid it sometimes, and since she had the place to herself . . .

I just talked with Spider-Man. And I'll probably talk to him again! This is so cool!

Sighing, she sat back down at her desk, wiggled her mouse to reactivate the screen—which had gone into standby mode while she talked to Spider-Man—and stared dolefully at the run-sheet file. After a moment, she started typing again, determined to get the thing to the sarge and out of her hair ASAP.

Can't wait to tell Shapiro about this . . .

• • •

As he swung amidst the buildings of the condominium complex that took up the space between 97th and 100th Streets on Central Park West, Spider-Man couldn't help but grin under his mask. *A cop who's a super hero groupie. I've now officially seen everything.*

Still, he knew more than he did before he made the trip to the Two-Four, and he'd also given the cops a tip on the source of the Triple X. *Assuming, of course, that Hector's reliable. Only one way to find out.* Mary Jane would be busy all through the evening—VPC was having its roof repaired, but the director had apparently rented a space on Bleecker Street for the night, so they'd be rehearsing late—freeing Spider-Man to investigate the possibilities in the early evening. One of the reasons he'd gone to talk to the cops first was to narrow Hector's intelligence down a bit. Long Island City was, after all, a decent-sized neighborhood, so Spider-Man appreciated Detective O'Leary's giving him a couple of starting points.

Just as he swung out over Central Park West and prepared to shoot a line onto one of the trees in the park itself, his spider-sense tingled a warning. So ingrained had his spider-sense become to the way he functioned that his right arm swung around behind him and his fingers tapped on his web-shooters before he'd even consciously acknowledged that his spider-sense was buzzing. The web-line hit one of the tall apartment buildings that faced the park on the southwest corner of 97th, and acted as a fulcrum to bring Spider-Man around and back over the street instead of into the park.

Landing on another building on Central Park West, closer to 96th, Spider-Man had no trouble identifying the source of the warning.

Four people knocked over one of the ubiquitous hot dog stands that had been selling their wares on Manhattan street corners for longer than Peter Parker had been alive. These four all shared one feature: each of them had skin that was an emerald green.

Triple X strikes again, Spider-Man thought as he shot a web-line to one of the trees that was both across and down the street a bit, then slid down it, taking him toward the quartet.

As he slid, he noted that one of them, a female, was bigger than the others, and currently smashing the hot dog stand to little pieces. A second—also female—was jumping up and down and yelling. A third was male, and had an outsized head, and was yelling something at the fourth one, also male. That last one fired a green ray-beam out of his mouth (which struck Spider-Man as more than a little gross) at the hot dog vendor, who collapsed to the ground even as Spider-Man let go of his web-line to land on the cobblestone-like surface of the Central Park West sidewalk.

"Now, now, boys and girls, just because he put too much sauerkraut on your dog, is that any reason to get crotchety?"

"Spider-Man?" the big-headed one asked.

"See, I just *knew* that hiring a publicist would do me good."

"Your feeble wit indeed identifies you as the wall-crawler," Big-Head said in a mocking tone. "I had hoped to pit my considerable intellect against a worthier foe, but you shall have to suffice. Attack, my minions!"

His spider-sense warning him of danger even as it was being loudly announced by Big-Head, Spider-Man leapt straight up toward a bus stop enclosure, doing a front flip and landing square on top. Meanwhile, the bruiser jumped for the spot where Spider-Man had been standing, just as Ray-Beam Mouth spit out a blast at the same location. Sadly, this meant that the beam hit the bruiser, who grunted her great annoyance.

"I'm sorry," Ray-Beam Mouth said, but that just caused another beam to hit the woman. She stumbled backward, but, unlike the vendor, did not fall.

"Buffoons!" Big-Head cried. "I am beset by buffoons! How many times must I remind you never to speak, Adrian?"

"You know," Spider-Man said, "when you talk like that, you sound just like Stewie from *Family Guy*."

"I'm tired'a this," the other woman said, and she also jumped into the air, and then stayed aloft parallel to Spider-Man's position on top of the kiosk. "I'm takin' you *down,* Spidey-Man." She then thrust out her arms, and green needles shot from her fingers.

Leaping easily out of the way and landing back on the sidewalk behind Ray-Beam Mouth, Spider-Man said in a mock-exasperated tone, "Please, it's *Spider*-Man, or just *Spidey*. Really, don't you people read the papers? Kids today, I swear."

Spider-Man then grabbed Ray-Beam Mouth—or, rather, Adrian—and tossed him gently upward into one of the trees that overhung the park. As Adrian landed in the tangle of branches, Spider-Man shot a web from each wrist-shooter, sealing his mouth shut but leaving his nose free to breathe.

"That's some case of halitosis you got there, pal. This oughta do until you can find some mouthwash."

Then he leapt once again into the air, warned by his spider-sense even as the bruiser came running at him.

"Now, now, stop rushing, you'll all get your turn to be embarrassed by me."

Deprived again of her target, she kept going, crashing into the other woman, who was just coming in for a landing.

"On the other hand," Spider-Man muttered as he held on to a lower branch from the same tree Adrian was now in, "looks like you guys really don't need my help for that."

The one who could fly was now on the ground, dazed. The bruiser—who had yet to utter anything more coherent than a grunt—let out a moan of anguish.

Big-Head looked up at Spider-Man, one of the veins in his massive forehead throbbing. "You find yourself amusing, Spider-Man?"

"Well, I generally don't fly in the face of public opinion."

"You'll be laughing out of the other side of your—"

The rest of Big-Head's sentence was cut off by the webbing on his mouth. Spider-Man found that that was an even better use of webbing than the similar shot on Adrian in the tree.

Another spider-sense buzz prompted Spider-Man to jump off the tree just before the bruiser slammed a fist into it.

Oh no. As he landed on the sidewalk, Spider-Man looked up to see that Adrian had also been knocked loose by the bruiser's blow. Whirling around, Spider-Man spun his web-shooters frantically to form a web cushion for Adrian to fall on. It barely formed in time for him to land on it.

Unfortunately, the time he spent doing that gave the bruiser plenty of time to leap at him, and this time they collided, as the only way Spider-Man could have dodged was to stop making Adrian's web cushion. *I hate this job sometimes,* he thought as he found himself knocked to the ground by a gamma-enhanced crazy person for the second time in two days.

Now, though, he could cut loose. He kicked upward, sending the woman flying into the air and grunting in shock. Spider-Man then leapt to his feet and—hoping like hell that she had a concomitant invulnerability to go with her superstrength—stood under her, preparing to catch her and toss her into the wall that separated the sidewalk from Central Park.

As he did so, he noticed a dimming in his spider-sense. *The danger's passing,* he thought even as he noticed the woman's skin tone becoming less green.

This is gonna hurt. If the woman was reverting to normal, no way he could toss her into a stone wall with his strength—there was a very real chance he'd kill her. So instead he simply caught her and then buckled his knees to help cushion her weight.

Pain sliced through his shoulder as he caught the woman, then wound up dropping her to the sidewalk rather than have her collapse on top of him. True, he didn't want to kill her, but he wasn't going to go out of his way not to hurt her, either.

Not that much hurting would be going on at this point. Just as with Javier, all four of Spider-Man's foes started experiencing convulsions—Adrian's restricted by being tangled in the hastily spun web cushion—and turning back to their natural complexions.

My God, Spider-Man realized, *they're only kids.* These four couldn't have been much over eighteen. Then again, Javier was only fourteen, but Spider-Man knew his history from being his teacher.

Spider-Man focused his concern on the victim. The vendor was lying on the ground, drooling out of the corner of his mouth, and starting to mutter something. The kids could wait—they knew damn well what they were doing when they took the Triple X, and from the sounds of it, Big-Head had made plans relating to it.

People started gathering around. Their murmurs were just audible over the sirens approaching from the north.

"Hey, you see that? Spidey beat up those kids!"

"Nah, man, he be takin' them kids down—they was bustin' up Igor!"

"Spider-Man's the one who beat up Igor. Let's get 'im!"

"*You* get 'im!"

"Them children was whalin' on Igor somethin' fierce. Spider-Man saved us."

I love a mob. The only thing you can count on is that you can't count on them, Spider-Man thought, not for the first time.

Remembering his conversation with Detective O'Leary, Spider-Man went over to the one with the enormous cranium—now normal-sized and -colored—and riffled through the kid's pockets as best he could while the kid was shaking and muttering something that was muffled by the webbing covering his mouth. "Don't worry, kiddo, it'll dissolve in an hour. Hope you're still not doing the shtick when it does—it's bad enough when guys like Dr. Octopus use it, but at least he's *earned* the right to talk like an old movie serial. You, though? Nuh-uh."

Then he hit paydirt: in the kid's front right jeans pocket was a ziplock bag full of some small tabs. They looked like ecstasy tabs, except they were colored green. Spider-Man suspected that was less a by-product of their being irradiated and more a case of food coloring used for marketing purposes.

Two blue-and-white NYPD cars pulled up to the curb, each disgorging two uniformed police officers. All four cops unholstered their weapons. "Hold still, web-head," one of them, a young white man with a nameplate that read CARCETTI, said. Spider-Man also noted the number 24 in gold on both of his collars, as well as those of his four fellows—and, after a glance, on the two vehicles as well.

Holding up his hands, he said, "Easy, Officer, I'm on your side. And you'll want to call in your precinct's Triple X Task Force on this one. Groucho, Chico, Harpo, and Zeppo here just beat up this guy—" He pointed at the vendor, Igor. "—while all green and ferocious. And this—" He held up the ziplock bag. "—is, unless I miss my guess, some actual Triple X." He set the bag down on the sidewalk.

"I said hold still!" Carcetti yelled, but his partner, a Hispanic woman with RODRIGUEZ on her nametag, put her hand on his shoulder.

"Ease off, Mike, he's one of the good guys."

"Like hell—I don't know what happened here, and this guy's a witness."

Spider-Man, not really wanting to stick around, leapt back up into the tree.

"Hey! I'll shoot—"

"What, pigeons?" Rodriguez said. "Let him go."

Calling down from the tree as he shot a web out to another tree, Spider-Man said, "Talk to Detective O'Leary, she'll vouch for me—and tell her I'll call her to-morrow!"

Whatever Carcetti, Rodriguez, or their two comrades

might have had to say in response, Spider-Man did not hear. Sticking around would not have been a good idea, especially with the fickle crowd and Carcetti's itchy trigger finger.

As he swung through the trees like a latter-day Tarzan, Spider-Man mused on his tempestuous history with the NYPD. He'd had good relationships with several cops over the years—among them, Captains George Stacy and Jean DeWolff, both deceased, and more recently a lieutenant named William Lamont—but also plenty of bad ones. Cops, Spider-Man had noted over the years, didn't take kindly to people getting in their way or trying to do their jobs for them or making their job more complicated, and Spider-Man had at various times done all three. By the same token, he also could deal with threats that the cops were simply ill-equipped to handle. Once or twice, representatives of the NYPD even recognized that and he'd cooperated with them. But that was rare— it was far more common for him to be met with Carcetti-style disdain.

Still, he thought as he swung over to the Metropolitan Museum of Art, ran across its roof, and then leapt out over Fifth Avenue, snagging one of the snazzy apartment buildings across the street from the Met, *I'll probably get some good brownie points with O'Leary by giving her those tabs. With luck, their lab can identify it properly, maybe get a clue as to who did this.*

Not that there were a lot of candidates. Top of the list was probably Dr. Bruce Banner—the identity of the Hulk when he wasn't big and green, and the foremost authority on gamma radiation—but Spider-Man couldn't imagine a circumstance under which he would manufacture a designer drug.

Of course, just because I can't imagine it doesn't mean it's untrue. And it wouldn't even make the top fifty list of Crazy Stuff I've Seen Since That Spider Bit Me. So he reluctantly put Banner at the top of the short list of people who had this capability.

Working his way south-southeast through the East Side of Manhattan toward the Queensboro Bridge, a second name came immediately to mind: Otto Octavius, better known as Dr. Octopus. He was a more likely choice than Banner, truly, given not only his credentials in the field of radiation, but also his criminal bent. *Still, drug trafficking isn't Doc Ock's usual MO. And if he was trying to set himself up as a new drug kingpin, he'd be proclaiming it to the world—his ego wouldn't allow anything less. Subtlety ain't his strong suit.* Nonetheless, he was a likely candidate.

Some other names—including some of the faculty at Empire State University under whom Peter Parker had studied as an undergraduate and a grad student—came to mind, and he made a mental note to investigate them. Or, possibly, pass their names on to O'Leary as well. *The cops have better resources for this sort of tracking than I do, and since O'Leary likes me, I might as well take advantage.*

The detective hadn't been wrong when she'd suggested that closer cooperation between him and them wouldn't be a bad thing, for all the reasons she gave. But so many people distrusted Spider-Man both on and off the force that he wasn't sure if that was really practical.

Attaching a web-line to the cable-car station that took passengers to Roosevelt Island, Spider-Man swung around in an arc that took him to the top spire on the Manhattan side of the Queensboro Bridge, which would take him right into the Long Island City section of Queens.

It was still light out, and Spider-Man suspected that, in his bright red-and-blue bodysuit, he'd have an easier time spying around the two housing projects O'Leary suggested at night, but he didn't want to waste any more time. The rampage on Central Park West highlighted how widespread this drug was becoming, and the consequences for it would be dire—not just for the users, who risked radiation poisoning, but for the poor schlubs who got in their way while they were using their super powers in a drug-induced haze.

The Bridgeview Houses were just north of the Queens end of the bridge, so Spider-Man went there first. The red brick buildings extended into the sky, all close to each other, linked on the ground by courtyards that had patches of greenery—bushes and trees—fenced off. Perching on the roof of one building, he saw one gray-uniformed person dolefully picking up litter off the ground with a stick and putting it in a bag slung on his shoulder. Groups of kids and smaller groups of adults wandered around, most of them heading to a particular doorway of a particular building. Nobody looked up at Spider-Man—his spider-sense was quiet—which wasn't a shock.

So how am I supposed to find the dealers in here?

He took a moment to restock his web-shooters with fresh cartridges from his belt, which he hadn't done in a couple of days. He'd gone through a lot of webbing against the four kids, and he wasn't sure how much he'd need once he found the Triple X market.

As he restocked, he paid closer attention to the walking patterns of the people below. He soon realized that several kids were standing alone. Some talked to people as they passed by. *I'm guessing those are the barkers.* Of the ones who stopped to listen to what the barkers had to say, some then went around to a spot Spider-Man couldn't see. He saw a few people playing that barker role, and after about twenty minutes, he noticed that all of them were sending people to an area behind the easternmost of the buildings that made up the Houses.

Staying low on the rooftops, Spider-Man made his way over to that building, leaping across when necessary. Peering over the edge of the south wall, he saw the ones sent by the barkers handing money to a person leaning up against a Dumpster. They were then directed to a staircase that probably led down to the laundry room—or storage, or whatever it was that the Bridgeview Houses kept in their building basements. People were going in there, but Spider-Man didn't see them leave.

There's gotta be another way out of there. He ran over to the other side of the building. The east wall was alongside 21st Street, and Spider-Man doubted that so careful a setup as what they had here would have any business being done on an open street. Obviously the crews dealing the junk were trying their best to avoid surveillance by the police. The offer of drugs, the payment, and the providing of the merchandise took place in three different locations. Each was handled by three different people, the last in a place out of plain sight in the windowless basement of a building. *Very efficient,* Spider-Man thought dolefully.

The west wall was up against another one of the buildings, which left just the north wall.

Sure enough, when he got there, Spider-Man found another staircase just like the one on the south wall, and people were climbing the stairs. He even recognized one of the buyers.

Okay, enough recon. Let's get some confirmation. Spider-Man followed an unsteady-looking man with light brown skin who could have been either black or Hispanic, and who looked like he had neither bathed nor changed his clothes since the Carter administration, as he made his way through the courtyards and then out onto the street. After a few minutes of following him down 21st, Spider-Man realized they were heading toward Queensboro Plaza. He figured that the tangle of overpasses, elevated subway trains, and streets leading to the bridge was an ideal place to lose oneself and have a snort or smoke or whatever in peace.

Spider-Man stayed on the rooftops of the tall industrial buildings that made up most of the area near the bridge, keeping a close eye on his junkie.

His guess had been correct. The junkie found a spot wedged in behind a support beam for the subway tracks. Spider-Man leapt down from one of the buildings to the underside of the inbound tracks, even as an outbound W train was going by on the other side, shaking the support beam a bit and rattling his teeth.

Jumping over to the support beam on the other side, he saw the junkie lean against the beam and slide down into a sitting position. He pulled something out of his pocket and studied it.

Deciding to pull the same trick on the junkie that he pulled on the two sergeants at the 24th Precinct, Spider-Man webbed the underside of the subway track above him and let the line hang down to just over the junkie's head. Spider-Man then slid down to the end of the line, hanging upside down.

"That stuff'll kill you, you know."

The junkie looked up. This close, he looked even

worse than he had from the rooftops. He had thatches of hair on his cheek and neck, sores on his nose that hadn't been cared for, and a bleary look in his eyes that Spider-Man was sure was the result of too many days spent doing what he was about to do.

"You ain't got no face, boy."

Spider-Man almost laughed. "Nah, I got one, I just hide it."

"You must be pretty goddamn ugly then, 'cause I ain't never seen no one who covered up his face like that, 'less it was winter." He frowned. "We didn't hit winter and nobody told me, did we?"

Shaking his head, Spider-Man said, "Nah, it's still spring."

Relieved, the junkie said, "That's good. You got a name, boy?"

"I'm called Spider-Man."

"What kinda name that be?"

Again holding back a laugh, Spider-Man said, "It's what folks call me."

"Well, folks be doin' some right foolishness, you ask me. Now as for me, I got me a proper name. It's Albert."

"Pleasure to meet you, Albert. That Triple X you got there?" Even as Spider-Man asked, he knew it wasn't— this close he could see that it was white, not the trademark green.

"You know, I'm thinkin' you really ain't got no face, 'cause you can't see worth a good goddamn. This look like Triple X to you? If this be Triple X, it be green."

"So it's heroin?"

"When you gonna start making sense? It's blow, son. Heroine's what they call those ladies in the Avengers and the Fantastic Four and those people."

"Okay, then, Albert, say I wanted to get some Triple X."

Albert frowned. "Don't see what good that be doin' you with no mouth or nothin'."

"All right, say *you* wanted some Triple X. Would you get it in the same place?"

Shaking his head, Albert said, "Naw, they don't be havin' that at Bridgeview. If ol' Albert want him some Triple X, he got to be sendin' one of them young'uns over to get it for him. See, they don't like Albert in Robinsfield."

The Robinsfield Houses. "Persona non grata, huh?"

"If that means I can't go there no mo', then yeah, persona no greater. Ray-Ray's boys be throwin' me out on account'a my bein' short two bills last month. Them boys got *no* sense'a respect for a junkie tryin' to make a livin'." Suddenly Albert shot Spider-Man a hopeful look. "You got five bucks?"

That surprised Spider-Man. "Why?"

"When them narcos be askin' Albert for tips, they usually give me five, ten dollars. Uniformed police, too. Now you, you ain't got no face, so I settle for five. And if you *ain't* payin', then I gotta ask you to move along and leave me be."

Spider-Man couldn't bring himself to actually pay Albert. In fact, he was seriously tempted to take Albert's drugs away, and the only thing restraining him was the same thing that kept him from giving Javier detention for mouthing off at him: it would do no good. All he'd be doing was denying an addict his fix, without giving him any viable alternative. That wasn't being a good guy, that was just making a bad problem worse.

Instead, he asked the question that had preyed on his mind since he first started observing the movements inside the Bridgeview Houses. "Albert—why are you doing this?"

"Askin' you for money? Don't you know what kinda world we live in? Don't nothin' cost nothin', you know what I'm sayin'?"

"No, no," Spider-Man said quickly, "I mean why do you do *this*? Why take the—the blow while sitting against a subway support beam?"

Albert snorted. "You got a better idea, you let me know. I ain't got no skills, I ain't got no looks, and I ain't got nothin' else. Oh, I had it once, but that was a long time ago. *Long* time ago. Ain't nothin' left for ol' Albert. I expect to be dyin' sometime soon. Least this way it don't hurt all the damn time. So if you don't mind, ' less you got Mr. Lincoln hidin' in that no-face body of yours, you best be movin' along and leavin' me be."

Spider-Man found he had nothing to say to that. Instead he reached out his left hand and shot out a webline, heading eastward toward the Robinsfield Houses.

6

"Red caps! Red caps! We got red caps, yo!"

"WMD! WMD!"

"Triple X here, Triple X, Triple X."

Hector Diaz walked through the big courtyard at the center of the Robinsfield Houses. The tall buildings formed a square donut around this courtyard, with an archway on the 34th Avenue side to let folks in and out on foot.

The courtyard made it easier for all the slingers to do their business. Hector didn't pay attention to none of the crazy-ass names the slingers came up with. All the names were bullshit—just like commercials on TV, lying so people will buy it. "WMD" tried to make folks think of a weapon of mass destruction like what they heard about on the news, and "red caps" made it sound like it was the good stuff from the old-school times. That was back when Hector's cousin was slingin' for "Bell" Ring, before Bell got caught by them narcos. He was doing his twenty in Ryker's, unless he got him some parole. Meanwhile some fool was trying to make like he had Bell's package by using his old name: "red caps." Only thing the fool's dope had was the same as Bell's product was that it was covered in red.

Hector didn't care. Dope was dope, and that was what

he wanted. Regular dope, not no WMD, not no fake red caps, and sure as hell no Triple X.

Walking up to the guy barking for Triple X—some skinny kid in a white hat whose name Hector didn't remember—he asked, "He around?"

Without saying anything, the kid took a cell phone out of the pocket of his baggy pants, flipped it open, and held down one button. "It's me. Hector's here, wants to talk to the man. A'ight." Closing the phone, he nodded to Hector. "He in B39 today."

Hector nodded back and went over to Tower B. Ray-Ray always moved around where he'd keep the stash—always belonged to someone in his crew who lived in the Houses. It was never Ray-Ray's own place. In fact, thinking on it, Hector didn't even know where Ray-Ray lived.

The elevators in Tower B were busted—again—with three white folks from the city trying to fix it. Hector didn't know why they bothered—just be broken again tomorrow. *Good thing Ray-Ray ain't in 154 like he was last week,* Hector thought. Walkin' fifteen flights of stairs *hurt.* But three flights were cool.

Each floor had nine apartments, and 39 was way the hell on the far side of the hallway. He knocked twice when he got there, pretending not to notice the rat that scurried along the floor. Hector remembered when this place was built—was supposed to be better than the old housing projects, better kept up, and whatever. That's why they called them "Houses." That lasted for about the first year, then it was just back to being the projects, except they don't call it that no more. It was just like the names for the drugs—fancy new name for the same old shit.

Cap opened the door. Taller than the doorway, and all

thin, Cap kept his short dreads hidden under a backwards Yankee hat. Hector heard that he wasn't called Cap because he wore no cap, but because he busted a cap in Big Junior back in the day.

Holding out his hand, Cap said with a big grin, "Hector Diaz in the house! What up, yo?"

Hector grabbed his hand. "Doin' a'ight. He in?"

"Yeah, come on back."

Three guys Hector didn't know were counting money in the living room. Hector knew the dope was in the bedroom, and that door was closed. Ray-Ray was sitting at the kitchen table, talking to some young'un.

"I ain't tellin' you again, boy, if you come up short one more time, Cap's gonna take you *out,* you feel me?"

The boy nodded.

"Get your ass outta here."

Before Ray-Ray had finished talking, the boy was practically out the door. Hector wasn't sure his little feet touched the floor.

Raymond Johnson had been called Ray-Ray for as long as Hector knew him, and that went back to when Hector was in nursery school and Ray-Ray was a third grader. Where Cap was tall and thin, Ray-Ray was short and round, but it was all muscle. Ray-Ray didn't have no neck, and had a goatee that made him look even fiercer. Ray-Ray always wore big-ass sunglasses. Hector knew it scared the young'uns, but still thought it was stupid. Since Hector saw him last, he'd shaved his head.

Ray-Ray had dropped out of high school and taken over Bell Ring's package when Bell got busted last year. Hector figured that the Triple X came from one of Bell's old connections, since Ray-Ray didn't have that kind of weight on his own yet.

"What up, Hector?"

"You heard about Javier?"

"I heard. So?"

"He in the *hospital,* yo."

Speaking more slowly and menacingly, Ray-Ray repeated, "I *heard.* So?"

"We can't be puttin' this stuff out there. I heard he got radiating poison and he might die."

"Yeah, or the fool might catch a bullet tomorrow when he pisses off the wrong person like he *always* do." Ray-Ray stood up from the kitchen table and looked down on Hector. "What you askin' me, Hector?"

Hector shook his head. "I don't know, it's just—this Triple X, it's *bad,* yo."

Ray-Ray grinned. "Bad? You crazy? I got the only package anybody *wants.* That little knucklehead with his 'red caps' that he done stole from Bell, he gonna be *history,* you feel me? Robinsfield'll be *mine,* yo, and I'll be movin' to Bridgeview next, and I'm takin' blocks all over the city. This my *ticket.* And you come runnin' up in here tellin' me it's *bad?* What, that people be droppin' *dead?* Hell, they be droppin' dead anyhow. Gonna happen no matter what, but in the meantime, I'm gonna make me some cash *money.* And look, yo, you wanna be part of it, just say the word." Ray-Ray sat back down. "You smart, Hector—you always been smart, even when you was a young'un, and I could use smart. Blowback, he good at the details, but he ain't got the brainpower, you feel me?"

Hector shook his head. Bernabe Martinez—"Blowback"—was Ray-Ray's second-in-command, but that was mainly because he did everything Ray-Ray told him to, was as tough as anyone, and remembered stuff better than anyone. But he wasn't smart.

It was precisely because Hector had brains that he said, "Nah, man, I can't be doin' that. I start spendin' all my time here, my Moms'll be all up in my face. I shouldn't even be here now, yo, but after what happened with Javier—"

"Don't be worryin' 'bout Javier. Look, I 'preciate you carin' an' all that, but *don't* be, a'ight? It's all cool."

"A'ight," Hector said, even though he didn't really believe it.

"Yo, Cap!" Ray-Ray called out into the living room.

Cap was watching ESPN on the TV. "Yeah?"

"Call De, tell 'im that Hector here get half off whatever he want."

Nodding, Cap pulled out his cell phone.

That surprised Hector. Ray-Ray didn't give discounts. "Thanks."

"Nothin' to it, little man. Like I said, you smart. An' the offer still stands, yo, if you change your mind or your Moms gets off your ass."

"A'ight."

Ray-Ray held out his hand, and Hector clasped it.

But even as Cap opened the door to let him out, he didn't feel no better.

When he got outside, he headed back to the barker who'd called up before—*De, that's his name,* Hector thought, remembering that his first name was DeCurtis.

"Cap says you get half off, yo," De said as soon as Hector walked up. "You want blow, you gotta wait for the re-up. H, we got right on—"

"*Cape!*"

Hector looked up. The voice had come from somewhere above him—probably one of the small terraces where they kept the lookouts. "Five-oh" meant the cops. "Cape" meant a super hero.

Given a choice, Hector preferred the capes. They actually played nice more than the cops, maybe because they didn't have to. Hector knew that lots of folks—himself included—broke the rules 'cause the rules sucked and were a pain all up the ass. But capes didn't have to play by the rules in the first place, they did this 'cause they *wanted* to—so that meant they followed them pretty close. Meant folks didn't get beat as much.

As soon as the word "Cape!" rang out across the courtyard, the barkers all stopped. Two people started running off. Hector saw that they were from one of the new crews. *Fools.* Most slingers knew better than to keep the stash out here like that.

Then Hector saw the red-and-blue figure of Spider-Man swinging down on some kind of rope into the courtyard.

Hector didn't know much about Spider-Man except for his name. Didn't care much, neither.

The cape landed right on the bench next to where De was standing and started crouching. Hector had never seen a cape up this close before. It startled Hector when he started talking, since his face was covered by his mask.

"I hear this is the place to get Triple X," the cape said, his voice muffled by the mask. It was hard to tell, but Hector felt like he was looking right at him.

"We just hangin', yo," De said.

"Right. And that guy on the terrace over there yelled 'Cape!' when I showed up because he was expressing his appreciation, not so you guys could hide the drugs."

"Ain't no drugs, hero-man. We just two citizens havin' us a conversation, which you intrudin' on."

Now Hector knew that Spider-Man was looking at him. "That true, Hector?"

Oh, man. "My name ain't Hector, yo."

"Yeah, sure. I know everything, Hector. I know about Javier Velasquez. I know about Valerie McManus. I know about those kids on the Upper West Side. I know about the radiation poisoning. And I know about Ray-Ray and that he's dealing Triple X."

Hector didn't have no idea who this Valerie lady was. But Spider-Man knew who he was and who Ray-Ray was and that Ray-Ray was dealing in Manhattan now. That scared him. The reason he didn't care nothing about capes was because they didn't care nothing about him. He saw them in the sky a lot, but that wasn't anything either.

"Now, you gonna tell me what I want to know?"

"Sound like you know everything." Hector cursed to himself; he sounded all scared.

De lifted the bottom of his windbreaker, showing the Sig Sauer he had in the band of his pants. "You best be movin' along, hero-man."

"Or what? Kid, I eat punks twice your size for breakfast every morning."

"Yeah?" De didn't look impressed, though Hector'd heard that Spider-Man could take out twenty guys without trying too hard.

"Yeah."

"Well, bring it, bitch. But ain't no drugs here, and ain't no Ray-Ray here, and ain't no Triple X here. You got a problem, then step to me. Otherwise, get yo' red ass outta here 'fore I call the cops an' tell them you trespassin' on city property."

Spider-Man just stared for a second.

"Fine." Then he thrust out one arm. Some kind of gooey rope shot out from his wrist and hit De's gun.

Before De could do anything, the cape yanked his arm back, pulling De's gun out of his pants.

Spider-Man then held the weapon in his right hand and brought his left hand down on the barrel, smashing it.

He threw it to the ground at De's feet. "It's for your own good—you could put an eye out with that thing. Toodle-oo!" Then he jumped straight up toward the wall of Tower D and started running *up* the side of the building. After he got to the roof, Hector lost sight.

"Hey, he done busted my gun, yo!" De sounded like someone'd killed his pet cat or something. "That was my *gun!*"

"So tell Ray-Ray to get you another one," Hector said.

"What, I'm supposed to tell Ray-Ray that some dude in *tights* broke my gun? Are you flippin'?"

"Whatever." Hector turned to walk away. "I'm gone, yo." He wasn't in the mood anymore, even at half off.

First Javier, then Mr. Parker, then Spider-Man. This Triple X is bad. I don't care what Ray-Ray says, I'm staying the hell away from this.

Under any other circumstances, Mary Jane Watson would have simply gone straight from rehearsal to the West 4th Street station to hop a subway home. Or perhaps she would have taken Anne up on her offer to join the rest of the tech crew at the Back Fence to decompress. Dmitri had put them through a brutal rehearsal, made worse by the fact that there were three understudies coming in—not just Mary Jane for Valerie, but Regina for Mary Jane, and the male understudy, Mike Rabinowitz, substituting for Lou, whose broken leg was keeping him off the stage as well.

But circumstances *weren't* different. Mary Jane was worried about Valerie. Nobody had heard from her—she hadn't called anyone, and calls to her cell phone were greeted with a message saying her voice-mail box was full. Valerie worked at a Starbucks on 14th Street, but she had taken this week off in order to gear up for *The Z-Axis* opening, so while nobody there had seen her, that wasn't really indicative of anything. From what Peter had told her, the powers Triple X gave its users were temporary, so Valerie couldn't have stayed a green harpy for long.

Mary Jane had tried calling Valerie's live-in boyfriend, Greg, but he wasn't answering his cell or returning messages, either. He and Valerie never bothered getting a landline installed, since they both had cell phones and could get Internet access via cable modem. Unfortunately, that meant that if Greg left his cell off, he couldn't be reached. Greg was famous for forgetting to turn his phone on, and for not checking his messages on those rare occasions when he did.

So Mary Jane took a brisk walk across Manhattan to Alphabet City, so named for the names of the avenues east of First Avenue that made up the neighborhood: Avenue A, Avenue B, and so forth. Apartments were small and cheap in this area, and many actors had taken up residence here due to both that factor, and its proximity to many of the small theatres where they plied their trade.

I just hope that Valerie's okay and she's just all weirded out because of what happened, Mary Jane thought as she walked up the steps of the crumbling stoop that led into the small apartment building. None of the names on the buzzers matched the names of the tenants, of course, but Mary Jane remembered that they were 4W, and she pushed that button.

A burst of static followed, with the vague hint of a voice under it.

"It's Mary Jane Watson," she said slowly, hoping the other end had better speakers.

The dirty glass door to the building emitted a low buzz, and Mary Jane pushed the door open. As she entered the dark, narrow hallway, she had the usual New Yorker's concern that she misremembered the apartment number and some stranger just let her into the building. Still, it was a common enough occurrence that it didn't really elevate above a concern to a worry.

Local zoning laws stated that any building six stories or higher had to have an elevator. For that reason, there were a lot of five-story apartment buildings in New York, and many were like this one: a corridor no wider than the doorways, a winding staircase wedged into the back of the building to allow access to the higher floors. Mary Jane trudged up the four levels—trying to maintain her footing on stairs that hadn't been swept in months, and trying not to think about the odd smells from the second floor—then went to the door on the west side of the building and knocked.

A muffled voice from behind the steel-and-wood door said, "S'open!"

Mary Jane turned the knob—sure enough, the door was unlocked. She'd been here only a few times before, but the door had always been locked; Valerie had always been paranoid about someone robbing her place. Then she recalled that Greg had been more blasé about it. *Which means that Greg's probably home alone, which doesn't really bode well.*

The door opened to a small living room. A battered old couch was against one wall, opposite a television that was currently tuned to the Discovery Channel. Wearing only a T-shirt and boxer shorts, Greg Halprin sat on that couch amidst several remotes, empty food wrappers and bags, and unopened pieces of mail. His short brown hair was spiked upward in a manner that suggested he hadn't combed it since he'd slept awkwardly on his pillow, and he hadn't shaved anytime recently. Greg was supposed to be an actor, too, but it didn't look like he was in any physical shape to audition. He was also "between jobs," as Valerie had put it.

" 'Ey, MJ, how's it hangin'?" Greg's words were so slurred, Mary Jane could barely distinguish the consonants. "What brings your babelicious face to the humble abode?"

"I was looking for Valerie. She—well, disappeared from rehearsal yesterday."

"Ain't seen her." Greg sounded wholly unconcerned as he looked back at the television. "Dude, can you *believe* all this stuff about dinosaurs? I mean, it's so totally out there, y'know?"

"You haven't seen her in over a day?"

Greg shrugged. "Figured she was out partyin' or somethin'. Wouldn't be the first time."

Mary Jane walked over to Greg and sat down on the vinyl ottoman with the splits along the side that sat randomly placed in the middle of the living room floor. Greg's eyes looked awfully vacant. "Greg, have you guys been doing Triple X?"

Now those vacant eyes lit up. "Is that what that's called? Valerie was talkin' 'bout scorin' some kinda special X. Our guy, he said it'd make her brain work better an' stuff. She thought it'd make her 'member her lines better. But I ain't seen her since then, so I don't know if she did score it." He frowned. "Bitch is probably hoardin' again. She always does that with the good stuff."

"Who's your guy?" Mary Jane asked.

"I dunno, the *guy*. Valerie knows 'im from back when they was in college. He had some weird lady with him. What're you, the cops or somethin'?" He grinned. "Or you tryin' to score, too?" Laughing, he added, "Knew that Ms. Perfect thing was just a thing, right? You're startin' to 'preciate the fine qualities of a good—"

Getting up quickly, Mary Jane said, "I gotta go."

"Naw, c'mon, MJ, stick aroun'. I got some weed 'round here somewhere." He looked on the floor in front of the couch and on the couch itself, rooting around the detritus, but not actually getting up. "Get some MJ for MJ—hey, get it?" He tittered at his own stupid pun.

"Hilarious." Mary Jane had never been all that thrilled with Greg, and now she actively wanted to run screaming for the nearest shower. "Look, if you see Valerie, tell her to call me right away, okay?"

"Fine, whatever." Greg sounded disappointed that Mary Jane didn't stay to get high—with him. "Dude, those dinosaurs really *rocked*."

Mary Jane exited the apartment, closing the door behind her, and walked as fast down the filthy stairs as her legs would carry her.

7

"I'm sorry, Peter, I can't help you. And I must say, I'm disappointed that you're even asking."

Peter Parker squirmed in the guest chair in the Midtown High School principal's office. The chairs were designed to be uncomfortable, something Peter had always ascribed to the principal's wanting to keep any students in here ill at ease. He was learning now that it applied to the employees under the principal's supervision as well. "Mr. Harrington, I wouldn't ask, but I met his mother at the hospital, and—"

"Peter, Peter, Peter." Harrington shook his white-haired head in a manner that made him look for all the world like a grandfather reproving a grandson who didn't know better. "I realize that you're comparatively new to teaching—although you did put in a certain amount of time as a TA at ESU, so I would think you wouldn't fall for these kinds of things."

"I'm not falling for anything," Peter said defensively, "I—"

"They *all* have mothers, Peter. And the ones that don't, have fathers. Some are even lucky enough to have both. And they've *all* got a story, they *all* have extenuating circumstances, but none of it matters."

"It does matter. We're talking about *people,* Mr. Harrington, and—"

"And I'm talking about abstract concepts, is that it?" Again he shook his head. "Peter, this *is* about people—specifically about the people who attend this school. I cannot keep a student enrolled in this school who takes drugs and then inflicts harm upon his fellow students and the employees of this school—including, I might add, you. Now I appreciate that young Mr. Velasquez has a mother. But so do Pablo DeLaVega, Lourdes Escobar, Peter Bain, Ian Chantal, and David King."

Peter frowned. "Who're they?"

"Mr. DeLaVega is the one Mr. Velasquez punched. The other four are the ones Mr. DeLaVega landed on. You say that it's not fair to Mr. Velasquez's mother to saddle her with a son who has been expelled from this school just because of some arbitrary rule in a book somewhere. I counter by pointing out that while people are affected, people also wrote that rulebook, and they were not imbeciles—and also that it's not fair to the parents of Mr. DeLaVega, Ms. Escobar, Mr. Bain, Mr. Chantal, and Mr. King to allow their children to remain in a school that has a shape-changing, rampaging drug addict among their fellow students." Harrington let out a long breath. "I'm not unsympathetic, Peter, but I'm also not going to fall for a sob story I've heard several thousand times before. And I certainly can't change the rules because one woman loves her child and one brand-new science teacher vouches for her. Am I making myself clear?"

In fact, he had made himself clear several sentences earlier, but Peter didn't think it was appropriate to mention that to his boss.

Especially when he's right. Harrington had been very

kind to Peter, and he had hoped to prevail upon that kindness. But Peter found himself unable to argue with anything the principal said. *Not that that'll make talking to Eileen Velasquez any easier.*

He got up from the guest chair. "Thanks, Mr. Harrington. I, ah—I had to give it a shot. I promised Ms. Velasquez, and—"

"I understand," Harrington said, leaving Peter to wonder how often people ever got to finish their sentences when in this office. "And I'm glad to see you taking such an interest in your students—though I would recommend your time be given over to the students who've actually earned it."

"The ones who've earned it aren't always the ones who need it—or the ones who get it," Peter said without thinking. *Ouch.* He would have given anything to take the words back. *Why can't my spider-sense warn me when I'm about to say something stupid?*

To Peter's relief, Harrington took the rebuke sportingly and laughed. "A fair point, Peter. I'll see you tomorrow."

Peter nodded and turned and left the principal's office. His shoulders slumped, he meandered through the empty halls toward the exit. Most of the students had left for the day, with only those involved in extracurricular activities still around, and most of those were in whatever room they performed those activities in.

He had sleepwalked through most of his classes today. After his trip to the drug markets of Long Island City, he had gone on his usual nightly patrol, which involved a dustup with a would-be jewel thief on West 4th Street. It was almost 4 A.M. by the time Peter stumbled in through the apartment window, at which point Mary Jane woke up and told him about her failed attempts to track Valerie down. As a result, he'd taught today on precious little sleep.

He walked down the streets of Forest Hills, the late-afternoon spring sun shining pleasantly on his face, looking for a pay phone. He had a few phone calls to make, and at least one of them needed to be made from a public pay phone, as opposed to a cell phone that was easily traceable to Peter Parker.

Reaching into his sport jacket pocket, he retrieved his cell phone and turned it on. As soon as it acquired a signal, the phone played the theme music from *The Simpsons,* which indicated that Peter had voice mail.

Opening the phone as he continued walking down the street, he called the voice mail to find two messages. The first was an I-love-you from Mary Jane. The second was from Eileen Velasquez, informing him that Javier had recovered from the heart attack, but had lapsed into a coma and Dr. Lee was concerned about whether or not he'd survive. Apparently Peter's theory—that the strain of changing size had put a strain on Javier's heart—was correct.

Peter returned that call but, to his disappointment, got only Eileen's voice mail. "Hi, Ms. Velasquez, it's Peter Parker. Thanks for your message, and I'm really sorry—and, uh, I'm afraid I don't have any better news for you. I talked with Principal Harrington, but he's pretty adamant about there being no exceptions. I'm afraid Javier's no longer a student at Midtown High. I'm, ah, really really sorry. Call me back when you get a chance. Uh, bye."

He hit the END button, then let out a long sigh. *Wish I could've talked to her in person—that's lousy news to have to give in a voice mail message.*

Turning a corner, he saw a bodega that had a pay phone outside it. Better yet, the phone was at least twenty feet from the entrance, which cut down on the likelihood of eavesdroppers. He pulled Detective O'Leary's card out of the belt he wore with his Spider-Man suit under his clothes and the change that had originally been earmarked for laundry. After depositing the coins, he dialed the number. Using his calling card number would have had the same security risks as the cell phone—better to play it safe.

"O'Leary."

"Hi, this is, uh, this is Spider-Man," Peter said, realizing too late how ridiculous it would sound.

"Yeah, sure."

"It really is me—you did say to call when we met yesterday. I told you about Triple X coming from Long Island City, and you told me it started on Amsterdam in the 90s with a telekinetic, and you didn't know what that word meant."

"I did *too* know what it meant!" O'Leary said indignantly. "Whatever—it *is* you, I guess."

"I did say we'd talk further," Peter said. "Wanted to know about that package I left for you guys yesterday afternoon."

"We just got the prelim on that from the lab. Oh, and before I forget, stay away from Officer Carcetti for a while."

"Yeah, I got the feeling he wasn't about to join my fan club," Peter said with a smile.

"Not hardly. Anyhow, we rushed the test, and they knew what they were looking for, so the prelim says it's probably a variant on ecstasy, with a heavy presence of gamma radiation. So much so that the lab techs are all wearing lead aprons when they work with the stuff."

That surprised Peter. "The rad levels are high enough to be toxic?"

"How the hell should I know? Christ, I'm not even sure what you just *said;* that's what we keep the geek squad around for. Unfortunately, we ain't keepin' a lid on this. The *Bugle* had a piece on it today."

That must be Betty's story, Peter thought. "Well, you shouldn't believe everything you read in the papers."

"I don't—it's what the great unwashed out there believe. I swear, this is gonna cause a panic. People are used to the guys like you and the FF—the people who've been around a while. But bring something new in, and everyone gets skittish. And this hits all the press hot buttons: paranormals *and* drugs." She sighed. "There's good news for us, though—they signed off on OT, finally. I guess when it's kids disrupting schools and articles in the *Bugle*, then it's worth paying overtime money for. I hate the bosses sometimes. Oh, and our first gamma-head, the telescoping kid?"

Grinning, Peter said, "That's telekinetic."

"Whatever—he's got radiation poisoning. Docs give him a week at best. And another one—a kid in Queens— just fell into a coma." Peter winced, assuming that to be Javier. O'Leary continued: "Hell, with that news, I'd be wearing a lead apron if I was in the lab, too."

"Yeah. Oh, listen—I think I know where the Triple X is coming from. The Robinsfield Houses."

Somewhat snidely, O'Leary asked, "You willing to come in and sign a sworn statement to that effect?"

Peter didn't answer.

"I'll take your sudden silence for a 'Hell, no.' Which leaves us right where we were yesterday, with Narcotics keeping an eye on Robinsfield like they always do. Problem is, the crews there are good. We can't get up on them without months of surveillance and wiretaps and things, and right now, that's not a priority in the department."

"Not a priority?"

"*Don't* get me started," O'Leary said in a long-suffering voice. "Besides, it doesn't matter. Even if you could sign that statement, it'd be weeks before we'd get anything off it. Unless those boys mess up—and these crews are too good to mess up that bad—there isn't much we can do except bang doors down. And we may do that, but we need better PC than a phone call from you."

Peter was suddenly reminded why he didn't work with the cops more often. He understood their need to follow procedure, but sometimes it really got in the way.

Before he could say anything else, an automated voice asked him to deposit more money for the next three minutes.

"You're on a pay phone?" O'Leary said incredulously after he'd deposited more quarters. "I'd think with the way you move around, you'd have a cell."

"Who says I don't? Cell phones are wonderful things—flexible, mobile, and they tell you the identity of who's calling."

"Ah, okay. Fair enough."

Another question occurred to Peter. "What about those four kids on Central Park West?"

"College kids," O'Leary said dismissively. "Thought it'd be cool to get super powers."

"They should try having them," Peter muttered.

"What's that supposed to mean?"

Regretting the words, Peter quickly said, "Nothing." *I need more sleep—I keep putting my foot in my mouth.*

But the detective wouldn't let it out of her teeth. "Like hell it's 'nothing.' C'mon, spill. Listen, I know Joll signed off on you talking to me, but Shapiro's in charge of this task force, and he'd go nuts if he knew I was talking to you on the phone—and worse, telling you lab results."

Smiling, Peter said, "Shapiro not fond of me, huh?"

"Don't take it personally—he hates all you costumes. Says you're all prima donna glory-hounds with delusions of relevance."

Peter rolled his eyes. It wasn't the first time he'd encountered that particular slur. "Well, as long as it's not personal."

"He's full of it, but he's good police. Anyhow, you got me offtrack—what do you mean 'they should try having them'?"

"Remind me never to be interrogated by you."

O'Leary chuckled. "Hey, I do this for a living."

"Yeah." Peter hesitated. A breeze kicked up, blowing some garbage out of the overfull public trash can at the curb toward him. "Let's just say Shapiro's dead wrong—I *don't* do this for the glory. A casual perusal of the *Daily Bugle* would show just how little glory I get in this business anyhow. No, it's not that."

"Money?"

"I should show you my Visa bill."

"Hey, for all I know you patented that webbing. No, actually, you couldn't have, 'cause then I'd see it all over the place. Come to think on it, why the hell *didn't* you patent it?"

"Long story," Peter said quickly. "The point is—I don't do this 'cause I want to. I do it 'cause I have to."

"Someone put a gun to your head?"

"No—to someone else's. And pulled the trigger, and I

didn't do anything to stop it." Peter's right fist clenched. After all these years, thinking about Uncle Ben—more to the point, thinking about the man who shot Uncle Ben, whom Spider-Man could have stopped if he wasn't being so self-absorbed—still made him feel wretched. And angry.

O'Leary said, "Okay, fine. So you've got an overdeveloped sense of guilt. Jewish or Catholic?" Before Peter could even attempt to answer that, O'Leary said, "What's that?" Her voice was more distant—talking to someone else. "Oh, okay." Her voice went back to normal. "I gotta go—keep in touch, okay?"

"Yeah, sure," Peter said even as a click on the other end indicated that O'Leary had hung up.

Why did I open up that much? Peter thought back over the conversation and realized he'd told the detective more than he'd told a lot of people who knew him only as Spider-Man about his life and his motivations. *I guess that's why they pay her the detective money.*

Peter walked over to the bodega entrance. Right by the door was a blue wire-frame stand that held copies of the *New York Times,* the *Daily Globe,* and the *Daily Bugle.* He grabbed a copy of the latter. While he doubted that Betty had put anything in her article that she didn't tell him yesterday, it didn't hurt to take another look.

As Mary Jane descended the staircase into the VPC lobby, the strains of the Beatles' "Norwegian Wood" hit her ears. She looked down the stairs to see that tonight's musical act had already started. Two men stood on the raised platform near the front door, both with long hair and beards. One (whose hair was red and beard was gray) played a guitar and sang Lennon and McCartney's song, the other (whose hair and beard were both a dark brown) sat and lay down a beat on a pair of bongos wedged between his knees. The crowd for this evening's performance of *Up the Creek Without a Fiddle* was milling about, most not paying attention to the music, which Mary Jane thought was a shame—these two guys weren't bad.

As they ended the song and then segued into "Under the Boardwalk," Mary Jane's cell phone started to ring to the tune of "Cool" from *West Side Story*. Removing her phone from her purse, she saw that the caller ID couldn't identify the caller.

With an apologetic look at the musicians for her disruptive ring tone, she dashed out the front door to the short stoop in front of the building that housed VPC. Opening the phone, she said, "Hello?"

A familiar voice said, "Oh, thank *God* you answered, MJ." It was Valerie. "Greg isn't answering his *goddamn* phone, and my sister's still in Michigan, and I didn't know *who* else to call, and—"

"Valerie, where are you?"

"What?" Valerie seemed confused by the question. "Oh, I'm at that homeless shelter on 39th and 10th—they *finally* let me use the pay phone, since I lost my cell. A shelter, can you believe that? The people here just smell *awful.*"

"How'd you get there?" Mary Jane asked, immediately heading down the stairs to the street and looking for a cab.

"I have *no* idea. I didn't even realize it was Friday until one of the volunteers told me. Look, I hate to ask you this, but I need you to come down here—and could you bring me some clothes?"

Mary Jane lowered her hand at that, waving off the free cab that was coming down MacDougal Street. "Clothes?"

"I don't know what happened, but I'm still in costume, and it's all ripped—Linnea's gonna have a cow. It's weird, it's like I was attacked or something, but I'm not bruised or cut or *anything*. MJ, I don't know what the hell *happened*."

Mary Jane walked down MacDougal toward a clothing emporium of a type common in the Village. She'd pick up something cheap and simple for Valerie to change into. "We'll talk when I get there, okay?"

"Is Dmitri pissed?"

Trying to sound jovial, Mary Jane said, "He's awake, so of *course* he is. Look, don't worry about it right now, okay? We'll talk when I get there."

"Thanks, MJ, you're a *goddess*."

Feeling several kinds of awful, Mary Jane closed her phone and put it back in her purse. She couldn't bring herself to tell Valerie the whole story over the phone—that she had turned into a green harpy, or that she had been replaced in *The Z-Axis*. Or, for that matter, that she was wanted for "questioning" by the police.

She picked up a cheap blouse, a pair of jeans that she was pretty sure would fit Valerie's slim legs and all-but-nonexistent hips, and a pair of crappy-looking moccasins, in case her shoes were trashed. Mary Jane had forgotten to ask, but the footwear was cheap and she couldn't call her back.

Once the purchases were made and placed in a bright red shopping bag with the store logo on both sides, Mary Jane hailed a cab and told it to take her to 39th and 10th. Then she flipped open her phone and called Peter.

"Good timing," he said when he answered. "I was just about to head out to do a little patrolling."

Mary Jane smiled, imagining him standing by the window in his Spider-Man suit, except without the mask on, allowing her to see his sweet face. There had been many times over the years when she hated that Peter was also Spider-Man, but ultimately she always came back to one simple fact: the qualities that made him Spider-Man were the same qualities she loved most about him. He'd tried to stop being Spider-Man on several occasions, both before and after they got married, and it never took. She knew now that it never would—and, more to the point, never *should*. If he were to stop being Spider-Man, he would stop being the man she fell in love with.

"You'll never guess who I heard from, Tiger."

"Ed McMahon, telling you you've won a major sweepstakes?"

Chuckling, she said, "No."

"The Avengers, accepting your application to become their spokesmodel?"

"Uh, no."

"Then I'm stumped."

"Valerie called—from a homeless shelter." She filled Peter in quickly. "My guess is that she came down off the high and someone from the shelter found her lying on the ground, convulsing, with her clothes ripped to pieces."

"Or a cop found her," Peter said. "Either way, she sounds like she's in better shape than some of the other gamma-heads."

"Gamma-whats?"

Letting out a bark of laughter, Peter said, "That's what Detective O'Leary was calling them. Guess it stuck."

Peter then told her about his conversation with the detective.

"I don't know," she said when he was done. "Sharing confidences with another woman—should I be worried?"

"She's a redhead, too."

"I know, I met her back at VPC when Valerie went harpy." Mary Jane chuckled again. God, it felt so good to talk to him. "It's a good thing I trust you, Tiger."

"Believe me, MJ, you have absolutely *nothing* to worry about."

"I love it when you're sincere. You're so *good* at it."

Peter's smile was almost audible as he said, "Years of practice."

Growing serious, Mary Jane said, "Look, Peter—don't tell O'Leary about Valerie, okay? I'll try to get her to talk to them on her own, but if not, I don't want Shapiro and his goons hassling her."

There was a long pause. "Okay, but if she doesn't go on her own, all bets are off."

"Fair enough."

"Look, I gotta go beat up some bad guys—and try to stop any more rampages by green-skinned addicts."

Mary Jane smiled encouragingly, even though the expression was lost over the phone. "Go get the gamma-heads, Tiger. I'll keep you posted about Valerie."

"Great. Love you."

"Love you, too."

As she closed the phone and put it away, Mary Jane wondered why she was being so protective of Valerie. *Maybe because I'd probably be her right now if it weren't for Peter.* She had been the original party girl when Peter first met her in college, but she had also stayed pretty clean, on the theory that modeling and acting required her body to be in pristine shape. On top of that, she and Peter had both lived through their mutual friend Harry Osborn's travails with substance abuse, which was enough to cure any sensible person of wanting to get hooked.

But she also lived the life, and she saw what everyone around her was doing. There were times when it was sorely tempting to join in the drinking, the snorting, the ingesting that everyone around her was enjoying.

Still, Peter was right—Valerie did need to talk to Shapiro and O'Leary and the others.

The cab pulled up in front of the shelter. Mary Jane paid the fare plus what she hoped was about a fifteen per-cent tip—she was never all that great at doing that kind of math on the fly—and then went in through the glass doors to the tall white building.

Her nose wrinkled as soon as she entered the waiting room. *There must be a dozen air fresheners in here,* she thought. The cloying artificial scents permeated the air; Mary Jane could almost taste them. *Then again, given the clientele, this smell is probably better than the alternative.*

A large Hispanic woman dressed in a sweatshirt and jeans was walking a short man wearing a winter coat and no shoes toward one door. The door buzzed and the woman pushed it open. Once they were gone, Mary Jane was alone in the reception area. A black woman was sit-ting behind a glass window—probably bulletproof—with a speaker's hole in the center and a tray in the bottom, reminiscent of teller windows at banks.

"Excuse me," Mary Jane said as she approached the window and placed the shopping bag on the floor next to her, "I'm here to collect Valerie McManus—blond, skinny, about five-four, five-five, wearing ripped clothes that look like Russian peasant wear."

The woman looked suspiciously at Mary Jane. "Just a second." She picked up the phone and dialed a four-digit number. "We got someone to see that skinny blond girl who came in yesterday. Yeah, she's a redhead. Bag'a clothes, too. Yeah, okay." She hung up. "Go on back."

Mary Jane nodded, picked up the bag, said "Thank you," and went to the door the other woman had gone through. It buzzed as she got near, and she pushed through it.

A small brunette waited for her on the other side. Mary Jane didn't think she looked old enough to be let out on her own.

"Hi, I'm Aimee. You must be Mary Jane?"

"Yes, I'm Valerie's friend."

"It's really good to see you, Mary Jane. I was kinda worried that, well, like, that you weren't, y'know, *real*."

Mary Jane couldn't help but laugh. "You thought Valerie was crazy?"

"Not really, but you never know. So many people come in here with all kinds of notions. When people lose their homes—"

"Well, Valerie didn't. She lives on Avenue C. She just had—well, something happened."

Aimee led Mary Jane back to the place where they kept the beds. There were more fresheners in the air, but now they didn't even put a dent in the problem. Mary Jane saw dozens of people of all races and both genders, with clothes in various forms of disarray.

The one thing they had in common was a lack of hygiene that was inevitable, given their circumstances.

"Oh, thank *God*."

Mary Jane looked over to see Valerie getting up off one of the pallets.

"Now do you believe me, you little *bitch*?" Valerie snarled at Aimee. "I *told* you I didn't belong here!"

Completely unperturbed by the abuse—Mary Jane supposed it was a regular thing around here—Aimee looked at Mary Jane and said, "Thanks very much for your help, Mary Jane. If you need anything, Carmen up front can find me."

"Thanks, Aimee."

As soon as Aimee turned to leave, Valerie muttered, "*God,* what a ditz. I so *hate* earnest little—" She shook her head. "Never *mind,* I just need to get out of these *clothes.* Can you believe this place?"

Mary Jane didn't say anything.

"C'mon, there's a bathroom back here."

If anything, the large bathroom smelled worse than the room they'd just left. Mary Jane immediately gagged, reflexively covering her nostrils with the sleeve of her denim jacket. She could feel her eyes watering. Seemingly unaffected by the stench—or so desperate to change clothes that she didn't care—Valerie eagerly took the red shopping bag and went into one of the stalls.

"So, MJ, can you *please* tell me what the hell happened?"

Mary Jane paused, and then said through her sleeve, "Look, Val—I know you're doing drugs."

"*Duh,* MJ, you were at Philo's party with me. I was the one trying to get you to—"

"I know you're doing Triple X, Val."

Silence. Then: "What're you talking about?"

"Val—"

"I don't even know what that *is.* Okay, look, Tuesday

night, Zeke and some lady came over with some X that was all green, and he said it'd make me know my lines better, but—"

Remembering what Peter had told her about the tabs he found on the kids on the Upper West Side, Mary Jane said, "Val, that's a new drug. It's called Triple X and it doesn't just get you high, it changes you temporarily. Wednesday night, as God, Lou, Dmitri, and the rest of the cast and crew are my witness, your skin turned green, wings grew out of your back—which is why your costume got ripped—and you flew out *through the ceiling* of the playhouse."

Valerie opened the stall door, now wearing the clothes Mary Jane had purchased. For a moment, Mary Jane allowed herself to feel pride at having guessed Valerie's blouse, pants, and shoe sizes properly.

"MJ, that's the stupidest goddamn thing I ever heard!"

"Val—"

Shaking her head and holding up a hand, Valerie said, "No, no, *screw* you, MJ. You just want the lead, right?"

Mary Jane felt her mind boggle. "What?"

"You made up some stupid-ass story so you could be Olga. Well, fine, I'm sure it worked." She thrust the red bag, which now had her old clothes in it, at Mary Jane and said with no sincerity whatsoever, "Thanks for the clothes. I'm going home."

As soon as Mary Jane's hand wrapped around the shopping bag handles, Valerie stormed out of the bathroom. "Val!" Gritting her teeth, Mary Jane went after her.

Valerie ignored Mary Jane's imploring her to stop as she made a beeline for the door that led to the lobby. It did not require someone to buzz it to let someone else out, only to come in, a design flaw that Mary Jane was not especially thrilled with.

"Val, will you wait a second, please?" Mary Jane yelled across the lobby as she followed Valerie to the glass door that led to the street.

Her husband had always joked about the "Parker luck," and how it was all bad, and it seemed that today being married to a Parker was enough for Mary Jane to have it as well—as soon as Valerie stepped outside, a free cab pulled up. She got into it without another word. *Probably going home to Greg,* Mary Jane thought with a sigh, *and to a nice buzz to take the edge off losing the part.* Naturally, all the other cabs in sight were occupied.

Had Valerie given her the chance, Mary Jane would've explained that she had never *wanted* the part of Olga, and that she certainly wouldn't make up a story like that. But Valerie wasn't being particularly rational on the subject—not that Mary Jane could blame her.

I didn't even get to tell her that the police want to talk to her.

She sighed and went back in. Aimee was in the lobby, a concerned expression on her face. "Is everything okay?"

"Yeah," Mary Jane said quickly, not wanting to drag her into this particular nightmare. She handed over the red shopping bag. "It's not much, but maybe it'll help someone here."

Aimee went back to her smile. "I'm sure it will do somebody some good. Thanks *very* much, Mary Jane. Have you ever considered volunteering?"

"I'm afraid I don't have the time right now." The words came out almost by rote. It was impossible to do everything kind and noble that she wanted to, and like so many others who didn't have enough hours in the day for what they *had* to do, much less wanted to, she had the stock answer perpetually on the tip of her tongue for when she was asked such questions.

Aimee didn't seem even a little put out. "That's fine. Thanks again!"

Mary Jane went back outside, opened her cell phone, and redialed Peter's number while heading eastward on 39th toward Times Square and the subway home.

Unsurprisingly, she got Peter's voice mail without a ring. He generally turned off the phone while patrolling. Shortly after first obtaining the cell phone, he'd had it on while in the midst of a fight with the Shocker. The ringing that emanated from his belt distracted him for just half a second, which was enough to keep him from ducking one of the Shocker's trademark electrical blasts.

"Hi, this is Peter Parker's cell phone. You've gotten this message because I've either turned the phone off, am on another line, or recognized your number on caller ID and don't want to talk to you right now, so there, nyah nyah. Leave a message after the beep and I'll get back to you as soon as I feel like it."

After the beep, Mary Jane said, "Bad news, Peter—Valerie not only denies that she turned into a harpy, she denies that she took Triple X. She thought it was regular X that was just colored green. She stormed out and went home, I guess, so, uh—I'd keep an eye out for harpies menacing Alphabet City in the next few days." She let out a breath. "I feel like I came all this way for nothing. I'll see you at home, Tiger. Love you!"

She closed the phone and continued down 39th, hoping that Valerie would be okay.

8

It only took a couple days to get them Russian boys off the stretch of Amsterdam.

Bernabe "Blowback" Martinez, Ray-Ray's second-in-command, had taken charge of the operation. Ray-Ray told his people to check out the major corners and projects and see who was hurting 'cause they didn't have no Triple X, then start moving their asses in.

Technically, them boys on Amsterdam weren't Russian, they was as black as Ray-Ray or as Hispanic as Blowback, but that's 'cause, on this part of Amsterdam, white boys didn't really blend. Only white folks you saw here were either buyers comin' farther uptown to score the good stuff, or cops.

Nobody wanted blow or crack or X or weed now. They just wanted Triple X, and Ray-Ray had the package. You got the package, you got the real estate, and now a block that was all Russians a week back was now all Ray-Ray all the goddamn time. *Supply and demand, baby,* Blowback thought with a smile that flicked the toothpick he always kept in his mouth upward, *supply and goddamn demand. Yeah.*

It was the slow part of Saturday—late morning, when the early risers, or them that ain't gone to bed yet, were done buying and the afternoon crowd ain't woke yet—so two of Blowback's slingers were on one of the stoops, waiting for the clientele. Sweet, who was tall and skinny and wearing a do-rag on his dome and a Yankees shirt with Derek Jeter's name and number on the back, was trying to get Lemonhead, a short round kid with a head that he kept shaved, to come up with somebody who could beat the Hulk.

Running his hands over his dome the way he always did when he thought—which meant, far as Blowback was concerned, he didn't do it near regular enough—Lemonhead finally said, "Iron Man."

"No *way,*" Sweet said, looking at Lemonhead like he was all nuts. "He just some guy in a suit. Hulk'll take that armor and crack it open, *pow!* Then Iron Man ain't shit."

"All right then, the Thing."

"Nah."

"What you mean 'nah,' you ever *see* the Thing? He big as shit, and all rocky, yo!"

"Nah, man, ain't gonna happen."

Lemonhead stood up all pissed off. "What you talkin' about? The Thing can kick his ass."

"Yeah, but the Thing ain't got that mean streak, yo. That's the edge. Maybe an even match, no problem, but Hulk's got that bad-ass temper." Sweet shook his head. "Try someone else."

Lemonhead climbed up onto the stoop's arm and sat up there so he could look down at Sweet. "You just gonna make shit up so you win."

"Am not, but you ain't comin' up with nobody that could do the job."

Blowback was about to chime in when he saw something.

Coming down Amsterdam was a big car that was slowing down as it got closer to them, even though it was still most of a block away from a traffic light that was still green. At first Blowback figured it was a customer.

Then he saw the gun muzzle.

"Get yo' ass *down!*" he shouted even as he ducked behind the stoop.

He saw one of the guns fire before he got out of sight, then he heard at least ten shots get thrown. A second later, the car was driving *mad* fast down Amsterdam, turning at the light with its tires screeching and heading off with serious speed. Only thing Blowback saw was that all three dudes in the car was white folks.

Goddamn Russians. Gotta be. Blowback hadn't even had time to get his Sig Sauer out. He stood up and looked over to see that Sweet and Lemonhead both had caught at least three bullets each. Sweet got one in the leg and two in the chest, both of them right on the interlocking NY of the Yankees logo on his shirt, which meant a heart shot; two of Lem's bullets were in the face, with the other one in his arm. Neither of them'd be slingin' no more. *And I gotta be tellin' Cutty that his little brother caught a bullet. Damn.*

Across the street, Blowback saw some citizen on a cell phone lookin' like he'd peed in his goddamn pants. *Probably callin' 911, which means I gotta get my narrow ass outta here.* He ran around to the other side of the stoop and removed the big brick that was hiding the stash—no sense in letting the cops take their product.

Blowback's ride was four blocks down the street—nearest goddamn parking space—so he ran that way after shoving the bags in his jacket and pants pockets. He had to tell Ray-Ray *now,* which meant heading back to

Robinsfield. Ray-Ray didn't talk on the phone—cops got wiretaps all the time, and Ray-Ray wasn't taking no chances—and Blowback wasn't about to do this through one of those knuckleheads he had in the Houses. Nah, he had to tell him in person that Sweet and Lem was dead and them Russians was starting a goddamn war.

Janna didn't even know what club they were *in*.

Laura and Terri had dragged her out of the dorm practically kicking and screaming. "It's Saturday night," they said. "You need to get out," they said. "Have some fun once in a while," they said.

Okay, it was true she hadn't been going out much since she broke up with Steve, and yeah, she was mopey because Steve started dating that skank Katie Turner within, like, five *minutes* of her breaking up with him.

But she really didn't want to be here. Sure, Terri and Laura loved coming to these places because they were ohmygod *so* hip, but as far as Janna was concerned, they were just *incredibly* loud, *way* overcrowded, *much* too dark, and were playing music that Janna thought sucked. They called it "dance music," which Janna just didn't get, since she never wanted to dance to it. *Play some Red Hot Chili Peppers or Queen or Led Zeppelin if you want me to dance, not this techno crap.*

She had every intention of telling Laura and Terri this, but it was so *loud* in here that she couldn't make herself be heard without shouting at the top of her lungs, and she just didn't *feel* like it.

So she sat on the curved couch that the three of them had taken over in one corner of the club. And she drank. The drinks weren't even any good. The only tequila they had was José Cuervo, which was the tequila equivalent of drinking Budweiser. Decent enough if that was all that was available, but not something anybody who appreciated the drink would go near.

More than anything, Janna wanted to go back to the dorm, open her own private stash of Patrón Añejo tequila, and come up with ways of murdering Steve with a fork.

She had gotten up to dance a few times, which involved barely moving while being pressed on all sides by sweaty, icky people. If Janna wanted to do *that,* she'd ride the 4 train at rush hour. She couldn't believe that she had to stand on line and pay a cover charge for the same experience here. When Terri or Laura got up to dance— they never all went up together for fear of losing their couch—they had each made sexy dancing gestures in the vicinity of two guys, but nothing came of it. *Thank God.*

Laura came back from her latest dance and then went to the bathroom. Terri leaned over and said, "Isn't this *great*?" Janna only knew she said that because she read her lips.

"No," Janna said honestly.

Terri scootched over right next to her so she could be heard more clearly. "You're not having fun?"

"Hel-*lo*? I've been, like, totally miserable since we *got* here!"

Looking crestfallen, Terri said, "But we were doing this so you'd have *fun*!"

Before Janna could answer that, Laura came back, holding a bag. She said something, but Janna couldn't make it out.

"What?" Janna prompted.

Laura sat down on the other side of Janna from Terri and held out the clear plastic bag. Inside were three ecstasy tabs, only green. "I said I scored this from a girl in the ladies' room. Triple X, baby!"

Janna wondered how, after the cover charge and the drinks, Laura had any money to pay for this stuff. "What's it do, make you wanna be in a porno movie?"

Terri laughed. Laura said, "The girl said it was twice as fast and twice as good as regular X."

At this point, Janna was willing to do *anything* that might at least have a chance of making this night not suck, so she eagerly took the tab. Terri took one, and Laura dropped one into her vodka tonic.

I think Laura got robbed, was Janna's first thought after taking it and waiting several seconds. She found that it just increased her bad mood because she had grabbed onto the concept of a buzz like a drowning person grabbing onto a life preserver and it just wasn't coming and it was driving her nuts and why couldn't anything go right and wow the lights in here are so incredibly bright and shiny and loud and pretty and her fingers started to tingle a little bit and suddenly she wasn't so much sitting in the chair as she was floating in the air above everyone and God she felt so incredibly good and this was the greatest thing she'd ever experienced in her whole entire life and nothing mattered whether it was stupid Steve or skanky Katie or anybody else because everything was just wonderful and the floor was so far away it was like she was flying through the air and maybe she really was since she was really really close to the strobe lights and her fingers were even tinglier and look at that something came out of her fingers like a laser beam only green and now everyone was screaming and why was Terri all big and muscular and green all out of nowhere and Laura was nowhere to be seen though there was a green blur in the room and why was everyone screaming and running all over the place all of a sudden weren't they all having a great time like Janna was?

Janna decided to ignore the shouting, ignore the screaming, ignore Terri ripping the bar up off the ground, ignore the green blur that looked a lot like Laura knocking things and people over, ignore *all that,* and just *fly.* Because she could fly, like that cute guy in the Fantastic Four who got on fire, he was a hottie in *every* sense of the word and maybe now that Janna could fly they could go out on a date or something together, he had to be better than Steve, but *anybody* would be better than Steve.

She had to get out of this place. There wasn't room to *fly* in here! So she thrust her tingling fingers out and then there was more green and then a big hole in the wall and Janna was free to fly wherever she wanted . . .

For Spider-Man, the best part of web-swinging was the apogee—that moment at the end of the swing on one web-line before the double-tap on his web-shooters to send out a new line, when he hung in the air unfettered. He'd never gone skydiving, but he wondered if that moment was what it was like for divers in freefall before they opened their chutes: the total freedom from physical attachment to anything, just *being* in midair.

Just at the moment, though, he was in no position to appreciate it as he swung out through the cool evening air over Union Square, his web-line attached to the big bookstore on the north boundary, coming around and landing on a large apartment building on the southeast corner.

Over the course of a Saturday afternoon that he should have been spending doing a lesson plan, or maybe finally grading the pop quiz he'd given a week and a half earlier, not to mention the previous day's test, Spider-Man had been on the lookout for gamma-heads—and finding them. He'd stopped three of them who were harassing families and scaring animals in the Central Park Zoo, another who had gained telepathy with his X high and was using it to force everyone in Madison Square Park to walk out onto Broadway into oncoming traffic, and yet another who came very close to breaking the Bronx-Queens leg of the Triborough Bridge in half. Somewhere in there, he'd taken the time to check out the Robinsfield Houses again, but found nothing useful. *At least I didn't see Hector around, either.*

Each time he'd found something, he'd left a message with Detective O'Leary from a pay phone. This strategy was proving less efficacious than he'd hoped, as he was running out of quarters. *Maybe I should just head up to the Two-Four and hope for the best.*

Before he could do that, though, he had to fulfill a promise to Mary Jane to swing around Alphabet City and make sure that Valerie hadn't gone harpy again. Jumping off the apartment building, he shot out a web-line to the Con Edison building to the east and leapt out over the 14th Street traffic.

The one thing he hadn't been able to devote much thought to, focused as he was on stopping the gamma-heads' assorted rampages, was the party responsible. He had left his theories on one of his messages to O'Leary, but to the best of his knowledge, there was no forward movement beyond that. *Of course, O'Leary hasn't actually returned* my *messages—mostly by virtue of my not leaving a number—so that's not indicative of much of anything.*

He hadn't had time to check out his old ESU professors, though he assumed that to be a dead end in any case. *Still, probably a good idea to eliminate them, if nothing else.* The two most likely candidates remained: Banner and Octavius.

By the time he worked his way over to Tompkins Square Park, though, such thoughts were banished by the buzz of his spider-sense, which enabled him to barely get out of the way of the green-skinned woman with bat-wings flying down toward the park's tree line.

Yup, she's gone harpy again.

Doing a quick forward flip, Spider-Man landed on the park's fence and saw that Valerie—assuming it was her, and not some *other* gamma-head who got turned into a harpy—was heading toward a group of kids, plus one adult, who were kicking a soccer ball around. She was also terrorizing the pigeons, a large group of which flew out of the park in a huff, with the exception of one that Valerie had nabbed in her hands. Spider-Man also noticed that those hands were more like talons now. *Mary Jane didn't mention that. Could be a further mutation from repeated exposure.*

While biochemist Peter Parker was fascinated by the process, the super hero Spider-Man had to deal with more immediate concerns—like those kids, some of whom were now panicking at the sight of a green winged lady with a pigeon in her clutches. Leaping down at Valerie, he said, "Hey, c'mon, you don't want to eat that, you don't know where it's been."

He tackled Valerie head-on, and they both went down and over into a nearby tree—an oak with a crowded tangle of branches that ripped at Spider-Man, making him rethink the efficacy of his plan. On the bright side, she let go of the pigeon, which took off at great speed toward one of the apartment buildings across the street.

Valerie screamed and slashed at Spider-Man's chest. He tried to jump back, but his progress was impeded by the branches of the oak, so the talons sliced through his shirt and scratched his chest.

"Ow! Hey, that hurts! You may want to see your manicurist." He kicked outward as he said that, trying to make it more of a push than a kick. He didn't want to hurt Valerie, just stall her and keep her from hurting anyone, or anything, until she came down off the high.

Unfortunately, all the kick did was clear her of the tree, allowing her to fly off.

Great, there she goes again. At least she's decided not to bother with those kids.

As he extricated himself from the oak and shot out a web-line to a building in order to give chase after Valerie, who was now flying northeast toward the river, a thought occurred to him. *She has wings, idiot. Web the wings.* He'd been going for several days straight, both teaching and heroing, without enough sleep, and it was obviously affecting his ability to think things through.

By the time he caught up to her, she was over 14th Street, heading toward the East River and the FDR Drive. Leaping onto a streetlight, he shot webs upward out of both shooters, waving his wrists in a long-practiced motion that would cause the webbing to wrap around what he hit.

As planned, the webbing snared Valerie's torso and the wings on her back. Screaming, she flailed her arms about even as she started to plummet toward the pavement. Spider-Man then launched himself off the streetlight with sufficient force that the metal rod vibrated with a clang as he pushed off, on a path roughly parallel to the height of the streetlight. If he got his angles right—and after all these years of web-shooting, he rarely screwed up such geometric calculations—he would catch her as she fell.

This would have worked perfectly had Valerie not spoiled the plan by ripping through the webbing with her talons, thus freeing her wings.

The Parker luck is running true to form, I see. Spider-Man shot out a web-line to snag a fire escape on a nearby building, and swung up and around to land on Valerie's back. *Sometimes, you just gotta do it the old-fashioned way.*

What Valerie had in strength she lacked in hard experience—and possibly brains, given that her vocabulary in this state consisted entirely of snarls and grunts. An experienced flier like, say, the Vulture could knock Spider-Man off his back like a bronco disposing of an inexperienced rodeo hand—and in fact had done so several dozen times. But Valerie had never had someone riding on her back, much less one with super strength and the ability to adhere to whatever he held on to, and so she found him impossible to shake.

Not for lack of trying, mostly in terms of bucking and weaving in a manner that would've made someone who didn't spend most of his time on a roller-coaster ride through the rooftops and canyons of Manhattan throw up. He sometimes wondered what would've happened if that spider had bitten an agoraphobe or someone with a weaker stomach than Peter Parker's. For now, though, it meant that no matter what Valerie did—and she did plenty—Spider-Man did not let go.

Then, all of a sudden, they started to descend slowly—heading right toward the FDR Drive's 34th Street entrance ramp. Looking down at Valerie's back, he saw that the wings were shrinking and her neck was growing pale. *She's coming down—in more ways than one.*

Reaching out, Spider-Man shot as much webbing as he could, simultaneously kicking his legs into Valerie's stomach in the hopes that it would force her to lift up a little so they'd overshoot the entrance ramp and land in the gas station beyond it.

Sure enough, it worked, if only for a second, before the wings shrunk away completely and he and Valerie became two dead weights falling through the air carried forward by momentum alone.

By that time, however, Spider-Man had made a handy-dandy web pillow that they both landed on—not softly, but at least it was a superior alternative to the hard pavement.

A customer was pumping gas into her car, and cried, "Jesus!" when they landed.

Spider-Man extricated himself from the web pillow. Valerie—and it was definitely her, for she had reverted to normal—was in no shape to do likewise. Just like Javier and the kids on Central Park West and the other ones he'd dealt with, she was barely conscious and twitchy inside her torn clothing.

He glanced around the gas station for a pay phone, but the only one he saw was dangling loosely off the hook, the earpiece having been broken off. *No luck there.*

Looking over at the woman pumping gas, he asked, "You have a cell phone?"

"Uh yeah—why?"

"Call 911."

"I can't do that!" The woman sounded aghast.

Spider-Man frowned under his mask. "Why not?"

"You crazy? I use a cell phone in the gas station, it'll blow up!"

"That's an urban legend," Spider-Man said with a

sigh. "Don't you watch *MythBusters*? Trust me, it'll be fine."

He then leapt up to the top of the gas station's kiosk, shot out a web-line to one of the tall buildings on the other side of the FDR, and swung westward in search of a working pay phone. Even if the woman didn't call 911, he could still let O'Leary know. But he was down to the last of his change, so he wouldn't be able to do this for much longer.

To his amazement, O'Leary answered her own phone this time. "This is Detective O'Leary."

"Detective, it's Spider-Man, and *please* don't make me go through the same rigamarole again, just trust that it's me, and that we've got another gamma-head at the gas station by the northbound 34th Street entrance to the FDR. There'll probably be a 911 call about it soon."

"Nice job," she said. "I hear you've been all over everywhere today."

"Just doing my bit. I can do one bit better on this one, though—her name's Valerie McManus."

"Valerie McManus?" O'Leary sounded surprised. "Greenwich Village Valerie McManus? Turned into a flying green thing or whatever?"

Spider-Man nodded, though the gesture was lost over the phone. "That's the one." He was about to tell her that she was stronger this time, but the only way he could explain how he knew that was to say that he was married to one of the witnesses to Valerie's first transformation.

"Good. We've had a hell of a time getting ahold of her, and her actor chums were all stonewalling."

That caused a wince, since Spider-Man knew that Mary Jane was one of the stonewallers.

"Listen, can you come up here?"

"I thought Detective Shapiro didn't like 'costumes.'"

"He doesn't—but there are other detectives in this house who feel different. Especially after what's been going on the last couple of days." She let out a long breath. "Look, just get your webbed ass up here, okay?"

"All right, all right." Spider-Man was a bit taken aback by O'Leary's insistence, and wondered what it was she wasn't telling him. "I can be there in about twenty minutes or so—assuming I don't run into any more gamma-heads."

"Or shoot-outs," she muttered.

That took Spider-Man even further aback. "Shoot-outs?"

"Yup. We got us a bona fide drug war on our hands."

Una O'Leary nursed what she figured had to be her thousandth cup of coffee in the past hour as she sat in the coffee room of the 24th Precinct. When Jerry Shapiro had called a meeting of the whole task force, he'd put it in here, since the second shift was now on and using the squad room. Shapiro was standing on one side of the refrigerator, with Fry towering over the other side of the appliance. *It isn't bad enough he has to be taller than everyone else, but he never sits down,* O'Leary thought uncharitably, not in the least because she was the shortest person in the Two-Four's detective squad. Fry's presence at least kept her from being the youngest, as the immense black man was six months younger than she, though his appearance tended to mute any cracks about his age.

Shanahan, by contrast, was always sitting down, complaining about his knees the whole time. The old, fat, bald detective was just six months from being on the job for thirty years, and he was counting the microseconds until that day came so he could "get the hell away from this job and live a real life" with a veteran's pension to live off of. He sat opposite O'Leary at the large table. Between them, and perpendicular to both, was Petrocelli, who was chewing and popping his omnipresent bubble gum.

They were waiting on two people. One was Wheeler, who finally came in holding a ream of paper. Wheeler was tall, young, well-built, and good-looking, which would've been fine if he himself hadn't been so overwhelmingly aware of all four qualities. If she saw Wheeler in a bar, she'd think about talking to him, but five minutes after meeting him, she probably would've been inclined to throw a drink in his face. At least he was good police . . .

The other, known only to O'Leary and Fry, was Spider-Man.

O'Leary had confided in Fry, because she figured he'd be reasonable. Petrocelli had his head too far up Shapiro's ass to do anything Shapiro wouldn't like, and O'Leary neither trusted nor liked Shanahan or Wheeler.

Meanwhile, Wheeler held up his ream. "Just got the faxes in from the One-Oh about that club mess. Two people were killed when they got trampled and a whole lot more were hurt, a few more were injured when one of the girls ripped the bar out of the floor, a few more by the super-fast one who knocked people over, and the last one bruised a bunch with her ray-beams. The girls were ID'd as Laura Silverstein, Terri Bowles, and Janna Gilman, all students at ESU. Silverstein's the one who bought the Triple X, but she didn't know the girl she scored it from—just someone else in the club." Wheeler shrugged.

Shanahan shook his head. "This is outta hand."

"That's why we have a task force, Pat," Petrocelli said. "You wanna contribute somethin' useful, do it, or shut the hell up."

Pointing an accusatory finger at Petrocelli, Shanahan said, "Shut your yap, you little—"

Petrocelli just laughed. "'Shut your yap'? You're Damon Runyon all of a sudden?"

"*Both* of you, shut *up*!" Shapiro didn't raise his voice often, but when he did, the windows shook. The coffee room went silent.

After a moment, Shapiro looked at Fry. "We got anything from any of the other gamma-heads?"

Shaking his head, Fry said, "Nah, most of 'em are unconscious or ain't talkin'."

"We got somethin' else," Petrocelli said. "I talked with Narcotics, and they ID'd the two vics up on Amsterdam from this morning as well as the one who got shot at over on 110th—all three are part of a crew run by a dealer named Ray-Ray, and the one on 110th had a whole lotta bags of Triple X on him, so we're talkin' dealers here, since street yo's like that don't buy in bulk, usually."

O'Leary perked up. "This Ray-Ray work out of Long Island City?"

Petrocelli nodded. "In the Robinsfield Houses."

Looking at Shapiro, O'Leary said, "That matches—"

Before she could finish, Shapiro held up his hands. "*Don't* start that again, Una."

"Spider-Man told me this stuff was coming out of LIC."

"I don't really care, Una, we're not dealin' with no costumes."

O'Leary looked over at Fry. He was about to say

something when Shapiro looked back at Petrocelli. "Anything else off that shooting we can use?"

Again, Petrocelli nodded. "Yeah—the guy I talked to at Narcotics nearly blew a gasket when he realized they were all Ray-Ray's crew. Both blocks that got hit belonged to a buncha Ukrainians for the last year or two. Now we got new crews in both locales and matching shoot-outs. And the witness up on Amsterdam says he saw white guys in the car that threw the shots."

"Yeah, that's probably the Ukrainians," O'Leary said. "Ray-Ray's taking their territory, now they're hitting back."

"Makes sense." Shapiro sighed. "Christ, this is only gonna get worse."

There was a pause. O'Leary gave Fry a significant look, since she knew that if she said anything, it would be dismissed out of hand. Picking it up, Fry turned to Shapiro. "Jerry, I think Una's right—we need to bring the web-head in on this."

Shapiro shot Fry a look—diluted by having to look up so far at the tall detective's face. "What're you, high?"

"Jerry's right," Shanahan said. "We don't need no costumes screwin' us up."

To O'Leary's surprise, it was Wheeler who said, "How's he screwin' us up? Right now, he's the only one containing this. We've got seven incidents involving gamma-heads in the last two days. A bunch of them had people injured and about half a dozen fatalities. You know how many of them ended with *nobody* hurt? Three—the three that Spider-Man's been involved in. He saved those people down at Madison Square Park and in the zoo, and one that just got called in to the One-Seven with some lady in a gas station."

O'Leary smiled. *Looks like I didn't give Wheeler enough credit.* "He called me after that one—Spider-Man did," she amended quickly. "Said that's Valerie McManus, from that theatre downtown."

Shapiro almost snarled. "And that means I'm supposed to let some costume into my house? No way."

"Aw, but I promise I'm housebroken."

O'Leary turned around to see Spider-Man sitting on the wall by the door to the coffee room, his back and feet flat against the wall, his knees bent. Standing in the doorway was the corpulent form of Sergeant Green.

Shapiro stepped forward and looked accusingly at O'Leary. "What the hell's he doing here?"

Before O'Leary could try to defend her decision to invite him, Green spoke up. "*I* let him in, *Detective.* You have a problem with that, *Detective?*"

Transferring his look to the sergeant, Shapiro started to say something, then thought better of it, knowing what Green's reaction would be if he said the wrong thing. "I'm just peachy with it, Joll."

A broad grin spread on Green's round face. "Good. I like 'peachy.' 'Peachy' is good. 'Peachy' means harmony and happiness and, best of all, a task force that can bring a case in, necessitating a nice press conference in which the commissioner sings the praises of the fine detectives of the Two-Four and makes us all look good to the bosses. It is my considered opinion that the presence of this costumed gentleman"—he pointed a pudgy finger at Spider-Man— "will make that happy outcome considerably more likely. It is also the opinion of Detectives O'Leary, Fry, and Wheeler, three detectives that you specifically requested for this detail, leading me to think that maybe you trust their judgment. Am I making myself entirely clear here, *Detective* Shapiro?"

"Yeah." Shapiro looked over at Spider-Man on the wall. "You got something useful to tell us?"

"A couple things. I—"

"Before you do that," Shapiro said, "I just want to say one thing for the record. I don't like you. I don't want you involved in police work." He looked over at Green. "My sergeant says otherwise, so I'm letting you help us out, but I just want you to know up front that I think you're an asshole who hides his face and doesn't deserve to be in the same room with real police."

Spider-Man sounded nonplussed in his reply. "Sorry you feel that way, Detective. But I'm here to help however I can. You don't want me, I'll go back out there and keep those gamma-heads from tearing up the city."

Petrocelli said, "We got Code: Blue for that."

Rolling her eyes, O'Leary said, "The same Code: Blue who had their budget slashed last year? The same Code: Blue whose equipment is breaking down?"

"Detective Shapiro," Green said, "you seem to be having some difficulties focusing your task force."

Shapiro smiled insincerely at the sergeant. "Just a free exchange of ideas, Joll. Keeps the police work fresh."

"Good rationalization," Green said. "Spider-Man, welcome to the Triple X Task Force. That's the task force commander, Detective Jeroen Shapiro. We all call him Jerry, mainly 'cause Jeroen's a sissy name."

Normally that got a smile out of Shapiro, but he was too busy staring daggers at the new arrival.

Green continued. "The landmass to Detective Shapiro's right is Detective Jimmy Fry, who looks down on all of us." Moving over to the sink: "Over there is Detective Ty 'Pretty Boy' Wheeler—I believe the nickname's etymology should be self-evident. Seated at the table are Detectives Lou Petrocelli and Pat Shanahan. And, of course, you know Detective Una O'Leary."

O'Leary smiled at him.

"Pleased to meet you all," Spider-Man said with a nod and sounding much more polite than O'Leary expected. *I guess his momma raised him right.*

"It ain't mutual," Shanahan muttered. "What the hell you gonna tell us we don't already know?"

Spider-Man actually seemed to consider Shanahan's mouthy words. "Well, for starters, I can tell you that this Ray-Ray kid who's dealing the drugs isn't the supplier. I've checked out his HQ, and he's got mostly teenagers working for him. To make ecstasy do what this stuff is doing requires a level of smarts that very few people have."

"We're already looking into that," Shapiro said.

O'Leary snorted.

"Something wrong, Una?" Shapiro asked snidely.

"Not at all, Jerry," O'Leary said quickly. She had suggested looking into it two days ago, but Shapiro kept taking her off it every time she started. To be fair, that was in part because so many gamma-heads were turning up, combined with the sudden drug war, so there were more immediate things for her, and the rest of the task force, to be involved in.

"Most of the users seem to be students," Spider-Man said.

"That don't mean nothin'," Shanahan said. "X is a kids' drug. If you really belonged in this room, you'd know that."

Looking at O'Leary, Spider-Man asked, "He always this cheery?"

"We keep him around for morale," O'Leary deadpanned.

"Good work." Spider-Man gave Shanahan a thumbs-up.

Shanahan gave Spider-Man the finger.

Shapiro looked at his watch. "Christ, it's after midnight. All right, we all need some sleep. Una, keep checking those possibilities on the supplier. Ty, Jimmy," he said to Wheeler and Fry, "keep on the hospitals where the gamma-heads've been taken. Maybe one of 'em'll decide to talk. Lou, Pat," he said to Petrocelli and Shanahan, "do the same for the families of the three shooting vics."

Petrocelli looked at him like he was nuts. "You really think they'll talk?"

"They sure as hell won't if you don't talk to them," Shapiro snapped. He then looked up at Spider-Man. "As for you—do whatever it is you do. You find out anything useful, tell us."

"Unfortunately, I'm running out of change to call you guys—and if you have something for me—"

"Like *that's* gonna happen," Shanahan muttered.

Ignoring him, Spider-Man continued: "—it'd be nice if you could call. Like if you hear about a gamma-head rampage that your guys can't handle."

"You think we can't handle this?" Shanahan asked.

Spider-Man stared at him with his featureless mask. "You ever take on someone who was high on X and could bench-press the Empire State Building, Detective? I have, several times over the past few days."

To O'Leary's amazement, that shut Shanahan up.

Then she rose from her chair. "I got an idea. We can give him Ursitti's phone."

Shapiro frowned at her. "Ain't Ursitti too busy usin' it?"

O'Leary shook her head. "He left it in his desk when he went on vacation so nobody could reach him."

"Figures," Petrocelli muttered.

"Fine, that'll work," Shapiro said.

"Thanks," Spider-Man said to O'Leary.

"No problem."

"All right," Shapiro said, "let's get moving." He looked over at Green. Green just nodded and turned and left the coffee room.

Aside from Shanahan, just Spider-Man and O'Leary were left in the coffee room after a moment, and she was only staying to finish off her coffee before going to Ursitti's desk to retrieve his phone. O'Leary assumed that Shanahan wanted to take his time getting up from the chair.

However, he apparently wanted to fire a few more verbal shots at Spider-Man. "No way I'm callin' this guy on no police phone."

"You have a problem with me, Detective Shanahan?"

"I got lotsa problems with you, but the biggie is that thing on your face."

"What, my mask?"

Shanahan nodded. "Yeah. I don't like somebody who claims to be on this side of the fence who can't stand behind what he does."

"Look, Detective—I really kinda *have* to hide my face. Occupational hazard."

"Bullshit."

"Excuse me?" Spider-Man said.

"Look," O'Leary said, "we're—"

Shanahan ignored her, like usual, instead turning around to look at Spider-Man. "I said 'bullshit.' You *have* to hide your face? That's the biggest load'a crap I ever heard in my life, and I been alive a lot longer than you."

O'Leary found herself jumping to Spider-Man's defense. "If people knew who he was, there would be all kinds of consequences to his family and—"

"Was I talkin' to you, girlie?" Shanahan snapped.

"Hey, watch it," Spider-Man said, a defense that O'Leary appreciated, but didn't really need. That Shanahan was a sexist jerk was hardly a news flash.

Shanahan turned back to Spider-Man. "You think, 'cause you deal with scumbags all the time, that you gotta hide who you are? You wanna know somethin'? I deal with scumbags all the time, too. An' when I arrest one of 'em, I'm wearin' a badge with a number on it that belongs to *me*. An' when I bring 'em back here, I type up a report that has *my* name on it. An' when that scumbag goes into the system, *my* name gets attached to his sheet. An' when it goes to trial, if it goes to trial, then I get on a goddamn witness stand in front of a judge an' a jury an' lawyers an' whoever the hell else is in the courtroom, and I give my name an' address an' testimony that's entered in the public record." He stood up slowly. O'Leary could hear his knees crack. "Ow! Goddammit!" He put one hand to his left knee, then turned back to Spider-Man. "You don't stand behind what you do, then what you do ain't worth shit."

With that, he hobbled out of the coffee room.

O'Leary was almost afraid to look at Spider-Man. "You didn't deserve that."

In a low, bitter tone, Spider-Man said, " 'Deserve' got

nothin' to do with it." He shook his head. "Guess that's part of his job as morale officer. C'mon," he said snidely, "let's get that phone so I can go back out and keep people safe."

"Point taken," O'Leary said, and led him into the squad room.

9

Peter Parker awoke to the smell of bacon.

It was his second-favorite aroma in the world to wake up to. The top spot was, naturally, taken by the smell of his aunt May's wheatcakes, which were about as close to heaven as Peter ever figured himself likely to get in this world.

But bacon did the trick in a pinch.

He climbed out of bed, only then noticing that he was still in the pants of his Spider-Man outfit. He had removed the shirt, mask, gloves, and footwear before collapsing on the bed at whatever ludicrous hour he had come in. After the oh-so-charming meeting at the Two-Four, he'd done another run around Manhattan and Long Island City—and not finding anything, which was something of a surprise for a Saturday night—before coming home to collapse beside his slumbering wife. She woke up long enough to kiss him, then fell back asleep. Mary Jane had long ago grown accustomed to his hours, and she knew that he'd wake her if something really terrible had happened. Since he didn't, she assumed it was a normal night.

Of course, for us, "normal" is a night of me beating up bad guys and risking life and limb. . . .

Padding into the kitchen, he saw a spread of waffles,

bacon, sausage, toast, home fries, coffee, and orange juice, with Mary Jane moving from the stove to the serving plate, holding a pan full of scrambled eggs.

"Wow—you did all this?"

Mary Jane grinned. "Nice try, Tiger. I did the scrambled eggs and the toast. The rest is way beyond my culinary capacity, as you well know, and came from the diner."

"That'll do. I can eat a whole henhouse right now." Peter sat down at the small kitchen table and started wolfing down the eggs. "Mmm, nice and fluffy, the way I like 'em."

"I figured a nice Sunday brunch was the right way to go for both of us after the week we had."

"I didn't get a chance to ask you," Peter said as he chewed. "How'd rehearsal go?"

"Don't talk with your mouth full, Tiger—I *know* May raised you better than that," she said with another grin. "Oh, that reminds me, May called. She said we're welcome to come over for dinner tonight unless, and I quote, 'Peter's trying to stop that awful drug I heard about on the news.'" She sat down and dug into her waffles. "Anyhow, I told her you probably would be, and she said that was fine, and to feel free to stop by for leftovers since she knows you forget to eat."

"That's my aunt." Peter smiled warmly as he popped a slice of bacon into his mouth. *Best thing I ever did was confide in her.* May Parker had only recently found out that her nephew was also Spider-Man, and from Peter's perspective it was like a giant weight had been lifted from his shoulders. Rather than proving too big a shock for the elderly woman to handle—which had been Peter's rationalization for not telling her for so many years—it was instead a huge relief, since she had thought there was something terribly wrong with Peter, the way he kept sneaking around. In retrospect, keeping the secret from her all these years had been horribly selfish and unfair of him, especially since it meant he had to constantly lie to the woman who raised him. Such behavior was unbecoming of someone who tried to live up to the ideal of being a hero. While Peter had good reason to keep his identity secret from the world at large, he had come to understand that deceiving his loved ones was not always such a hot idea.

That train of thought led him to Detective Shanahan's diatribe. "MJ—I went to the 24th Precinct last night."

"Really?" Mary Jane sounded surprised.

"Detective O'Leary asked, and her sergeant signed off on it, even though Shapiro, the head of the task force, didn't like the idea."

"Shapiro's the one I talked to at the theatre," Mary Jane said through a mouthful of waffle. "He's a jerk."

Grinning, Peter said, "Don't talk with your mouth full. Anyhow, one of the detectives, a cranky old jerk named Shanahan, started ripping into me after the meeting broke." He summed up the gist of Shanahan's comments to Mary Jane.

Mary Jane chewed thoughtfully on some sausage when he finished, swallowed it, then finally spoke. "Like you said, he's a jerk."

"Yeah, but let me tell you, he definitely struck a nerve. I can't help but wonder if he's right. I mean, I originally only wore the mask as a way of creating a new identity for myself as a showbiz performer separate from Puny Peter Parker, the Geek Supreme of Midtown High. After that, it just kinda got to be a habit. Maybe I'd've been better off—"

"Stop right there, Peter." Mary Jane was pointing her

fork at him. "I know you've been feeling a little weird about the whole secret identity thing since May found out—hell, since *I* told you that I knew about it all along. But I only have three words to say to you: Green, Goblin, Venom."

Peter shuddered, the home fries turning to ashes in his mouth. Venom was, in many ways, Spider-Man's deadliest foe, in part because he was immune to his spider-sense, in part because he knew Spider-Man and Peter Parker were one and the same. His first encounter with Venom was when the latter showed up at the apartment he and Mary Jane shared shortly after they got married, where he proceeded to terrorize her.

And then there's Osborn . . . The first person to don the costume of the Green Goblin was a lunatic industrialist named Norman Osborn. He learned that Peter was Spider-Man, and his knowledge of that fact led to more hardship and strife than Peter could have imagined. Osborn killed Gwen Stacy, as well as a man who was very much like a brother to Peter. For a time, he made Peter believe Aunt May was dead. Plus there was the abuse he heaped on his own son, and Peter's best friend, Harry, which led to his losing his mind and also taking on the mantle of the Goblin until he died as well.

Spider-Man had made many enemies in his career, but those two were arguably the worst.

"Point very much taken," he said, dolefully scooping some eggs into his mouth. "Still, Shanahan wasn't entirely wrong, either. It's not like these guys don't take risks, too. And they don't have the proportional strength and speed of a spider to protect them."

"That's their choice. And they do actually get *paid* for this."

"Second point taken." Peter sipped his coffee. "I guess he just got me thinking is all."

Before the conversation could continue, the strains of the theme to *Rocky* could suddenly be heard from the bedroom.

"What is *that*?" Mary Jane asked. "You change your ring tone again?"

That jogged Peter's memory. *Ursitti must be a Stallone fan.* "That's my temporary phone." He dashed into the bedroom, saw the name O'LEARY on the display, and flipped it open. "Yo."

"Look, Shapiro doesn't know I'm calling you, so don't tell him, okay?"

"What is it, Detec—"

"We got word from the Two-Eight that some slingers are gathering on 113th Street on one of Ray-Ray's blocks. Nobody's doing anything right now, 'cause it's Sunday morning, but—"

"Sunday morning? What's that got to do with anything?"

Sounding like she was talking to a five-year-old, O'Leary said, "It's *Sunday*. There's always a truce on Sunday morning—*nobody* messes with that."

"Are you serious?"

"No, I risked my task force commander reaming me out *again* for talking to you without cause just to make a joke. Will you just shut the hell up for a minute? It's already a quarter to twelve, and as soon as it hits noon, the truce is off, since most people are back from church by then. You gotta get over there. I don't trust those boys at the Two-Eight to do much of anything, frankly."

The detective put a lot of disdain into that last sentence, making Peter wonder what exactly the officers of the 28th Precinct did to deserve such treatment. *Then again,* he thought, *there's always a level of interdepartmental rivalry and disdain in any profession. No reason for cops to be any different.*

O'Leary continued: "That's why I'm telling *you*. You're there, maybe no bodies."

Peter swallowed. *But no pressure.* "Yeah, okay, I'll get right over."

"Good." She hung up without another word.

Turning around, he saw Mary Jane standing in the doorway. "Your cop phone has a loud volume—I heard the whole thing."

"Yeah, so I better get going." He placed the phone back in his belt and put it on, followed by the shirt.

Mary Jane walked into the bedroom. "You know, I think she has a crush on you."

"MJ, c'mon."

"Seriously, she's definitely hot for you. I think I may have to get a restraining order." She was grinning ear to ear. "At the very least, you may want to read one of those tell-alls that groupies have written—get some idea what you're dealing with."

"She's not a groupie, she's a detective who's putting up with enough garbage from her fellow officers, and who's trying to make my job easier, and that's sounding *way* more defensive than it should, isn't it?"

The grin had fallen a bit, though not entirely. "A little bit, yeah."

"Sorry." He sighed as he put his boots and gloves on. "It's just that she really thinks I can contribute, which is a nice change from the usual. I mean the best I generally get, even from the cops who *like* me, is a yeah-okay-we'll-deal-with-you-'cause-we-gotta attitude. And then there's folks like Shanahan and Shapiro."

Mary Jane kissed him before he could put his mask on. "Don't sweat it, Tiger, I was just teasing. And I think it's good that you've got someone on your side for once. Now get your cute little butt over to 113th before the truce ends." She hesitated. "They really have a Sunday truce?"

"Apparently." Spider-Man pulled the mask over his face. "I love you, MJ."

She dazzled him with her best smile, the one that never once failed to melt his heart. "Love you too, Tiger."

As he leapt out into the sunny Sunday morning air, he realized that he never did find out how Mary Jane's rehearsal went. . . .

Jesus "Save" Martinez couldn't believe that them damn Ukrainians hadn't heard about Sunday morning.

Boris—he had a real name, but Save just called him Boris 'cause he didn't like having to remember no three-syllable name that was all Ds and Vs—was all shocked when Save told him that he had to wait to take out Ray-Ray's boys on 113th until noon.

"You don't be violatin' Sunday mornin'," he'd told Boris down at his crib in that crappy diner in Brooklyn. Save hated going there 'cause it was full of white folks who didn't speak English, but that was the only place Boris would meet, and as long as the Ukrainian dude was payin', Save'd go wherever.

"Why do you care?" Boris had asked with that accent of his that made him sound just like the guy in the *Bullwinkle* cartoon that Save had decided to name him after.

Then Save had finally figured out how to put it so Boris would understand it. "How come you don't order no killin's on no Friday nights?"

"It is the Sabba—Ah!" he had suddenly said, looking like someone shined a damn light on his face. "This is your Christian observance, yes?"

"Damn right. So we ain't shootin' nobody till noon. You violate Sunday mornin', then all hell breaks loose, know what I'm sayin'?"

"Not particularly, but I do not care that much," Boris had said while sipping that weak tea he always drank. "As long as it is done."

Now Save was sitting in the crappy Toyota he used for work—he only used the Lexus when he was taking out one of his ladies—and waiting for it to be noon so he could go around the corner to take out Ray-Ray's slingers and show them boys who they was messing with.

Next to Save, Bee was listening to his iPod. Checking his watch, Save saw that it was 11:58. "Yo," he said to Bee.

Bee was lost in the rhythm of his music.

Save reached across the front seat and ripped the earpiece from his left ear. "I'm *talkin'* to you!"

"What up with you, dog? I'm listenin' to—"

Save didn't want to hear it. "It almost twelve. You know what that mean?"

Bee's eyes went wide, as he looked at something behind Save. "Holy—!"

Whirling around, Save saw a dude carrying a nine-mill pointed right at the back of Save's head, saying, "Truce's over—*ow!*"

That last part was on account of he got kicked in the head by a red blur.

"Start the car, yo, start the *car!*" That was Bee, screaming his fool head off.

Instead, Save took out his own hardware, a Beretta he took off a security guard from a job he did a few years back. He'd been saving it for the right occasion, and he figured this'd be it, since he'd have to dump it when he was done.

Suddenly the blur turned into a man who said, "Hey, didn't your mother tell you it's not polite to point?" Then he did some kind of flip and landed on the hood of the car.

Damn. It was Spider-Man. *Hell with this, Boris don't pay me to deal with no capes.* Now he did turn the car on, but just as he was turning the key, glass came flying all *over* the place, and Save felt like a hundred knives done nicked his face. Then a fist grabbed his Jets jersey and yanked him forward onto the hood.

"Now now," Spider-Man said, "leaving so soon? The party just started. Word to the wise, by the way—if you're casing a joint, do it from a *little* farther away. *I* figured out you were planning to ice Ray-Ray's crew from way the heck up on the rooftops, and our friend who's sleeping on the floor over there"—he pointed to the pavement, but Save couldn't stop staring at Spider-Man's face, which was just *scary*—"figured it out, and I don't think he's much of a candidate for Mensa. And where're *you* going?"

With the hand that wasn't holding Save, Spider-Man shot out a web-line to his left. Save still couldn't look, but he heard the distinctive shouting of Bee, which meant Spider-Man probably got him with his webbing.

"Where was I? Oh yeah, Ray-Ray's people will probably be wondering why they haven't heard any shots yet, soooo . . ."

Save started feeling dizzy, and then he heard shots

being thrown. Spider-Man was leaping in the air, still holding on to Save.

Then a hot pain sliced through his shoulder, and he cursed loudly and repeatedly, realizing that he'd caught a bullet.

"Hey, c'mon, guys, the whole object of the exercise was to *stop* the shooting!" That was Spider-Man again. Save closed his eyes, unable to look, and in a lot of pain from the bullet hit. He heard more shots and the thwipping sound of Spider-Man's webbing, and then sirens.

Now the cops. Should've kept my damn mouth shut about the damn truce.

More pain pounded into his shoulder as he hit the pavement: Spider-Man must've dropped him. He decided to open his eyes.

He saw Spider-Man's feet, the feet of some cops, and voices yelling, "Get *down* on the ground, *now*! Move it, scumbags!"

Save tried to reach for Spider-Man's ankle with his good arm, figuring maybe to trip him up and get away— but *damn* if Spider-Man didn't dance out of the way. "Hey, none of that to the guy who kept you from getting shot in the head."

Save tried to speak, but he couldn't make his mouth move. And his vision was getting all blurry. *And, after all that, they got me anyhow.*

"Yo, web-head," another voice—sounded like a cop— said, "our sergeant says you're on our side for this one."

"I'm on your side for *all* of them, Officer—and this kid's been shot. I'm gonna get him to St. Luke's before he bleeds out."

"Fine, whatever. We got plenty to talk about, don't we, scumbag?"

That was the last thing Save heard before he blacked out.

It had only taken Spider-Man a few minutes to convince the emergency room doctors at St. Luke's to take the guy in the Jets jersey to one of their trauma rooms—he suspected it was more the way the kid was bleeding all over the floor than anything Spider-Man said. *Good thing the costume's mostly red,* he thought dolefully as he stared down at the bloodstains. He was about to turn around and head out—and maybe catch a nap, as whatever energy he'd gotten from MJ's brunch was wearing right off—when a familiar voice spoke.

"Good Lord, they'll let anybody in here."

Whirling around and leaping to the ceiling just in case, Spider-Man saw the tall form of Detective Fry, walking alongside the shorter Detective Wheeler. Fry was wearing the same suit he had worn the night before and hadn't shaved in the interim, whereas Wheeler was clean-shaven and wearing a rather snappy suit.

"Well well well," he said, "if it isn't Big Man and Pretty Boy."

Rolling his eyes, Wheeler said, "I'm gonna kill Joll, I swear."

"Yeah, yeah," Fry said. "What brings you here?"

"There was an attempted shoot-out on 113th. One of the shooters got himself shot, so I brought him here."

Fry asked, "He gonna live?"

Spider-Man shrugged as best he could while crouched on the ceiling. "Probably. He bled a lot, but the bullet only got him in the shoulder."

Looking down triumphantly at Wheeler, Fry said, "You owe me twenty bucks."

Grumpily, Wheeler said, "The kid could die yet."

Confused, Spider-Man asked, "What're you—"

"After Una called you," Fry said, "I bet Ty here that you'd keep anybody from getting killed if you got there before the bullets flew."

Looking at the shorter detective, Spider-Man said, "Your confidence in me is touching."

"Bite me."

"Don't tempt me," Spider-Man muttered.

"Actually," Fry said, "you should probably come with us."

"Oh?"

Fry started walking down the hall. Spider-Man followed by coming out of the crouch and walking upside down along the ceiling, avoiding fluorescent light fixtures as he went. Wheeler trailed a few steps behind, muttering something about how costumes were weird.

"Got a call from the attending. They got another gamma-head—he busted up a fancy restaurant on Columbus—only this is a middle-aged white guy in a suit."

Fry had said that like it should mean something. "So?"

"Like Shanahan said, X is a kids' drug, mostly. Anybody over the age of thirty who takes it is probably a junkie or homeless or something. This guy don't fit the profile. That makes him worth talking to, assuming he's out of his coma."

"Does our middle-aged white guy have a name?"

Before Fry could say anything, Spider-Man experienced a mild buzz of his spider-sense. He resumed the crouching position on the ceiling, which got him out of the path of the gurney that was coming down the corridor behind them at top speed, even as a nurse yelled, "Coming through!"

Fry and Wheeler dashed to the side of the corridor as the gurney went past, navigated by emergency medical technicians, nurses, and doctors toward one of the trauma rooms. One of the EMTs was saying, "GSW to the chest, BP eighty over thirty, pulse—"

The victim's pulse was lost as they went around the corner.

"Never a dull moment," Spider-Man said.

Fry nodded in agreement.

"I don't get that," Wheeler said, shaking his head. "Why do they say 'GSW'?"

"Same reason they say 'BP,'" Fry said. "It's an abbreviation."

"No it ain't. 'GSW' is five syllables; 'gunshot wound' is three. The whole point of the abbreviation's so they can convey the information faster and maybe save the guy's life. Those extra two syllables could make the difference between life and death."

Spider-Man smiled under his mask even as Fry said, "I doubt it."

"How the hell do *you* know? You catch a bullet—sorry, a 'GSW'—right in the heart, your life's down to nanoseconds. I don't want to die 'cause some EMT was too busy pronouncing all three syllables of the letter W."

Looking up at Spider-Man, Fry said, "I begged Jerry—*begged* him—to pair me up with Una. But he stuck her on phones talking to scientists all day, so I got stuck with *him*."

"*You* can bite me too, Jimmy."

"I ain't bendin' over that far. Here it is," Fry said quickly before Wheeler could reply to that. "This is the room where they're keeping the gamma-heads."

"You never told me the guy's name," Spider-Man said

as he skittered over the top of the door frame to enter the room. There were eight beds inside, all occupied. Spider-Man wondered how many other hospitals in the city had devoted entire rooms to victims of this drug.

"Right." Fry reached into his jacket pocket and pulled out his notebook. "It's, a doctor, named—hang on. . . ."

Spider-Man, however, no longer needed the detective's assistance in identifying the latest addition to the ranks of the gamma-heads. He recognized the pale man with the brown hair and matching mustache lying in the bed nearest the door, having first encountered him very shortly after he became Spider-Man. "Kevin Hunt."

Both Fry and Wheeler looked at Spider-Man with surprise. "You know this guy?" the latter asked.

"Yup. Brain specialist, right?"

Fry nodded. "He's working at the ESU Medical Center."

Nodding, Spider-Man said, "Yeah, I'd heard that. When I first met him, he was working at Bliss Private Hospital in Westchester. He was the physician of record when a man was checked in after being caught in an explosion at the U.S. Atomic Research Center." Spider-Man turned to the two detectives. "That patient was Dr. Otto Octavius."

"Oh, great," Fry muttered.

Wheeler asked, "Who the hell is Dr. Otto Octavius?"

"You probably know him better as Dr. Octopus," Spider-Man said. "I know I do."

Hunt was still in a coma, from the looks of it. Spider-Man probably wouldn't have even remembered him if he hadn't appeared on television a while back to discuss Octavius. Specifically, he'd been recanting his initial diagnosis of brain damage—a diagnosis that had always been used as the explanation for Octavius's insanity. However, Hunt was saying, what he'd assumed to be damage might have been the synapses of his brain reordering themselves to accommodate the four new limbs that were now a part of Octavius's body, and ones that didn't follow the muscle-over-joint pattern of virtually every other human limb. Octavius had mental control of his metal arms, even after they were separated from his body, and that would probably have meant changes to his brain chemistry.

Spider-Man remembered that interview mostly because it drove home the very real possibility that Octavius *wasn't* insane—that he was that much of a creep normally.

Fry walked over to the bed. "I ran this guy before coming down here. No priors, no history of drug use—hell, according to what the woman at ESU told me, he doesn't even smoke or drink."

Spider-Man remembered what O'Leary had told him when they first started talking. "This isn't a beginner's drug."

"Right. Like I said, this guy doesn't fit the profile."

Hunt's eyes suddenly fluttered. Spider-Man leapt over the bed to the other side and grabbed the doctor's right hand, since the left one had various tubes and leads in it. "Doc, it's Spider-Man, can you hear me?"

In a very muddled voice, Hunt said, "Spi-Man?"

"Close enough."

"Dunno—wha' happen. Was jus' eatin' brunch like always an' somethin' happen." Then he drifted back to sleep.

Looking up at Fry, Spider-Man asked, "What was the restaurant?"

Checking his notebook, Fry said, "Place called Mark's on Columbus and 83rd."

Turning around, he saw that there was a window in the room—along with seven other patients, most of whom were asleep or staring openly at Spider-Man. He leapt toward it, causing one of those staring patients to bark out an astonished scream. "I'll meet you guys there."

"We already had units canvass the restaurant," Wheeler said. "Nothin' weird there."

Before Spider-Man could respond to that, a weak voice said, "Spider-Man? That you?"

Looking over at the bed closest to the window, Spider-Man saw a face that he hadn't seen in years. A pale, flat face, a nose that had been broken at least once, curly black hair—now receded a bit—and matching thick mustache, this was the face of a man who, among other things, was partly responsible for the death of Betty Brant's brother Bennett, as he'd been working with Dr. Octopus at the time.

"Blackie Gaxton, as I live and breathe."

"You know this guy?" Wheeler asked.

"Yup. Haven't seen him in years, though."

"That's 'cause I'm *clean,*" Gaxton said.

"Sure you are," Wheeler said as he and Fry walked over to Gaxton's bed. "That's why your sheet in Philly's as long as my arm."

"In Philly, yeah," Gaxton said. "After I went up against *this* guy, I went straight, moved to New York. I been workin' as a store manager since then."

Spider-Man had to admit to a certain pride, and a desire that more lowlifes would decide, after facing

Spider-Man, to go straight the way Blackie had. *At least that explains why I haven't heard boo from him since Bennett's murder.*

Fry asked, "So how'd you wind up in the Triple X ward?"

"The what?" Gaxton sounded confused. "Look, all's I know is I got sick, felt something weird on my legs, and then I woke up here."

Spider-Man checked his chart. "You took Triple X, Blackie—it's a new drug that's like X, only with super powers."

"What the hell's X? Oh, wait, ecstasy, that garbage the kids're doing? Jesus, I don't *do* that stuff. Talk to my parole officer, I been *clean.*"

Looking up at the detectives, Spider-Man said, "I believe him."

Wheeler looked at him like he was nuts. "Mind tellin' me why?"

"Why would he lie?"

Fry said, "Using illegal narcotics would qualify as a parole violation."

"Jesus Christ, I'm *clean,*" Gaxton said.

"What if he has been?" Spider-Man asked. "What if somebody fed him—and Hunt—the Triple X?"

Wheeler rolled his eyes. "Gimme a break. Maybe you costumes are big on conspiracies, but in the real world, things ain't that complicated. This hump's a gangster with a sheet who ain't exactly outta the profile."

"I told you, I'm *clean!*"

Ignoring Gaxton, Wheeler pointed back at Hunt's bed. "*That* one's a doctor who sees drugs all the time, and works in a medical research center. For all we know, he *made* the stuff. It ain't any more complicated than that."

"What if it is?" Spider-Man asked.

Before Wheeler could say anything else, Fry asked, "What're you saying?"

"If Blackie here has been clean—"

"I am!"

Looking over at Gaxton, Spider-Man said, "Shut *up*, Blackie, willya?" Turning back to the detectives, he said, "These two guys have one thing in common: Doc Ock. And he's one of the top suspects for creating this drug in the first place. He's got the smarts to create it."

Fry nodded. "And he's enough of a sociopath not to care about distributing it."

Wheeler looked up at his fellow detective in shock. "You're buyin' this, Jimmy?"

"No, but I'm not dismissing it, either. You were the one who said he'd be useful."

"For keeping the gamma-heads in line, not for police work. He's a thug, we're detectives—*we* should be doin' the detecting!"

Fry looked away from his partner. "Say it is Octavius. What's the next step?"

Spider-Man shrugged. "Find him."

"He's got half a dozen warrants out on him already," Wheeler said. "We're already lookin' for him." He shook his head. "This is nuts. Why's it always gotta be costumes with you people?"

"Occupational hazard. Look," Spider-Man said, turning to Wheeler, "I'm gonna head out and do my thug thing by keeping the gamma-heads in line. I'll also press some of my contacts, find out if anybody knows what ol'

Ockie's up to these days. Who knows? Maybe I'm wrong. But it's worth checking out."

"We'll keep in touch," Fry said.

"Speak for yourself," Wheeler muttered.

As Spider-Man opened the window and leapt out it, he heard Gaxton say one last time, "Goddammit, I told you guys, I'm *clean*!"

10

The last person Hector Diaz expected to see in the lobby of his building on Monday morning was Biggie, but there he was, standing in the corner by the mailboxes. As soon as Hector came out of the elevator, Biggie looked up and said, "Yo, Hector, time to be suitin' up."

"Suitin' up for what?" Hector asked as he and Biggie shook hands. *I swear, one of these times, I ain't gonna get my hand back,* he thought as Biggie's massive palm enveloped his.

"You been livin' in a cave, dog? There's a *war* on, yo, and we got to be retaliatin' on them Russians."

Hector was now completely confused. "Biggie, what you talkin' 'bout?" He headed to the dirt-streaked glass door that led to the lobby. Briefly, he wondered how Biggie got in without a key, but he probably just waited until someone came out and then walked in. Happened all the time.

"Ray-Ray been expandin' into the city, hornin' in on some real estate that used to belong to some Russians—till Ray-Ray came in with the product. So them Russians done gone and shot up Sweet and Lemonhead and Jay."

That drew Hector up short. "Sweet's dead?"

"All *three* of 'em, dog. And it's time for some righteous retributatin', know what I'm sayin'?"

Given their relative sizes, Hector figured it was best not to let Biggie know that "retributating" wasn't a real word. He walked down the street toward the bus stop that would take him to school. "So what's the drill?"

"The drill be, get yourself to them Houses soon as you're done with classes."

"Why we waitin' that long?"

" 'Cause them Russians ain't stupid, dog. They got boys workin' for 'em that might be noticin' if everyone in Ray-Ray's crew ain't in school today, you feel me?"

Hector nodded. "A'ight, I be there."

"Good." Biggie offered his hand, and Hector's got swallowed up in it again. "Later, dog."

Biggie stomped off in the other direction. Hector got to the corner just when the bus showed up. He dropped his MetroCard in, pulled it back out, and went to the seat in the back corner. He didn't know nobody on this bus, which was weird, but happened sometimes. Just luck and all.

Sweet's dead. Hector couldn't believe it. Elwood Candelario got the nickname "Sweet" when he was in grammar school with Hector, mostly on account of hating his first name. He was always going on about capes and their different powers, when he wasn't talking about baseball. Hector used to joke that if Sweet ever met Derek Jeter and Captain America on the same day, he'd just die right there 'cause he wouldn't have nothing else to live for.

And now he's dead.

Drugs was one thing. Hector didn't think he'd be able to get through life without drugs, and it didn't make no sense to him that people could buy all the booze and cigarettes they wanted, but couldn't get blow. Hector had seen people drunk and had seen people high. Drunks killed people and shot people and beat people, but when you was high, you was mellow.

But dropping bodies? *That ain't right. People shouldn't be dying.*

And there'd be more if Ray-Ray was talking war. He was starting to think that maybe he wasn't gonna be heading down to no Robinsfield Houses after class. *I ain't ending up like Sweet. No way.*

He arrived at school, said yo to folks he knew, and went to his locker. Martha was just closing her locker when he got there. " 'Sup, Martha. How's Javier doin'?"

Martha just shook her head. "Still in a coma." Then she went off to homeroom.

Hector headed to the bathroom before following her to homeroom. He pushed the big painted metal door open and sauntered in. Nobody else was inside, which suited Hector fine. He didn't want to deal with nobody right now.

Instead of going to a stall or a urinal, though, he walked over to one of the tiny white sinks, dropped his bookbag on the tile floor, and stared at his reflection in the dirty, cracked mirror.

This ain't right.

"Hey, Hector, got a sec?"

Hector turned to see that Mr. Parker had followed him into the bathroom. "What, this gonna be a thing with you now, Mr. Parker?" Then he looked at the teacher more closely. He had bags under his eyes and he was walking slowly, like his legs hurt. "The hell happened to you?"

"Rough weekend," he said quickly. "Listen—I need your help."

"*You* need *my* help?"

"I know you're involved in this, Hector. It's bad enough that people are winding up in the hospital by the dozens—"

"Dozens? What you talkin' 'bout?"

His voice getting harder, Mr. Parker said, "Every hospital in this city has at least three or four people who are sick and dying because of Triple X. Or they've got people who've been beaten, bashed, zapped, or mind-controlled *by* someone on Triple X. And on top of that, you see the papers this morning? There's a drug war on—Spider-Man stopped a major shoot-out on 113th Street yesterday, right before he kept five other gamma-heads from tearing up the town. This is getting out of control, and it has to stop."

Hector had been thinking the same thing, but hearing it come out of some white teacher's mouth made him realize how stupid he'd been. "What, *you* gonna stop it? You makin' me laugh, Mr. Parker."

Mr. Parker shook his head. "Hector, you owe it to—"

"To what? What you askin' me to *do*? Roll over on my people? Ain't happenin', yo. They my *friends*. They *family*. I ain't flippin' them."

"Hector, you don't understand—"

"Oh, and *you're* gonna explain it to me? You makin' me laugh again, Mr. Parker, livin' the good life and trying to tell *me* how it is."

Then Mr. Parker laughed.

"Now *you* think it's funny?"

"I do actually, yeah—you really think *I'm* living 'the good life'?"

"You expect me to believe you ain't? Grew up in your house in the suburbs an' shit." Hector turned his back on the teacher and twisted the handle on the sink. Cold water dribbled from the faucet; Hector shoved his hands under it.

Mr. Parker laughed again. "I grew up right here in Forest Hills, Hector—and the house was barely big enough to fit me, my Aunt May, and my Uncle Ben."

That surprised Hector. "No parents?" he asked as he walked over to the paper towel dispenser.

"They died when I was a kid. My aunt and uncle were pretty old, but they raised me anyhow. And then Uncle Ben died when I was only a little older than you, so it was just me and Aunt May. I had to take on work as a photographer when I was still in high school just to pay the bills. To give you an idea how incredibly lucrative *that* profession is, I took on teaching instead, and I think you have a good idea how little *we* make. So don't think you've got the monopoly on a crappy life, Hector. And even if you did, that doesn't mean you or your friends should just throw your lives away for a drug that's *killing people*—whether it's the users, the people they're hurting, or the pushers who're shooting each other over it."

Hector didn't say anything as he finished drying his hands and balled the cheap paper towel up into a ball.

"Fine," Mr. Parker said. "Stand by and watch people die, knowing you could've done something about it."

After tossing the towel into the trash bin, Hector whirled around and pointed a finger. "Yo, don't be *puttin'* that on me, Mr. Parker!"

"Who else am I supposed to put it on?"

With that, Mr. Parker turned around and left the bathroom.

Hector stared after him for a few seconds, then picked up his bag, slung it over his shoulder, and went back into the hallway.

He spent the rest of the day in a kind of daze, wandering from class to class without paying much attention, except in Mr. Parker's class. For some crazy reason, he wanted to act natural in his class. Not draw attention or nothing.

As soon as school let out, he practically ran out the door, not even bothering to stop at his locker. He hopped the bus that would take him to them Houses to talk to Ray-Ray. He went to the back, and saw somebody left a copy of the *Daily Bugle* on the seat. Picking it up, he started flipping through it. On page ten, he saw a story about Triple X. It was written by a reporter named Betty Brant, and it talked about the task force the NYPD formed, and people who'd been put in the hospital 'cause of Triple X. It also talked about how Spider-Man was keeping the folks high on it—"gamma-heads" is what Mr. Parker called 'em, and now Hector knew why, since that's what the article called 'em, too—from going too crazy or hurting people. He couldn't be everywhere, but he was doing his best.

And he was up in them Houses last week trying to find out.

It took almost half an hour 'cause of the damn traffic, but Hector finally made it to Robinsfield, walking through the grafitti-covered archway on 34th Avenue that led to the courtyard.

Nobody was barking today. No other crews were slinging. Hector looked for De, so he'd tell him where Ray-Ray was holed up, but when he saw De over at Tower A, he also saw Ray-Ray, along with Blowback, Biggie, Cap, and some other folks he didn't know by name, though one of 'em was the kid Ray-Ray was chewing out last time Hector was up in here.

When Hector walked up, Ray-Ray said, "My *man!* Glad you could join the party, dog!" He held up his hand, which Hector clasped. "We be takin' down some Russians, yo."

Hector winced. "Takin' down?"

Ray-Ray stared at him through his big sunglasses. "They got Sweet, they got Lemonhead, they got Jay, and they *almost* got Blowback. Time for some *pay*back!"

Everyone around Ray-Ray made all kinds of "Yeah" and "Damn right" noises.

"This is *wrong,* yo," Hector said. "Where is it gonna end?"

Holding up a hand, Ray-Ray said, "Back up off me, Hector. Ain't nothin' to be doin' but unto them what they doin' unto us, you feel me?"

"This ain't right. Look, you give people dope, that's cool, nobody gives a damn 'cause everybody be dopin', but now you killin' folks! With the Triple X and now this." Hector shook his head. "Forget that, what about the cops? You start droppin' bodies, them cops gonna be out here, yo. In force. They already got a task force."

"Say what?" Ray-Ray was looking at him like he was buggin'.

Hector shoved the *Bugle* in his face. "Was in the paper, yo, they formed a *task force* just for Triple X. You know what that means?"

Knocking the paper to the ground, Ray-Ray said, "Don't mean *shit,* a'ight?"

Cap said, "We wastin' time, Ray-Ray. We gots to be *goin'.*"

Shoving his hand at Hector's face, Ray-Ray turned around and said, "Let's be movin'."

They all started to walk away from Hector into the

courtyard toward the exit. Hector could see that they all had bulges in their pants or jackets—they all was carrying.

He only had one thing left to say. "What about Spider-Man?"

That stopped all of them about twenty feet from the archway. Ray-Ray turned around and said, "Spider-what?"

"He came by here the other day—broke De's gun."

Ray-Ray whirled on De, who started backing up. "Yo, you told me you *lost* that gun."

De didn't say nothing.

Hector kept talking. "He all over this, and he ain't gonna be lettin' up. What happens when—"

Whatever Hector was going to say next was cut off by the squealing of tires. He looked over and saw that two cars had pulled up onto the sidewalk and were in the archway, blocking it.

Four white guys got out and started shooting.

Hector thought he heard shouting, but he wasn't sure 'cause Ray-Ray and his crew opened up, too, and the guns was so *loud*. He fell down to the ground, but he wasn't sure why except that everything was so *loud* and his stomach hurt and then he couldn't breathe and *what the hell's going on, is that blood, oh. . . .*

Then everything went black.

Spider-Man swung across the North Lawn of Central Park en route to the 24th Precinct, having spent the day trying desperately to keep his eyes open while teaching. After leaving the hospital yesterday, he'd stopped five different gamma-heads, as he'd told Hector, as well as stopping some kid from breaking into a synagogue. Apparently the kid had the mistaken impression that there'd be valuables inside. Spider-Man took a certain bitter amusement out of educating him to the fact that the only thing he'd find in there worth anything was the Torah scroll, but that had more spiritual than monetary value. Besides, he probably wouldn't find a fence for it. *Though in this town, you never know.*

He'd also been digging through his contacts, but nobody he found knew anything, and he hadn't seen any of his usual Octopus-related stoolies. *Then again, Sunday night's not usually the best time for seeking out lowlifes.*

All this meant yet another late night. He'd gotten a message on Ursitti's phone from O'Leary to come by the Two-Four for a meeting in the afternoon, which he'd barely be able to make if he came straight from Midtown High. He had been hoping for an opportunity to tail Hector after class—since direct questioning and a guilt trip weren't doing the trick, and right now Hector was all he had—but he didn't want to squander what little goodwill he had with the NYPD. *If nothing else, it might come in handy later.*

He leapt out over the 100th Street exit to the park and swung around the face of the tenement-style buildings on the north side of the street, then the buildings of the condo complex on the south side, then took a big swing off the Health and Human Services building across the street from the precinct house before landing on the roof. This time he came in through the same window by which he departed on his last two trips here: the one that led to the detectives' squad room. Sure enough, all six members of the Triple X Task Force were present, as was Sergeant Green and a Hispanic man wearing a pink shirt and yellow tie. O'Leary, Shanahan, Wheeler, and Petrocelli were all seated at their desks, with Green sitting in the guest chair at O'Leary's desk; Shapiro was standing, as were Fry and the other man.

"Sorry I'm late," he said as he came in and climbed across the big pipe on the ceiling. "Couldn't catch a cab."

"Inspector," Green said, indicating the man in pink, "this is our civilian assistance."

"Cute way'a puttin' it." The man looked up at Spider-Man. "Esteban Garcia. I command this precinct. I appreciate the help you're giving us."

Both surprised and pleased, Spider-Man said, "Thanks—glad to do it. I just wish I could do more than knock around the gamma-heads." He said that last with a look at Wheeler.

"Actually, you have." Shapiro sounded like he would've liked anything in the world more than to have to say those words. "Una?"

Sounding much more excited, O'Leary said, "We've got two more gamma-heads that don't fit the profile. One was on Ryker's, a kid named Jeff Haight."

Spider-Man frowned. Ryker's Island was the largest prison in New York City, located on the East River between the Bronx and Queens. The name sounded familiar, but it took him a few seconds to finally place it. "Oh, jeez, Haight? He was an idiot, but I never pegged him for a druggie."

"He isn't," O'Leary said. "Somebody offered him a hit of Triple X in the cafeteria and when he didn't take it, he got the shit kicked out of him."

"Figures. Haight can't even do something intelligent right." Haight was a photographer who wanted to become Dr. Octopus's personal shooter. All it got him was busted for conspiracy and harboring a fugitive, a term he was still serving.

O'Leary continued: "The other one's a man named Nat Fredrickson. Also no history of drug use, though he has a couple of DUIs. The kicker here is, he's the ex-husband of Carolyn Trainer."

Spider-Man winced. "This just gets better and better." Trainer was a devotee—one might say a groupie—of Otto Octavius, having followed his career even before the accident. When Ock was killed, Trainer took on the mantle of Dr. Octopus for a time, before figuring out a way to resurrect Octavius through means Spider-Man still had to admit to not entirely understanding. Then again, Ock was hardly the only bad guy in his rogues' gallery who'd cheated the Grim Reaper.

Fry said, "Looks like you were right—Octavius may be involved in this."

"And like I said before," Wheeler said, "so the hell what? We still can't find the sonofabitch."

"We can look harder," Spider-Man said. "I've already put a few feelers out."

"To who?" Shapiro asked.

Chuckling, Spider-Man said, "Gee, Detective, you gonna give me a list of your CIs?"

O'Leary laughed, but broke it off at a stern look from Shapiro. "We have contracts with our CIs."

"And I have understandings with mine."

Shanahan said, " 'Understanding' my ass. You bust their heads, right? Hell, we should arrest him for brutality."

"That's enough," Garcia barked. "Detective Shanahan, you're out of line."

In a wholly unapologetic tone, Shanahan said, "Sorry, sir."

"Something I don't get," O'Leary said.

Shanahan muttered, "There's a surprise."

Somehow, Spider-Man resisted the urge to punch Shanahan in the face—or, at the very least, web up his mouth.

"Octopus has never had any kind of underworld contacts." O'Leary turned to Spider-Man. "Right?"

"Just the usual rent-a-thugs. He was never a player in the same way that other guys have been. He wouldn't lower himself, to be honest—the only times he's worked with other people, it's been a marriage of convenience in order for him to achieve his own ends." He was thinking in particular of the times Octopus hooked up with some of Spider-Man's other regular sparring partners to form the so-called "Sinister Six," mostly in an attempt to do together what none of them had managed alone: kill Spider-Man. There'd been several incarnations, sometimes with more or fewer than the usual six, and they'd mostly been done in by their mistrust of each other—and, in Ock's case, by his own massive ego.

Petrocelli asked, "If that's the case, how does he hook up with a Long Island City slinger?"

"He doesn't," Spider-Man said, "but he doesn't have to. Look, we know that Ock's involved because there are people being hit here who don't have a history of drug use, but who *do* have a history of getting in Ock's way. Hunt's the doctor who worked on him after the accident—Ock thought Hunt was trying to imprison him in the hospital. His deal with Gaxton went south when I stopped them. Haight was an annoyance. There may be others, for all we know."

"What about Fredrickson?" Fry asked.

"That's the key," Spider-Man said. "Carolyn Trainer doesn't have Octavius's book smarts, but she's got plenty of street smarts, and I know she *did* develop the kinds of contacts that Octavius would consider beneath him. I can't see him being able to facilitate a deal with Ray-Ray, but I can see Trainer."

"We still gotta find Octavius," Petrocelli said.

"Yeah," Wheeler said. "Question is, how?"

"Let me work my angle."

Shapiro pointed at Spider-Man. "If you do find him, you *call us,* you understand? I'm not having my case trashed because some costume can't follow procedure again."

Frowning, Spider-Man said, " 'Again'?"

"You know how many times we find a guy webbed to a lamppost for no reason? You put your cute little *'courtesy your friendly neighborhood Spider-Man'* card on it, but there's no stolen merch, no witnesses, no victims, just a couple of knuckleheads webbed to a lamppost—and *they* ain't talkin'."

"Detective—" Spider-Man started. He'd heard this complaint before.

However, Garcia interrupted. "All right, Detective, you've made your point."

Glowering at Spider-Man, Shapiro said, "Yeah."

"As for you," Garcia said to Spider-Man, "if you're gonna keep cooperating, you will cooperate. That means following the rules, understand? I don't want a glory hound screwing our case."

"Inspector, the next time I seek glory will be the first. Like I've already told your detectives, that's not why I do this."

"Fine." Garcia walked to the door. "I want this drug war ended and this case *closed,* people. Do a job."

As soon as the door to the squad room closed behind

Garcia, Shanahan said, " 'Do a job,' Jesus. Knute Rockne, he ain't."

"All right," Shapiro said, "enough. Let's get to the hospitals, keep trying to get *something* out of the vics. Maybe one of 'em knows their dealer." To Petrocelli, he said, "Narcotics is keeping an eye on Ray-Ray, right?"

Petrocelli nodded. "It's been quiet, though. That in itself is scary."

Oh man, Hector, why couldn't you talk to me? Spider-Man shook his head. Hector was a good kid, but Spider-Man couldn't entirely blame him for not rolling on his buddies. How many secrets had *he* kept to protect his friends and family over the years, after all?

"Keep in touch with them. I wanna know—"

The desk sergeant Spider-Man had met on his first trip here burst in all of a sudden. "Jerry, we just got a call from the One-Oh-Eight—shots fired in the Robinsfield Houses. There're some narcos there, and they told the One-Oh-Eight to call you."

Without hesitating, Spider-Man leapt for the window. "I'll meet you guys there." He was out the window before anybody could object, swinging across the street and through the condo complex to the park, making time as fast as he could to Long Island City.

Now, Spider-Man wished he had tailed Hector. True, it would've meant not getting the confirmation on the Ock connection right off, but if that kid wound up dead . . .

With great power comes great responsibility. That was something Uncle Ben had told him, something that had become his lifelong credo. *But sometimes the responsibility really sucks. And I just can't be in two places at once.*

It took about fifteen minutes to wend his to LIC, and

by then it was all over. Ambulances and blue-and-whites were surrounding the Houses, lights flashing, casting a red glow on the entire area. Spider-Man could smell the gunshot residue as he approached, which meant a *lot* of gunfire.

"Yo, web-head!"

Spider-Man saw a short black woman waving at him. She was dressed casually, but had a badge on her belt. He twisted in midair to do a backflip onto the top of an ambulance, then leapt over to the roof of the car next to where the cop was standing. "Can I help you?"

"Joan Barnes, Narcotics. Una O'Leary called and said I should talk to you when you got here."

Making a mental note to buy O'Leary flowers when this was all over, he asked, "What happened?"

"Drug hit. We got one of the shooters, but the rest rabbited. Two of our guys got hit—the one shooter we got laid down cover fire for his buddies."

"They okay?"

Barnes nodded. "We're stakin' out a drug market, you *bet* we're all wearin' Kevlars."

Looking closely, Spider-Man noticed the impressions of the Velcro flaps of a bulletproof vest under Barnes's sweatshirt. "Who's the shooter you got?"

"White guy—talks with an Eastern European accent. I figure it's a Ukrainian crew working out of Brighton Beach. They're the ones getting pushed out by Ray-Ray."

"Anybody else hit?"

At that, Barnes actually smiled. "That's the fun part. Ray-Ray took one in the chest—and he wasn't wearing a Kevlar."

"Anybody else?"

Opening her notebook, Barnes started flipping pages.

"Lessee—two of Ray-Ray's crew. Ambo took 'em to Parkway." She got to the right spot. "Robert Billinghurst, street name 'Cap,' and a new kid, Hector Diaz."

A fist of ice clenched Spider-Man's heart. "They took 'em to Parkway?"

"Yeah, why, you—"

But Spider-Man didn't hear the rest of the sentence, as he leapt off the roof and made his way to the hospital. *I should've tailed Hector. I knew I should've tailed Hector!*

11

As opening night fast approached, the minds of the cast and crew of *The Z-Axis* were turning to thoughts of homicide.

Mary Jane was working out just fine in the role of Olga, if she did say so herself. The part was, after all, less challenging than that of Irina, so plugging into it wasn't too difficult. Dmitri had been effusive in his praise—which, for Dmitri, meant that he only told her that she was awful and was ruining his show once or twice, as opposed to constantly.

The problem was with Regina in the role of Irina. Regina was also, after all, playing Fiona, the lead female part in *Up the Creek Without a Fiddle,* the about-to-close show currently running at VPC. Fiona was a not-too-bright prostitute with a drug problem who was the victim of the men around her; Irina was a smart, prim young woman who believed in the best of people. Thus they were two radically different parts of the type that most actors would be thrilled to have on their resumé in order to show off their range.

The problem was, Regina was having a hard time getting out of Fiona mode and into Irina mode, as it were.

This had a domino effect on everyone else. Dmitri

was so frustrated that at Sunday's rehearsal, he actually succeeded in ripping his prized Dodgers cap in two (it had since been replaced with a Mets cap). Regina was annoyed at herself for not getting Irina down pat, and was taking it out mostly on the crew, who proceeded to take it out on the entire cast by screwing up cues and set changes. This in turn got the cast members annoyed and upset, which they took out on each other and Dmitri, who was aggravated at all of them. *Thank God we have Monday off,* Mary Jane had thought after Sunday's disaster.

That union-mandated off-day on Monday was a huge help, as Tuesday afternoon's rehearsal—the last one before previews began Wednesday night—went swimmingly. They were going through the climactic scene in Act 2 when Irina chews Olga out for being an idiot. Regina put her all into the chewing-out, and Olga's response—during which she emerges from her shell for the first time in the entire play—was as intense as Mary Jane could make it.

When they were done with the scene, and the lights went out, Mary Jane was stunned to hear clapping from the audience.

The houselights came up, as they did after every scene so Dmitri could nitpick them to death before going on to the next scene, and she saw that it was Dmitri who was clapping.

"Now *that,* my good friends, *that* is acting. Jane Mary, Regina, for the first time in a week I believe that you quite possibly might not be ruining my play."

"Gee, thanks, Dmitri," Mary Jane said dryly.

Regina touched Mary Jane's shoulder. "God, MJ, I'm so sorry I've been such a bitch."

"Don't worry about it," Mary Jane said quickly, even though Regina had, in fact, been one. "It's the usual pre-opening jitters."

"Yeah, but I don't *get* those. It's just—I don't know, what happened with Valerie is *so* totally weird. It's got me so *totally* freaked out."

"I know." Mary Jane tried to sound understanding, though her own tolerance for weirdness was higher than that of most folks who didn't actually wear super hero suits.

"Excuse me?"

Mary Jane looked to the rear entrance to see a good-looking man in a suit, holding a small pad of paper.

Dmitri turned around and threw up his hands. "This is closed dress rehearsal. You cannot be here!"

Regina whispered to Mary Jane, "I don't mind if he stays a while." Mary Jane tried to hide a smile at Regina's sudden switch to flirt mode.

The man opened his jacket far enough to show a badge on his belt, as well as a shoulder holster. " 'Fraid I can. I'm Detective Ty Wheeler. I need to talk to, uh"—he checked the pad—"Ms. Regina Wright."

"Lucky me." Regina sounded like a cat about to pounce on a mouse. But then, Regina tended to go through men the way buzz saws go through trees. Remembering Peter's description of Wheeler's lousy behavior at the hospital, she decided not to say anything and just let Regina loose on him.

Regina jumped down off the stage, but Dmitri moved to stand between her and Wheeler. "What is this about?"

"You're Mr. Voyskunsky, right? This is follow-up on Ms. Valerie McManus."

"Ms. McManus is not in this play anymore, so you have no business here."

"No, but Ms. McManus's boyfriend said that Ms. Wright might be able to help us with our inquiries. I'm afraid I have to insist, Mr. Voyskunsky."

Regina put her hand on Dmitri's back. "It's okay, Dmitri. I want to help Valerie." She then walked past Dmitri, and Wheeler led her over to the back corner seats to talk.

"Okay," Dmitri said. "We will take five."

Fat chance it'll only be five minutes, Mary Jane thought with a smile. "I need something to drink. Anybody want anything?"

Mike Rabinowitz, who had taken over for Lou Colvin, said, "I would just *kill* for an apple juice."

"I think we can avoid murder, especially with a cop in the room," Mary Jane said with a smile as she grabbed her purse from the front-row seat where she'd left it.

She walked downstairs to the small counter behind the box office where nonalcoholic drinks were served, and asked the volunteer whose name she couldn't remember for an apple juice and a diet soda.

Then her cell phone rang. Cursing herself for forgetting to turn it off during rehearsal, she reached into her purse, pulling out both wallet and phone.

To her surprise, it was Valerie's number showing on the display. Flipping open the phone, she said, "Val, you okay?"

"It's Greg." Valerie's boyfriend sounded absolutely awful. "I'm calling from Cabrini, I—oh, *God.*"

Cradling the phone in her shoulder, she paid for her drinks while saying, "Greg, what is it, what's wrong?"

"It's Val—the doctors—they say she's *dying*, MJ! I don't know what—"

Then he stopped.

"What is it?" she asked after a second.

"Sorry, the nurse just said I can't use the cell in here. Look, MJ, I gotta talk to you, okay? Can you come by here tonight?"

Peter would probably be spending most of the night trying to keep a lid on the Triple X problem, so Mary Jane didn't hesitate to say, "I'll be there as soon as rehearsal's done, okay?"

"Great. We're in Room 310 at Cabrini."

"Got it," she said as she walked back upstairs, juice and soda in hand.

God, she thought as she ended the call and turned the phone off before putting it back in her purse. *She's dying. This is insane. Please, Peter, find out who's doing this, and stop them. . . .*

Eileen Velasquez had just finished leaving her tenth message on Orlando's cell phone voice mail when the doctor walked up to her in the waiting area.

Dr. Lee wasn't, in Eileen's opinion, a very nice woman. If she'd met her under any other circumstances, Eileen probably would've walked across the room to avoid the doctor. But she had been very straightforward and honest with Eileen about what Javier was going through, and Eileen appreciated that right now. The doctors who had treated Manuel always danced around with fancy words and false hopes and fake promises. Dr. Lee didn't do any of that.

"I'm afraid the news isn't good, Ms. Velasquez. Javier has a brother with bone marrow edema, yes?"

Eileen winced. "Had a brother—Manuel died in a car accident a few years ago."

Lee shoved her hands into the pockets of her white lab coat. "Has Javier been tested for it?"

Nodding, Eileen said, "Every year, I always make sure Javier and Jorge are tested. They've been clean." Eileen did not like where this conversation was going.

"Javier isn't showing any signs of radiation poisoning," Lee said, "but it looks like the radiation in the drugs he took is having an effect on him. He's tested positive for the edema. By itself, it's probably treatable, but his heart is still weak—the treatments for the edema would probably trigger another heart attack. In fact, it's pretty likely that he'll suffer another one in due course anyhow. He's not coming out of his coma, and I'm not sure he's going to."

The doctor said some more things, but Eileen didn't hear them. At some point, Lee walked away but Eileen didn't notice that, either. All she could think about was that she was soon going to lose another member of her family.

She was startled out of her nightmare by the chirp of her cell phone. To her amazement, the display indicated that it was Orlando.

"Orlando, baby, thank you for calling m—"

"What do you *want*, Ma?"

The hostility in Orlando's voice was like a slap. "Didn't you get my messages?"

"Yeah, I got 'em. I know what's goin' on, so—"

"Javier's *dying*, Orlando."

"And I'm supposed to give a damn *why*, exactly?"

Eileen tried to gather up outrage, but found she couldn't. The fact of the matter was, Orlando's behavior was completely consistent with how he'd been for years. Why should he act any different now?

Still, she gave it a shot. "He's your *brother.*"

"He never gave a damn about me—don't see why I gotta be returning the favor. Look, I got homework, okay? I gotta go. I got your messages, so stop calling me."

Orlando cut off the connection.

Eileen held the phone to her ear for several seconds. She felt a tear roll down her cheek.

"Hey, you okay, Ms. Velasquez?"

Closing the phone, Eileen looked up to see Peter Parker standing over her, looking concerned.

"I'm fine, Mr. Parker. Just trying to keep my family together—and like usual, screwing it up."

He sat down next to her. "What happened?"

She told him what Dr. Lee had said about Javier. "And I've been trying to reach my oldest boy, Orlando, but he wants nothing to do with me or Javier."

Putting a hand on hers, Parker said, "I'm sorry. I wish there were something I could do."

Somehow managing to get her face to form a smile, she placed her other hand on top of Parker's. "Unless you're willing to fly down to Florida and kick Orlando's butt, there isn't much you can do." She and Parker both got a quick laugh out of that, then she added, "You did enough just by caring, Mr. Parker. Thank you."

"No problem. And like I keep saying, it's Peter." He extricated his hand and stood up. "I gotta go—another of my students wound up here in a drive-by yesterday."

"You're not careful, you'll be spending all your time in here." Eileen found the words to be bitter ones, given how much time she herself was spending in this messed-up place.

"Yeah, I know. See you later."

What kind of world is this where a teacher Javier can't even stand cares more about him than his own brother?

When Hector woke up, he panicked, because he couldn't feel anything below his neck.

He tried moving, and then got pins and needles all up in his chest and legs. And everything smelled funny. . . .

Looking down at his body, he realized he was in a hospital gown—in a hospital bed. He could feel bandages on his chest.

Then he remembered everything. *They shot me!*

"About time you woke up."

Hector saw Mr. Parker standing in the doorway. He turned over so his back was facing the teacher. "What do *you* want?"

"Heard you got shot."

"Yeah. You gonna be puttin' *that* on me, too?"

"No, I put that on the guys who shot you. Ukrainians, from what I heard."

Wondering how a science teacher knew so much, then deciding that he really didn't care that much, he said, "Yeah, you know everything, don't you?"

"What's your problem, Hector?"

Hector turned back over and shot Mr. Parker a look. "What's my *problem*? My problem is that I *listened* to you, and I got *shot*! The hell you *think* my problem is, yo?"

"I'm sorry about that, but—"

"Only reason I *went* down there was 'cause I listened to you. I was just gonna go home an' stay low, but naw,

I gotta listen to Mr. Teacher Man who knows all about how baaaaad my life is when he really don't know *shit!*"

Mr. Parker just stared right back at Hector. "So now what, Hector? You're just gonna lie here and feel sorry for yourself?"

"*Hell,* no. They done *shot* me, and I'm gettin' back at them!"

"Oh, *good* idea!" Mr. Parker walked up to the bed. " 'Cause as much fun as getting shot at is, dead is so much better."

"And you got all the answers, right?"

Putting his hands on the metal railing, Mr. Parker said, "I know that if you'd told me—or the police, Spider-Man, *anyone*—about where the Triple X was coming from, it wouldn't have come to this."

Hector turned back over again, not wanting to look at Mr. Parker's stupid white face. "I don't roll on family, yo."

"Family? The people who got you shot are family now?"

Turning his head around, he said, "*You* the one who got me shot!" Then he looked back at the wall. "Ray-Ray'll take care'a me, then there'll be—"

"Ray-Ray's dead."

Hector turned around again. "What?"

"Took one in the heart."

"Fine, then Blowback take over. So what?" Even as Hector said that, though, he wondered what it would mean. Blowback didn't have Ray-Ray's head.

"And Javier's dying, too. Doctors figure he won't live out the week. And then there's all the other Triple X cases, and—"

"I told you, that ain't on me!"

Mr. Parker kept talking all calm. "Maybe not, but you *can* do something about it. And if you don't do something to stop this when you have the means, then you become just as bad as whoever it is who's making this drug. Then you *are* responsible." The teacher turned his back on Hector and walked to the door. "You live with that, Hector."

And then Mr. Parker left.

Good goddamn riddance, Hector thought. His chest started to ache.

Greg Halprin didn't look much better today in Room 310 of the Cabrini Medical Center than he had when Mary Jane visited him last week, although he was better-dressed. Now wearing a Columbia University sweatshirt and faded jeans, he still had slept-in hair, and even more beard stubble.

When he looked up, Mary Jane saw one other change—his bloodshot eyes indicated someone who was most definitely not high on anything, but who also hadn't slept in a few days.

Valerie McManus was lying in the bed next to the chair Greg was sitting in, which was the one of the three beds in the room closest to the door. The other two were occupied by elderly men who slept and had no company.

"Hey, MJ." Greg's voice was much weaker than it had been last week. "Can you believe this? She's *dying*. The docs say it's some kinda radiation poisoning."

Mary Jane stood behind Greg and put a hand on his shoulder. "I'm sorry."

"It's crazy. I mean, we been doin' everything, you know? Weed, coke, blow, X, you name it, and all we got was high. But this—" His voice broke. "The guy said it'd make her smarter. He didn't say it'd make her dead."

Remembering what both Greg and Valerie had told her, Mary Jane said, "Greg, you told me that Zeke—the guy—he had a woman with him."

Greg nodded. "Yeah, some purple-haired lady."

Jackpot, Mary Jane thought, clearly remembering a purple-haired woman with mechanical arms who had taken on the mantle of Dr. Octopus after the first one died, and who later went on to resurrect her predecessor. Peter had filled Mary Jane in on the working theory that the source of the Triple X was Otto Octavius and Carolyn Trainer, and if Greg and Valerie's supplier had a purple-haired lady with him, that went a long way toward proving the theory right.

She walked around to face Greg. "Listen to me, Greg—you need to go to the police and tell them about your suppliers."

Looking at her like she was nuts, Greg said, "Are you out of your *mind,* MJ? I ain't talkin' to no cops about no suppliers. I ain't rattin' the guy out, okay?"

"Fine, then, don't rat the guy, just the purple-haired lady. *She's* gotta be the one who came up with the Triple X, right? Zeke didn't have the stuff until she showed up?"

"Yeah," Greg said, "that's true."

"So just give her up. Keep Zeke in the clear." Mary Jane knew she was encouraging at the very least that Greg commit a misdemeanor, but the important thing was to get *someone* to corroborate that Trainer was the one pushing the Triple X.

Shaking his head, Greg said, "No way. Nuh-uh. She'll kill me."

Oh, God, Trainer threatened them. "Look, the cops can protect you from the purple-haired lady, you just—"

"I don't mean her, I mean Val! If I talk to the cops—" Again, his voice broke. He looked over at Valerie on the bed.

Mary Jane followed his gaze. Right now, Valerie looked peaceful, as if she was sleeping, even with the IV in her arm and the oxygen tube in her nose and wrapped around her ears. *God, she may never wake up from that.* There were no outward signs of radiation poisoning yet, but Mary Jane knew that was only a matter of time.

"Jesus, she looks so peaceful," Greg muttered, his words echoing Mary Jane's thought. "She ain't gonna make it, is she?"

"I can't answer that," Mary Jane said honestly. "But if she isn't—do you really want the person responsible for killing her to stay free?"

Greg closed his eyes. "Dammit, I don't know. It's usually Val who decides this stuff, I'm just—" He hit the arm of the chair weakly with his fist. "I'm just a guy, y'know? Just doin' my thing, I don't know nothin' 'bout—" He slumped.

Reaching into her purse, Mary Jane pulled out the card that Detective Shapiro had given her at VPC. "Listen, after Val changed the first time, I talked to this detective. He's up at the 24th Precinct on 100th Street, and he's in charge of the whole Triple X thing. You can talk to him."

It took a few seconds for Greg to take the card. "Yeah, okay. I'll go tomorrow."

Mary Jane didn't like the sound of that. "Greg, go tonight. I'll stay with her."

"Okay, but—let me sit with her a few more minutes, all right?"

Looking around the room, Mary Jane found another chair and brought it over next to Greg. She sat down and said, "Okay. I'll sit with you."

"Yeah, thanks." Greg kept staring at Valerie. "Jesus." They sat alone in silence after that.

12

Spider-Man was very grateful for the fact that wearing a mask meant nobody in the Triple X Task Force could see that he could barely keep his eyes open.

He'd slept in today, having called in sick to work Monday night right before collapsing in a heap on the bed and sleeping until two on Tuesday, then heading to Parkway Hospital to visit Hector. Then Mary Jane called him from Cabrini saying that she had stuck Greg in a cab that would take him uptown to the 24th Precinct, and he should get his red-and-blue butt over there.

Monday he had made a wholly futile attempt to find Dr. Octopus. Unfortunately, Sunday's run through his usual stoolies proved prophetic for Monday's: nobody knew anything, and those that might have were nowhere to be found. Spider-Man was starting to get a complex.

The closest he got to good news was hearing that Elias Kitsios would be at Amsterdam Billiards for a tournament Tuesday night. Kitsios was one of the go-to guys if you wanted to buy equipment, usually stolen, of the type needed by guys like Dr. Octopus. When Ock needed anything, from lab equipment to an air conditioner, there was a good chance that Kitsios would be the one to get it for him.

The good news was, at least Spider-Man was able to stop a few more gamma-head rampages, though several straight days of keeping super-powered druggies from doing too much harm, while trying not to do too much harm to them, was taking its toll on even his enhanced stamina. The extra sleep this morning and afternoon had helped, but not nearly enough. As he sat on the wall of the Two-Four's detective squad room once again, he felt the bones of his arms and legs turning to liquid. He hadn't had a decent meal in days, though he had promised Aunt May, in a hasty phone call right before he webbed over to the precinct house, that he and Mary Jane would come over for a late dinner tonight. Thrilled at the prospect, Aunt May said she was heading out to the Associated Supermarket on Queens Boulevard to get all the fixings.

Shapiro, Shanahan, and O'Leary were present. Petrocelli was out chasing a lead. Shapiro and Shanahan studiously ignored the wall-crawler, leaving O'Leary to do all the speaking. Given their hostile attitudes, compared with O'Leary's friendliness, this suited Spider-Man fine.

Fry and Wheeler came walking in, the latter with two mugs of coffee in his hand. To Spider-Man's surprise, he handed one of those mugs to Spider-Man.

"Heard you been goin' full tilt. Figured you might need this," Wheeler said with a small smile.

"Thanks, Detective." Spider-Man took the steaming mug, figuring this to be a peace offering from Wheeler.

Lifting his mask up to his nose, he took a sip, and then

had to gather up all his willpower not to spit it out. This was even worse than Midtown High's faculty lounge coffee, and that stuff was often mistaken for sewage. *Maybe it's not so much a peace offering as revenge.*

Wheeler looked at Shapiro. "So who's this guy comin' in?"

"Greg Halprin," Spider-Man said. "He's the boyfriend of Valerie McManus, and he's giving up his supplier."

Shapiro shot Spider-Man a look. "How'd *you* know that?" He looked at O'Leary. "Did you—?"

Quickly, O'Leary said, "I just told him we had a possible witness."

Sitting down at his desk, Wheeler said, "Hang on— Halprin? I talked to that guy today. He sent me back to the theatre, said one'a the other actresses had somethin' to say." He grinned. "She didn't, turns out, but, *man,* what a babe."

Fry shook his head. "You hitting on witnesses again, Ty?"

"Didn't need to—this one was coming on to me."

O'Leary laughed. "Well then, she couldn'ta been much use as a witness, 'cause if she was hitting on you, then she's gotta be blind."

Wheeler good-naturedly tossed a paper clip at O'Leary, who batted it aside.

"If you kids are finished . . . ," Shapiro said. Everyone else settled down. "Petrocelli's following up on someone in Inwood who matches Octavius's description. Meanwhile—"

One of the uniforms walked in, along with Greg Halprin, looking pathetic.

O'Leary leapt to her feet, leading Greg over to her

desk. Mary Jane had said in her phone message that Greg was not handling Valerie's decline very well, and seeing him now, Spider-Man could see that clear as day. As Peter Parker, he had met Greg only once, when they were both in the audience during the callbacks for *The Z-Axis,* each of them, as Greg had put it, "lending our womenfolk some moral support." He'd seemed a nice enough guy— a little slow on the uptake, perhaps, but harmless. Based on what Mary Jane had told him, however, he'd been at his best at that callback.

He certainly wasn't now. When O'Leary asked him his name, he struggled with the concept, and his address took several seconds.

But once he got to the meat of the statement, the words started to flow better. "Look, we took stuff, okay? You try getting through an audition or a callback straight—or try sittin' around hopin' that they'll call you, even though you know they're gonna go for some-one else. You're too tall, too pale, not blond enough, too wide in the shoulders, not skinny enough, what-the-hell-ever. Can't expect a dude to face that straight, you just *can't.*"

Spider-Man found himself drinking the awful coffee just to cover the bark of derisive laughter he had on standby. He was married to someone in the same busi-ness—who'd also spent plenty of time as a model—and she faced it just fine straight. Apart from a bout with cig-arettes, Mary Jane had stayed clean.

Then again, not everyone has MJ's strength.

"So we met this lady. Dude, she was *intense.* Never got a name, but she had a hawk nose, and purple hair, I re-member that much. Wasn't even stylin' or nothin', just regular hair 'cept it was purple."

O'Leary, who had been typing Greg's words into the keyboard on her desk, stopped, nodded, then looked at Fry. The tall cop brought over a booklet and dropped it on O'Leary's desk. She flipped it open to the middle.

Peering over, Spider-Man saw that the page O'Leary opened to had five mug shots of women, all in color, each woman with purple hair. *Why does it not surprise me that there are four purple-haired women in this town besides Trainer with rap sheets?*

Greg didn't even hesitate. "That's her." His index finger landed right on the picture of Carolyn Trainer.

"All right," Shapiro said, "Detective O'Leary's gonna print out your statement. I want you to read it and sign and initial it everywhere the detective tells you, okay?"

Nodding, Greg said, "I just wanna get the people that did this to Val, y'know?"

"I know, son." Shapiro put a hand on Greg's shoulder, and spoke in as kind a voice as Spider-Man had heard him use.

O'Leary stood and led Greg over to the printer on the far side of the squad room.

Looking over at Shanahan, Shapiro asked, "We got an address on Trainer?"

"Yeah, but I dunno if it's current."

Spider-Man pulled the mask down over his face. "Where?"

"Hang off a second," Shapiro said, holding up a hand toward Spider-Man. "We take Trainer, I don't want you within a thousand feet of us."

"I beg your pardon? Detective, this lady *was* Doc Ock for a while, and she was actually pretty good at it."

Shapiro shook his head. "I don't care, this is the first real lead we've had since they formed this damn unit, and I ain't lettin' it get screwed up by some technicality 'cause we brought a civilian in a costume on the bust."

"What difference does it make?" Spider-Man asked. "Can't you just arrest her on old charges?"

Shapiro said, "There *are* no old charges."

Spider-Man blinked under his mask. "What're you talking about? She was wearing the tentacles, she—"

"Wearing metal arms isn't a crime," Shapiro said.

"But she was arrested, and—"

Fry spoke up, then. "And she was brought to trial, and a jury of her peers found her not guilty of any of the charges, mostly because the DA couldn't put a decent case together and her lawyer ripped the prosecution case to shreds. Not surprising, really, since their only witness was her father, who—"

Wincing, Spider-Man said, "Who was killed by the Green Goblin."

"Yup," Fry said. "No witness, no case, no conviction."

"Well," Shapiro said, "there was one other witness." He stared right at Spider-Man. "But he wears a big red mask and doesn't testify at trials."

"How do you like *them* apples?" Shanahan asked with a nasty smile.

Before Spider-Man could respond in kind—or web Shanahan's mouth shut, an option that was looking more pleasurable by the second—Shapiro went on. "So I can't take the chance of having you there on Trainer's bust. Hell, we don't even know if the address we got for her is current. But if it is, we'll take her in and get her to flip Octavius."

Spider-Man couldn't help it. He laughed.

"What's so goddamn funny?" Shanahan asked.

"You're not gonna get Trainer to give up Octavius. Not on a drug charge, not on an assault charge, not on the charge of being the second coming of Lucrezia Borgia."

Shanahan gave him a dirty look. "You think we can't flip some broad?"

"I know for a fact you can't flip this one. She's so devoted to Octavius *she had him resurrected from the dead.* You really think she'll give him up?"

"Even if she doesn't," Shapiro said before Shanahan could say something else stupid, "she's still in on this. Right now, we need an arrest. We need to show the inspector and the commissioner and the mayor and the newspapers that we're *doing* something. An arrest will go a long way toward keeping people calm."

"Maybe," Spider-Man said, "but I'm not about to just sit on my hands and let you guys—"

The desk sergeant—Larsen—burst into the squad room. "We just got a call from the One-Twelve. Some old lady in a supermarket's turned green and is firing ray-beams outta her eyes."

For the second time in two days, a fist of ice clenched Spider-Man's heart, but this one was bigger and colder. "What supermarket?" he asked.

Looking down at the Post-it he was holding, Larsen said, "An Associated on Queens Boulevard over by—"

The word "bouelvard" had barely escaped Larsen's mouth when Spider-Man was out the window.

Of all the people Ock would go after, Spider-Man had hoped, had prayed, that May Parker would have been left off the list. After all, she hadn't actually done anything to him. *Then again, neither did Gaxton, really, and that didn't stop Ock from hitting him with the drug. . . .*

Years ago, Dr. Octopus had learned that May was in line to inherit an island containing a nuclear power plant. When Spider-Man later learned the whole story, he had thought it an odd thing to bequeath, but May would only say that it was from the "side of the Reillys we try not to talk about." In order to get his hands on the plant, Ock had courted May, and got her to agree to marry him. Spider-Man hadn't actually stopped them himself, being beaten to it by a mob boss who went by the sobriquet of "Hammerhead." Between them, Ock and Hammerhead blew up the power plant and destroyed the island, though both somehow managed to escape with their lives. With the island gone, so too was Ock's interest in marrying Peter's aunt.

I guess, Spider-Man thought as he webbed across Manhattan in record time, *it was too much to hope that Ock would've forgotten about her.* May had been at death's door more than once since Peter Parker became Spider-Man, and he even thought her to be dead for a brief time, and he wasn't about to let her be taken from him by Ock's sick revenge scheme.

Queens Boulevard, one of the major thoroughfares of the borough for which it was named, had both a main road and a service road. Traffic on the eastbound side was snarled, as the cars couldn't get past the giant crater on the divider between the eastbound service road and main road, as well as the tree that had been knocked across the road, both right in front of a giant Associated Supermarket.

A green beam of light shot across and hit one of the street lamps. People were shouting and running away from the supermarket as Spider-Man swung into the parking lot, which seemed to be the source of the beam.

Several blue-and-whites were surrounding a single female figure, with over a dozen uniformed officers standing in a position that kept their cars between them and her.

Said figure was skinny, green, and shooting beams from her head. Even from this distance, and with the new skin tone, Spider-Man instantly recognized May Parker.

As he swung into the parking lot he saw another beam fired and heard a familiar voice yelling, "I'm sorry! So sorry!"

Spider-Man landed on a car behind one of the blue-and-whites. "Not your usual gamma-head, is she?" he said to the one cop not in a uniform.

Whirling around, the cop—a heavyset Latino man with a bald head and a thick mustache—said, "About time you showed up. Shapiro said you'd be here."

Nice to be wanted. "I think I can convince her to come quietly."

"Yeah, we tried that." The detective pointed at one of the blue-and-whites, which was missing its entire trunk. "But I ain't about to tell these guys to open fire on an old lady, even if she *is* green. Christ, she must be, like, ninety years old or somethin'."

"As it happens, she's a fan of mine. Wrote some nice letters to the *Daily Bugle* and everything. So I think I've got a shot here."

"Good—'cause if you don't, I do."

Nodding his understanding and silently swearing he wouldn't let any harm come to his aunt, Spider-Man leapt over to a car next to her. "Mrs. Parker, this is Spider-Man. Just take it easy."

"Spi—Spider-Man?" Another beam shot out and demolished a Dumpster.

"Easy, Mrs. Parker—listen, just close your eyes."

"But then I can't see."

His spider-sense buzzing, Spider-Man leapt just as another beam shot out of his aunt's eyes, totaling the car he was on. *Hope the owner's insured.*

Landing in front of her as she said, "I'm so sorry!" Spider-Man grabbed her arms.

"It's okay, Mrs. Parker, really."

"I don't feel very well," she said. "Ever since that nice woman with the purple hair gave me those free ice cream samples, I . . ."

Then she collapsed in his arms.

"Move in!" the detective cried, just as an ambulance pulled up.

Waving off the uniformed cops who ran toward him, Spider-Man said, "She's fine, I got her."

"Sir," one of the uniforms said, "we got to—"

"I said, I *got* her! Back off!"

Refusing to let any cop near her, Spider-Man waited until the EMTs rolled up with their gurney, at which point he gently placed his aunt on it, then let the pros take over.

He then tore into the supermarket itself, making a beeline for the frozen foods section. Sure enough, there was a table with some small spoons and empty cups on it, with a sign reading FREE SAMPLES.

The supermarket had been evacuated, of course, and somehow Spider-Man doubted that Trainer would hang around once her objective of poisoning Aunt May was accomplished. *I wonder if she just pushed it on everyone here, or had a special batch ready for when Aunt May came by.* Probably the latter, since Queens Boulevard wasn't being overrun with gamma-heads.

Spider-Man ran out the front door and leapt up to a nearby high-rise, being careful to avoid any of the cops or EMTs—or members of the press, for that matter, several of whom filmed his departure.

When he alighted on the roof, he took out Ursitti's cell phone and called O'Leary.

"Everything okay?" she asked.

"I want Trainer's address, and I want it *now.* I'm going to beat that woman until she bleeds."

"I can't do that, and you know why. Shapiro's getting the warrant on the address right now. It's gotta be a clean bust."

"I don't care! What she and Ock are doing—" Spider-Man cut himself off. He couldn't very well tell O'Leary that the latest target was the woman who raised him.

"You think we don't know what they're doing? But if we don't do this right, Trainer will *walk,* especially since our only witness is a drugged-out actor whose girlfriend is dying. We gotta be real careful with her." She paused. "But only with her."

"What do you mean?"

"Well, Trainer's clean, but Octavius isn't. Got about a dozen outstanding warrants, at least. Doesn't matter *how* he's brought in."

Spider-Man started to say something, then stopped. "What time is it?"

"About six-thirty. Why?"

Forcing himself to calm down, Spider-Man said, "I've

got a pool game to catch." He closed the phone without another word.

Shooting a web-line off to one of the trees on the Queens Boulevard service road, Spider-Man thought, *The tournament isn't starting until nine, but if Kitsios is playing pool for real tonight, chances are he's at that place on 8th that has the cheap booze he likes, so he can liquor up. . . .*

Elias Kitsios leaned over the crappy pool table and lined up a shot. He'd knock the seven in the corner and bank it off the side to sink the two. After that, the eight-ball would be all set up and he'd take this idiot's money.

This was all just a warm-up for Kitsios. Tonight was the tournament, playing on a *real* regulation table, not the dinky thing they put in bars like this dump on 8th Street. Usually, he just came here for the drinks—this was the only place in Manhattan that had *ouzo* at what Kitsios considered a reasonable price—but when some black kid started trash-talking about how he was a pool god, Kitsios decided to make a little extra money. It'd be good prep for tonight.

And the extra cash didn't hurt. Not that he needed it. He had plenty of clients, including one who was rolling in it and spending like there was no tomorrow.

Now just gotta sink the last two and take this idiot for everything he—

"The important thing," a voice from above him said suddenly, forcing Kitsios to scratch his shot, "when you're playing pool is to focus, to *never* lose your concentration."

Slamming the stick down on the table, Kitsios whirled around. "Who—?"

But there wasn't anybody in the bar who hadn't been there before. The ones who were, though, were all looking up.

Kitsios followed their gazes to see Spider-Man hanging upside down from the ceiling.

"What do you want, *arachne*?"

"Dr. Octopus."

Letting out a breath, Kitsios asked point-blank, "I tell you where to find him, you let me get back to my game?"

"That's the idea. C'mon, I know Ock's hatching a scheme, and with him, schemes usually mean fancy-shmancy equipment, and fancy-shmancy equipment usually means yo—"

"He's at 91st Street—the abandoned subway station under Broadway. I got him the generators and lights and some lab stuff."

Spider-Man didn't say anything for a second. "That's it? I don't have to beat you up or anything?"

Kitsios sighed. "I got a game to finish and a tournament to play uptown. I don't have time for you. Besides, what can Otto do to me?"

"You really don't want to know the answer to that one, Kitsios."

Waving off Spider-Man, Kitsios picked up his cue stick. "Nobody can get what I can get. That makes me too useful to beat up, except by people like you. So the best way to keep you from doing that is to tell you what you want."

He walked toward the table, but his opponent used his own stick to block Kitsios's path. "Nah, man, it's *my* shot. You scratched."

Pointing at the ceiling with his thumb, Kitsios said, "That was because of—"

"I don't care if yo' Moms came in to tell me how much fun she had with me last night, you don't hit nothin', you scratch, *my* shot, got it?"

Kitsios looked up, only to see that Spider-Man was gone. *Good riddance. Those super heroes just get in the way of things.* Then he looked down at the table, seeing that his opponent had several good shots and might be able to take the table before Kitsios had another chance.

"Yes," he said slowly, "I 'got' it. Take your shot." He stepped off to the side and took his cell phone out of his pocket.

13

For Otto Octavius, it had begun three months ago when he visited his mother's grave.

Technically, one could argue that it had started longer ago than that. The notion of infusing gamma radiation into one of the many drugs of which the doltish members of the human race partook, thus increasing its potency and also imbuing the user with one of the common paranormal side effects, had first occurred to him several years ago. But he had never bothered to marry that thought to an action.

But Octavius had goals, ones that required resources he didn't have, and could only acquire with money that he also didn't have. Petty thievery of the type in which he had once indulged was no longer practical—too many banks and depositories were equipped with security designed to stop people like Octavius. Circumventing that, while possible, wasn't cost-effective given the actual monetary gain he'd realize from the theft.

On a winter evening three months ago, the anniversary of Mary Lavinia Octavius's death, he visited her grave. He wasn't entirely sure why he had chosen to visit on this particular anniversary. Several such had come and gone without his marking it, but this year, on the eve of his most recent plan's commencement, he had done so.

For the longest time, he had been devoted to his mother, particularly after his father, Torbert Octavius, died. Father was a thug, a construction worker who labored with his hands and had very little patience with people who used their intelligence. He was also good enough to die in a construction accident, thus freeing Otto from his endless tirades about how Otto should defend himself against the school bullies "like a man"—as if any but a simian would respond in such a manner.

Father was dead, so he no longer mattered. Liberated from his verbal and physical abuse, both Otto and Mother had flourished. Encouraged by Mother to excel, Otto had graduated at the top of his class both as an undergraduate and a graduate student, attaining his doctorate in the minimum time.

Though he'd taken many jobs, and developed a reputation as one of the premier atomic scientists in the country, it was as a project manager at the United States Atomic Research Center that he had come into his own. His cousin on his mother's side, Thomas Hargrove, worked there—one of only two competent people employed at the center. The other was Mary Alice.

Ah, Mary Alice.

Unlike the other dolts at USARC, Mary Alice understood his work. More to the point, she understood *him* in a way no one else but Mother ever did.

Sadly, their relationship was not to be. Mother was furious at the notion of Otto's abandoning her. Foolishly, Otto agreed, not wanting to disappoint the woman who raised him, who encouraged him.

To this day, Otto wondered what he had been thinking listening to Mother. With Mary Alice, he would have been happy. Instead, he shunned her, got Hargrove to fire her from USARC, and devoted himself fully to his work.

It had been all he had left.

Mary Alice went on to marry some other man. Eventually she died of complications resulting from a blood transfusion that was tainted with HIV.

Perhaps it was all for the best. The work was what mattered.

Certainly Mother didn't, even before her death. Otto came home early one night—a rare occasion when he *didn't* work a twenty-hour day—to find Mother dressed up, preparing for a date.

Otto, naturally, was livid. He had sacrificed his own happiness with Mary Alice for Mother's sake, yet she felt free to gallivant around with some imbecile behind his back.

They argued. Never a skinny woman, Mother couldn't handle the strain of her prodigious bulk and the stress of their contretemps. A cardiac infarction ended her life.

She no longer mattered, either.

Liberated from her simpering, he was able to accomplish great things. Already the world's leading authority on radiation, he had, months earlier, designed a set of four mechanical arms that allowed him to manipulate volatile materials from a safe distance. Then came the explosion that fused the arms to his body, granting him full mental control over the dexterous limbs.

On that day Otto Octavius—wretch, outcast, the prototypical "mama's boy"—died, and "Dr. Octopus" was reborn from his ashes. The nickname had been given to him as a sneer by those inferior minds at USARC, and Octavius took great pleasure in throwing it back in their faces as the name he took as a recognized genius.

True, the press insisted on labeling him a "super villain," but Octavius was far more than that. He'd been belittled, betrayed, and bothered by so many for so long. Lesser minds had kept him from achieving his goals.

And it had all started with dear old Mother.

What would my life have been like if she had died with Father? he had thought that night at her grave months ago. *Or if so many others who got in my way had not been present to ruin my plans? When people die, they stop mattering. So it's time some of them died. Especially that irritating arachnid . . .*

Spider-Man had been the one to stymie Octavius's plans the first time, and most of the times after that. Octavius's first jail sentence was light—Mother's final gift to him, as her recent death was cited by his lawyer as the main reason why the bench should take it easy on him, and the judge agreed—and what few prison stays he'd had since were short-lived.

No jail could hold a man of his superior intellect for long. Mother may have appreciated his genius, but she never understood it.

No one did.

Certainly not Spider-Man, despite his continued meddlesome presence, which was sufficiently routine that Octavius had, on this occasion, taken steps to prepare for it.

The phone call a few moments ago from Kitsios confirmed that those preparations were about to bear fruit, as did the sound of rending metal that signaled the door to the dome's caving in.

The dome had been constructed in the 91st Street station mostly by Octavius's arms at his direction, using material supplied by Kitsios. As a youth, Octavius had made a study of the various abandoned underground caverns located throughout the New York metropolitan area—abandoned military bases, unused land, power stations, and the like—which he had used in adulthood as bases of operation. Abandoned subway locales were also beneficial, whether the caverns constructed for the abortive attempt at a subway in the late nineteenth century, or places like the 91st Street station, originally built for the still-running subway constructed in the early twentieth.

Made of reinforced steel, the dome served to protect Octavius's ears from the din of the 1, 2, 3, and 9 trains that rattled by at high speeds on their way to and from the 96th Street station, and his sensibilities from the muck-encrusted, graffiti-covered, rat-infested walls and floors of the long-abandoned platform. Only someone with Octavius's strength could get through the dome's walls and single door.

Whatever the arachnid's failings, he was a creature of considerable strength. He stood now in the gap in the dome created by his rending of the door, his costume covered in a layer of soot and grime from traversing the subway tunnels in order to arrive here.

"It's over, Ock."

Smiling, Octavius said, "I doubt that very much."

Octavius had expected the arachnid to arrive much sooner. Kitsios had informed him that Spider-Man had spent the last several days in search of Octavius. Since Octavius's only outside contacts on this endeavor were Carolyn Trainer and Elias Kitsios, he instructed the latter to make his movements known and, when his and the arachnid's paths inevitably crossed, to provide Spider-Man with the 91st Street locale.

Now that he had been good enough to show up, Octavius attacked Spider-Man with two of his arms. Predictably, the arachnid jumped out of the way—and just as predictably, Octavius attacked with a third arm.

To his surprise, Spider-Man succumbed to the attack, the end of the arm colliding with his masked head.

However, Spider-Man recovered quickly, and ducked out of the way of the fourth arm, leaping onto the curved wall of the dome and projecting one of his tiresome webs toward Octavius's face. Octavius deflected it easily with two of his arms, the webbing sliding off the specially treated metal surface of his arms. Long gone were the days when Octavius would succumb to so minor an inconvenience as the arachnid's artificial web.

The remaining two arms had Spider-Man cornered near the floor of the dome, but he was able to grab each with one hand to stave them off. "It wasn't enough for you, was it, Ock?" Spider-Man asked through what sounded like clenched teeth. "You couldn't just poison the streets with your radioactive garbage, you had to target innocent people?" There was a tone in the voice that surprised Octavius: an anger, a resentment that was almost personal.

Octavius laughed. "Your definition of 'innocence' differs from mine. All those who were targeted offended me in some manner—a guilty charge in my own court."

His other two arms went for Spider-Man's legs. Octavius planned to grab one extremity with each arm and toss him aside like so much garbage. He hadn't defeated Spider-Man this quickly since their first meeting. *It can't be this easy,* he thought.

And, indeed, it wasn't. Still holding on to two metal arms, the arachnid leapt forward in a flip that took his feet around two hundred and seventy degrees to land with his feet on the wall of the dome. It was, Octavius had to grudgingly admit, an impressive move, one a normal human simply could never have made.

"Guilty, huh? What about May Parker?"

At that, Octavius snarled. In truth Mrs. Parker had done nothing bad to him—it was because of that foolish, deformed gangster that Octavius lost his chance at that power plant. Mrs. Parker had been kind and generous to him.

Just like Mother was . . .

No, she too had to die. Just like Gaxton, Haight, Hunt, and the others, including Carolyn's former husband.

They had to die so they would no longer matter.

"Cat got your tongue, Ockie?" Spider-Man asked as he pulled on the metal arms in his grasp, hoping to yank Octavius off his feet. However, the arms were not at their full extension, and all the arachnid's foolish pulling did was extend them.

Octavius commanded them to retract once again, in the hopes of doing what Spider-Man intended to do to him: pull him off the dome wall. However, Spider-Man simply let go of the arms.

"I have no need to justify my actions to anyone, arachnid, *least* of all the likes of you."

Leaping up to the top of the dome, Spider-Man spoke in the same angry tone. "It's over, Ock. The cops've got your groupie, and I've got you."

As Spider-Man dropped down, apparently hoping an aerial assault would prove more fruitful than a frontal one, Octavius raised all four arms and had them attack Spider-Man at different points in his descent. Even he would not be fast enough to evade all four.

I wonder if he speaks the truth about Carolyn, or is simply trying to bluff me. No matter—she has served her purpose. The funds from peddling the gamma-irradiated drugs to the unwitting fools of this city had amounted to more than he needed to bankroll his latest endeavor.

Two of Octavius's arms collided with the arachnid's form, sending him flying across the dome. Spider-Man managed to recover enough to land feetfirst on the dome wall, using his ability to stick to surfaces to land safely. Octavius then tried to club him with two of his arms, but his foe managed to dodge them—and leave himself open for a blow to his ribs with a third arm. Spider-Man grabbed that arm, but Octavius simply yanked it out of his foe's grasp.

The dance continued for several more minutes, and Octavius had to admit to a certain disappointment: Spider-Man was barely holding his own. Octavius was not sure whether he was still reeling from the initial blow to the head, or not thinking straight due to the anger Octavius detected in his voice, or both. His enemy was also forgoing his usual attempts at wit—for which Octavius was frankly grateful—which alone bespoke an unusual state of affairs.

Perhaps I will be able to kill him as well. That was almost too much to hope for. Despite all his attempts over the years, he had never been able to deal the arachnid a fatal blow, and Octavius wasn't naïve enough to believe that today would change that—but that didn't mean he wouldn't try his best.

Spider-Man leapt about the dome like a dervish, but as fast as he was, Octavius's arms were faster, moving as they did with the speed of thought. The confined space of the dome did not permit the wallcrawler his usual freedom of movement, and Octavius was able to deliver several blows to the head, ribs, and stomach. For the arachnid's part, he was able to get anywhere near Octavius only twice, and both times, Octavius was able to use his arms to remove Spider-Man from proximity to his person.

Then, Spider-Man leapt to the ceiling once again and looked at the lab table at the far end of the dome from the entrance.

"Nice little setup you've got here, Ockie." Spider-Man's voice sounded slurred, as if he were too tired to go on, and he seemed unsteady. "What is it with you and underground holes, anyhow? It's no wonder you're so pale."

"My motives are not for such as you to divine, arachnid."

"Y'know, Ock, that's what I love about tussling with you—I mean, let's face it, most of the guys I throw down with have the cranial capacity of a fried egg. But you, you're the only one who uses 'divine' in a sentence—as a verb, no less."

Truly I was hoping to avoid the inane banter. Octavius snarled and thrust an arm toward the ceiling, but Spider-Man leapt behind the lab table. He kicked it hard enough to send it flying through the air at Octavius, who had to use all four arms to deflect it.

When he had done so, the arachnid was nowhere to be seen.

Turning and looking out through the opening left by the shattered door, Octavius saw a web-line swinging limply from the ceiling, obviously abandoned within the last few seconds. Spider-Man had used the desk as a distraction to make his escape. *No doubt he realized his defeat was imminent.*

Octavius at once considered and rejected the notion of

giving chase. It would be foolish to expose himself at this stage. *Let him make his futile attempts to stem the tide of the drug, or to find me again. He will fail at both.* This particular hideaway was simply a front for the inevitable confrontation with Spider-Man. The arachnid had no idea where Octavius's true base of operations was, nor would he ever find it.

Then Octavius smiled, remembering one of the arachnid's tired tricks. He quickly found one of those ridiculous "spider-tracers" on his back. Shaped like a small red spider, the device served as a homing beacon. Too many times in the past, Spider-Man had found Octavius by attaching one of the infernal devices to his person.

Smashing the small tracer to pieces with one of his arms, he thought, *Not this time, fool.*

The dome shook as an uptown train went careening down the tracks, headed toward 96th Street. With the door smashed, the dome had lost much of its usefulness, and Spider-Man's awareness of it—and subsequent thrashing—disposed of the rest of it. Grabbing his hat and camel-hair coat, he contracted his arms and headed toward the tracks.

All is going precisely according to plan.

Jeroen Shapiro stared at the purple-haired woman on the video monitor.

He was standing with Fry and Wheeler in the cramped video room, which had the monitors that got the feed from the video cameras in the two interrogation rooms. Anybody who watched television knew that interrogations weren't conducted in secret, and nobody was fooled by the old two-way glass anymore, so many precinct houses had just installed video cameras and had done with it. Besides, having a video record of interrogations was useful at times.

Carolyn Trainer had just been coming home when Shapiro and his task force, along with some uniforms, burst into her home, warrant in hand. They had found a stash of Triple X in her closet behind a false wall—Fry had been the one to notice that the depth of the closet didn't match the layout of the house—and had brought her to the Two-Four. Shanahan was continuing to supervise the search of Trainer's house, while Petrocelli was heading to Parkway Hospital in Queens to interview May Parker, the latest unwitting Triple X junkie. She was in recovery and, according to a rather peevish-sounding doctor, was eager to talk to the police even though the doctor said she should rest. Shapiro just wished all witnesses were so willing to help out.

O'Leary was walking in, putting her cell phone on a clip on her belt. "Just left a message for Spider-Man. No word from him on Octopus."

"We don't need to," Shapiro said, "we got her."

"What if Spider-Man was right?" O'Leary asked.

Shapiro whirled sharply on her. "He wasn't. Jimmy and I will get her to flip."

Shaking her head, O'Leary said, "I don't think you will, Jerry. She's devoted to him."

"And you're a little too devoted yourself."

Defensively, O'Leary asked, "What the hell's *that* supposed to mean?"

"You've had your nose in spider-butt this entire case."

Fry interposed his massive form between Shapiro and O'Leary. "That's outta line, Jerry—and you know it. Una's right—Spider-Man *has* been helpful, and he hasn't been wrong yet."

Shapiro looked up at Fry, then walked toward the door, pushing past O'Leary. "Let's go do our interview."

The fact was, Fry was correct, both about his being out of line and about Spider-Man and O'Leary's being right. As irritating as O'Leary's hero worship was, it hadn't interfered with the police work. What chafed Shapiro most was having that damn costume shoved down his throat by Green and the inspector. This was *his* unit; that should've been *his* call.

He shook his head. *Right, like the bosses have ever given a crap about that kind of protocol before.*

Speaking of which, he bumped into Green in the hallway between the video room and the interrogation room where they'd placed Trainer. "So, at last we have an arrest."

"Yeah, Joll. I'm on my wa—"

"Inspector Garcia is practically wetting his pants, he's so tickled by these joyous tidings. He's calling a press conference and everything, talking about the mass quantities of Triple X that the good Detective Fry here found in the suspect's closet. Of course, if he was also able to say that the aforementioned suspect had given up her partner in this endeavor, said partner being one of the most wanted fugitives in the country, I suspect that the inspector would be positively orgasmic."

"We're gonna go try that now," Shapiro said.

A huge grin bisected Green's round face. "Excellent news! I'll go inform the inspector now."

Shapiro watched the sergeant continue on his way down the hall, a noticeable spring in his step.

Fry asked, "Did he just skip?"

"Don't even go there, Jimmy." Shapiro shuddered. "I hate this."

"Hate what? Joll's happy."

"This kinda happy means he'll be *seriously* pissed off if we screw this up." He looked at Fry. "So let's not screw this up."

They entered Interrogation Room 2 to find Carolyn Trainer, still wearing the apron and all-maroon outfit she used to give free ice cream samples to the customers at the Associated at Queens Boulevard, including one laced with Triple X to feed to May Parker. She even wore a metal nametag that said HEYER, which belonged to an employee of the ice cream company who had called in sick that day, and who also had a substantial deposit recently put in her savings account. Uniforms were already on the way to Heyer's apartment to pick her up.

The interrogation room was painted an unfortunate shade of green, and no one had applied a new coat since Shapiro transferred to the precinct. There were no windows, and the only features besides the two rickety metal chairs and Formica table were the video camera in a far corner and the air vents. During some interviews, the detectives would alter the temperature to help put the suspect ill at ease.

"I gotta tell you," Shapiro said to Fry as they walked through the door, "I don't know why we're bothering with talking to her. We got the drugs, we got her, we got two witnesses that say she's dealing this crap. Why don't we just toss her into the cage and be done with it?" He closed the door behind him.

Fry, picking up the cue smoothly, said, "Well, y'know, Jerry, I was looking at this woman's background. I mean yeah, she's got a Ph.D., but that's in computer science. She doesn't have any kind of chemical skills."

Shapiro just stared dumbly at Fry. "C'mon, Jimmy, what's she need chemical skills for? All she's gotta do is get this stuff in the hands of some slingers, and she's set."

"I don't know, Jerry." Fry shook his head and folded his arms, leaning his tall frame against the wall. "You heard what the lab geeks said—somebody with some serious test-tube smarts made this stuff. That ain't this lady."

Sitting down in one of the two chairs opposite Trainer—who was held fast via a single handcuff that was bolted to the table—Shapiro said, "Yeah, that's a good point."

For the first time, Trainer spoke. She was smiling. "Cute act, boys, but you're wasting your time. I want my lawyer."

Shapiro winced. "Now, see, you really shouldn't do that. If you ask for a lawyer, this conversation ends."

"That was the idea. I know my rights. You were kind enough to read them to me earlier, after all."

"This is true, you do have that right. But if this conversation ends, we write this up like what it looks like."

Fry added, "And it looks pretty shitty for you."

Counting his points off on his fingers, Shapiro said, "We've got the Triple X drugs in your house. We've got a witness who admits you sold him Triple X. We've also got the crew you sold the drugs to—they got shot up by some Ukrainians who didn't appreciate the competition. Most of these guys are brain-dead, and their head guy got himself shot, so I can pretty much guarantee that one of them will be more than happy to shave off a few years so he can put in the one who sold their stuff. We got the lady from the ice cream company that you bought off to borrow her uniform. We got all that on you—plus, I'm pretty sure the old lady you gave the ice cream to will be able to ID you, too."

"You know, if you're gonna do this stuff seriously," Fry said thoughtfully, "I'd lose the purple hair. It makes it real easy to pick you out of a lineup, y'know? Even if you're a half-blind old lady like May Parker. And what's the big deal with her, anyhow? I mean, in order to have been there when she was, you would've had to stake out the supermarket, and maybe her house, too, for, like, *weeks.*"

Trainer shook her head and looked away. "I really wish I'd killed that old hag when I gave her that stuff."

Shapiro looked up at Fry. "What's this? Detective Fry, I do believe that I heard Ms. Trainer say something that can and will be held against her in a court of law."

"I believe you're right, Detective Shapiro."

Looking wholly unintimidated, Trainer said, "Nice try, boys, but the only way to prove that I said what I just said is to show the videotape that camera up there's feeding to, which will show that my statement came after the part where I asked for my lawyer. Which I'm asking for again. Until he shows up, you can't use a damn thing I say to you—which is why I'm going to tell you this." She leaned forward in the chair. "I will never say anything that will lead to Otto's being imprisoned. I don't care how much time I'm likely to get, either from the DA in a deal or from a jury. If it helps Otto, then I'll do it, and that's all there is to say."

Then she leaned back, a triumphant look on her face.

Shapiro stared at her for several seconds. She didn't have her mechanical arms—they hadn't been found yet in her house—and without them, she was just a normal woman. A very small part of Shapiro wanted to turn off the video camera and beat the living crap out of her.

And that would accomplish what, exactly? She's not gonna give Octavius up.

So without another word, he got up and left the room, Fry right behind him.

As soon as he shut the door behind him, Fry said, "Spider-Man was right, sh—"

Whirling on Fry and pointing a finger up at his face, Shapiro said, "Don't *ever* say those words in my presence again, Jimmy! You understand me? I put up with that costume 'cause Garcia said to, but I will *not* listen to that. Bad enough I'm getting it in both ears from Una."

Before Fry could reply, O'Leary came out of the video room. "I told you she wouldn't flip."

"So did I," Fry said, "and so did Spider-Man."

"Since when do we start consulting costumes about police work?"

O'Leary said, "It's the same as when we talk to any expert about a particular case. Spider-Man knows Dr. Octopus better than anyone."

"And, more to the point," Fry said, "he's better equipped to deal with the gamma-heads *and* Octavius than we are."

Shapiro had had more than enough of this. "So what? A bodybuilder's better equipped to subdue a brain-dead hopped up on meth, but we ain't about to start using one. He ain't trained, he ain't accountable—he doesn't have a badge."

"Maybe," O'Leary said, "but he ain't going anywhere, either. And I'd rather have him working with us, given a choice."

Although Shapiro had several responses to that, Green's arrival forced him to squelch them. "That was a remarkably speedy interrogation, Detective. I have to confess, your prowess in encouraging suspects to trade up continues to improve."

"No it hasn't," Shapiro said. "She lawyered up the minute we walked in. And even if she hadn't"—he gritted his teeth—"the costume was right, she ain't givin' Octavius up. We need to get him some other way."

Green stared at Shapiro for a few seconds.

Here it comes, Shapiro thought, dreading the thermonuclear explosion that was about to issue forth.

"Then we'll get him some other way. Meantime, we've got the redoubtable Ms. Trainer, and she'll make a dandy top story on the five o'clock news, and an even dandier headline. Nice work."

Green slapped Shapiro gently on the arm, and continued down the hall.

Silence reigned for several seconds before O'Leary asked Fry, "Did he just *not* kill Jerry?"

"Apparently not," Fry said dryly.

Shapiro let out the breath he hadn't realized he was holding. "Guess Trainer's good enough for Garcia's goddamn press conference. So let him have her. Like Joll said, we'll find Octavius some other way."

14

Pain sliced through Spider-Man's chest as he gingerly swung his way toward Central Park. *That's at least a couple of cracked ribs. Probably a concussion, too. I love my life.*

When he got to the park, he leapt from tree to tree, which was also painful, but not as much as raising his arms to swing on a web-line was. He'd have to do enough of that once he got out of the park, but he wanted to do as little of it as possible. To that end, he worked his way down to 59th Street, then leapt across to one of the trees hanging over the fountain in front of the Plaza Hotel.

"Mommy, look! It's Captain America!"

Spider-Man looked down to see a little girl pointing up from the sidewalk. The mother in question said, "That's nice, dear," in a distracted voice.

I've got too much of a headache to correct her, he thought with a smile, so he gave her a jaunty wave, then shot out a web-line and attached it to the FAO Schwartz building across the street, took a mighty leap, and swung around to alight on the side of Trump Tower.

Okay, that was a mistake. The action of swinging sent white-hot agony coursing through his entire torso. Leaping over to the Schwartz building, he climbed gingerly up to the roof and decided to simply run across rooftops until he got to the Queensboro Bridge, then run across that. *Anything else hurts too much.*

When he reached the bridge, he pulled out Ursitti's cell phone and turned it on. There was one message, from O'Leary: "We got Trainer—she was just coming home when we came to deliver the warrant. Was wearing some kinda weird apron or something."

Spider-Man sighed as he started running up the frame of the bridge. Trainer had obviously gone straight home from the supermarket after poisoning Aunt May. *Her bad luck,* he thought with a certain malice.

O'Leary continued. "She's already made it clear she won't give Octavius up. You're right, she's really devoted to that nut job. I'll let you know if anything changes—hope you're having better luck with Octavius."

As he reached the top of the first tower, Spider-Man put the phone away. There wasn't much point in letting the cops know about Ock's little hidey-hole—it wasn't his real base anyhow. It took him a while to really take a look at the equipment Ock had in his 91st Street abode, but once he did, it was obvious. All he had was a couple of test tubes and a Bunsen burner. It wasn't anywhere near enough equipment to do what Ock had been doing. Heck, it wasn't enough for one of Peter Parker's "Intro to Chemistry" students to work with, much less a scientist of Ock's caliber. *It was just a place to lure me and kick my butt. That's why Kitsios gave the location up so easily.*

Working his way to the second tower, he sighed and chastised himself. *Ock's one of your three or four deadliest foes, web-head—you should know better than to take him on when you're not thinking straight.* If he hadn't been so focused on his anger over Aunt May's being poisoned with the

Triple X, he might have questioned Kitsios's easy acqui-escence, or recognized the inadequacy of Ock's setup at 91st Street right away instead of after Ock used him as a punching bag for half an hour. *Which means the next time I face him, I won't be as aggravated, but I'll still be exhausted, and badly injured to boot.*

Gritting his teeth against the pain—the buildings were too far apart in Queens for his rooftop-running gag to do the trick—Spider-Man swung his way home.

To his surprise, Mary Jane was waiting for him. He thought she'd be at rehearsal. She got up and walked to-ward him as he came in the bedroom window—she had been lying on the bed reading a magazine.

"Tiger, you"—her nose wrinkled—"smell *really* bad."

He laughed, then clutched his side. She noticed that, walked more quickly to him, guided him to the bed, then went straight for the first-aid kit.

Gingerly removing his costume shirt, mask, and gloves while seated on the edge of the bed, he asked, "What happened to rehearsal?"

"They're running the scenes I'm not in—Dmitri's fo-cusing all his energy on Regina—so I got to come home early."

"Lucky me."

Mary Jane came back with the kit and started taping his ribs. "So what happened to you *this* time?"

"Good news and bad news. The good news is, Greg gave his statement, and it was enough for Shapiro and his band of loonies to serve a warrant on Carolyn Trainer."

Emphatically, Mary Jane said, "That's *great* news."

Peter smiled wryly. Mary Jane didn't exactly have good memories of Trainer's brief tenure wearing the tentacles. He continued: "The other good news is that I tracked down Ock."

"And the bad news is he kicked your butt all over Manhattan?"

"No, just all over the little dome he built in the old 91st Street station. Thing is, he was waiting for me so he could beat the daylights out of me." He shook his head, an unwise move with the concussion, and he had to steady himself on the bed. "I can't believe I let him walk all over me like that."

As she finished taping his chest, Mary Jane said, "As I recall, the first time you and the good doctor met, he cleaned your clock, too."

"Yeah." Peter remembered the day clearly. It was the first time he'd ever been defeated in his nascent super heroic career, and he had been convinced that he'd have to hang up his webs forever. Only when he attended a lecture by the Human Torch of the Fantastic Four—who revealed that the FF had been defeated themselves a few times, but always got up off the mat, as it were—did he regain his confidence and go back after Octopus. He said to Mary Jane, "I don't think I'll be able to fuse his arms together again like I did then, though."

"No, he'll expect that." Mary Jane put her hands on his shoulders and stared at him with those beautiful green eyes of hers. "So you'll have to do something he won't expect."

"God, MJ, the two of us have gone 'round and 'round so many times, I don't think either one of us can really surprise the other, unless—"

Suddenly his face brightened. He had the perfect solution. It would take a bit of work, and he'd need to track

Ock down via the spider-tracer. *But it's so crazy, it just might work.*

He stood up. Mary Jane stared up at him. "I know that look, Tiger. It's the I've-got-an-idea-that's-so-crazy-it-just-might-work look."

Grinning, he said, "You know me entirely too well. I'm gonna need to swallow an entire bottle of aspirin, and then I need to make a call. . . ."

Otto Octavius had always been happiest in the laboratory. It was the only place on this wretched planet where he was able to exert total control. He was the master of it all: the chemicals, the isotopes, the equipment, the elements themselves.

And the plan had worked beautifully. Creating a designer drug was the work of only a few days, and most of that was finding the right proportion of radiation to infuse the drug with so that it would have the proper effect. The fools of the city would jump at the chance to give themselves paranormal abilities in addition to a high. Even better, the drug killed them that much faster, thus reducing the population, which was always a plus for Octavius. His eventual goal was to control everything outside the lab as well as inside it, and control was easier when the overall numbers were smaller. Carolyn's criminal contacts were more extensive than Octavius's—he never bothered with such minutiae, simply employing extra sets of arms when he needed them—and so he let her do the legwork. She was now rotting in a holding cell in the 24th Precinct for her troubles, but Octavius had decided to reward her when the time was right.

Targeting the others—Hunt, who had tried to imprison him after the explosion; Gaxton, who so ineptly mishandled the job in Philadelphia; Haight, who presumed too much; dear Mrs. Parker, the simpering old fool; and the others, such as Carolyn's ex-husband—was a two-edged bonus. For one thing, he was able to rid the world of those who had annoyed him—so they would no longer matter. For another, they were, to some degree or other, innocents, and therefore would push all the right buttons with the arachnid. Spider-Man was always at his sloppiest when bystanders' lives were in danger. Octavius had scored one of his greatest victories when he killed a retired police captain whose name Octavius could no longer remember. Spider-Man had been blamed by the fourth estate for the murder, and, though he won in the short term, the death of that old man had long-term consequences for Spider-Man, both personally and perceptually. Their recent tussle at the dome under 91st Street had also served that purpose adequately. *The only flaw was that I was unable to finish him off. But that will come in time. The arachnid is reactive, much like the creature he emulates—he waits until his prey comes into his web before dealing with it. I am proactive, and unlike him, I can afford to lose. He can lose only once—and that will be a good day indeed. . . .*

His current plan made use of the facility that once headquartered the United States Atomic Research Center in lower Westchester. Before it was shut down by the Department of Defense and left abandoned, the facility had had an isolation that appealed to Octavius when he started working there. Since the shutdown, an industrial park had been constructed nearby. Still, the location itself was ideal for Octavius's researches.

Selling the drug had given him the necessary capital, as well as a distraction for the police and Spider-Man.

Now, with the materiel and equipment he'd purchased from Kitsios, he could start the next phase.

"Now this—*this* is a laboratory! Not like that kids' chem set you had at 91st Street."

No. It cannot be! But when Octavius whirled around and looked up at the ceiling, he saw the hated arachnid hanging from it. "How did you find me? I destroyed your infernal spider-tracer!"

"Correction, Ockie—you destroyed *one* of my infernal spider-tracers. I left two on you, in case you found one."

Octavius sometimes forgot that the arachnid, while limited in so many ways, was still cleverer than most. "No matter. I will defeat you as easily as I did before."

And with that he came at Spider-Man with all four arms.

Okay, Spider-Man thought as he leapt off the ceiling to avoid Ock's attack, *this really has to work now.*

This time around, he didn't bother with any kind of offensive maneuvering, for two reasons. One was that the plan called for him to lure Ock out to the industrial park. And the other was that he was in enough pain just dodging Ock's blows. One day later, his ribs felt better, especially taped up, but every move still gave him at best a poke of pain, and at worst searing agony throughout his entire thoracic region.

He just moved on instinct, letting his spider-sense warn him when the blows were coming and dodging out of the way, making sure to keep his distance, forcing Ock to stretch his arms to the limit.

"Cah-*mon*, Doc, is that the best you can do? The Scorpion can tag me with one tail more often than you're getting me with all four of those goofy arms of yours."

Even as he taunted Ock, he moved toward the staircase that led to the aboveground portions of the former USARC. Ock had holed up in the basement, which was where all the good labs were. Spider-Man had noted that the section which held the room where the explosion that created Dr. Octopus took place was still sealed off by lead blast doors. *Probably won't be safe for human life for a bunch of years yet.*

As Spider-Man ran up the stairs, his spider-sense buzzed a warning. One of Ock's arms was heading not for his head, but for the metal staircase in front of him. Leaping into the air even as the arm came down on the stairs, rending them into smaller pieces of scrap with the spine-vibrating squeal of metal on metal, Spider-Man flipped around over the smashed stairs and reached down to grab an arm.

That was a mistake, as Dr. Octopus retracted the arm with a jerk. Spider-Man didn't let go for a second, which was long enough for the motion to aggravate his ribs.

Stick with the plan, doofus, he thought, continuing upstairs and clutching his ribs with one arm.

"You will not escape me again, arachnid! You will die in this place, just as I was born here!"

"As usual, Ock, you're the master of cheap symbolism." Spider-Man leapt up to the top of the stairs, then ran across the wall of the giant hallway that served as the entryway to the USARC.

"You imagine yourself to have an advantage in the open spaces, do you?"

"Well, I've always had a healthy imagination," Spider-Man said as he kicked his way through the large doors and out into the open air beyond the facility.

He had gone about fifty feet toward the industrial park when his spider-sense buzzed, just after hearing the sound of rending metal. Unfortunately, he was in mid-leap, and was able only to curl himself into a ball to try to avoid the door, which Dr. Octopus had ripped from its hinges and tossed at Spider-Man.

His attempt was only partially successful—the door clipped his left arm, knocking his momentum off and sending him careening toward the ground.

Reaching out with his right arm, he shot out a web-line at a tree that was at least fifty feet off. He snagged it and used it to swing up in the air, shooting out another line to snag a different tree, which he pulled himself to-ward. All the while, his chest and arm were throbbing a conga-drum line in his head. He'd been going full tilt for days, with not enough sleep, plus his teaching duties (even with taking Tuesday off), he had cracked ribs, and now a bruised arm, and he was trying to avoid being killed by a powerful super-villain.

Just a typical Wednesday evening in the Parker life, he thought with a sigh as he shot a web-line from the tree out to the parking lot at the center of the industrial park.

There were only a few cars in the lot, but there shouldn't have been any, since the park was supposed to be evacuated.

Alighting for a landing in the northwest corner of the lot, as far from the few cars as possible, Spider-Man turned and waited for Ock to show up.

He didn't have to wait long. Using his arms to stride forward, Dr. Octopus entered the parking lot, the pincers on the ends of his arms smashing into the asphalt.

"This ends now, arachnid!" he said, his arms holding him still about thirty feet in front of Spider-Man.

Smiling under his mask, Spider-Man said, "You don't know the half of it. Look down."

"What are you playing at?" Dr. Octopus couldn't help but lower his head—only to notice two dozen red dots suddenly appearing on his chest.

Stealing a glance upward, Spider-Man saw that every roof of every building that adjoined the parking lot was filled with black-clad NYPD sharpshooters.

"It's over, Ock."

"Do you truly believe that this will dissuade me from killing you?"

"Get real, Ock—there are twenty-four guys up there. Yeah, you can deflect *a* bullet. But even you can't stop two dozen MP5s fired by experts."

A snarl formed on the doctor's face.

Nobody moved.

There was a very small part of Spider-Man's brain that wanted Doc Ock to make a move, to force the cops to take him down. It was no less than he deserved for all the deaths he'd caused, from Bennett Brant and Captain Stacy on down the line.

But that would mean placing myself above the law. And no matter what Shapiro and Shanahan and the rest of them might think, I'm not gonna do that.

Then, after several seconds passed, the snarl became a smile. He retracted his arms, bringing him down to the ground. "Well played, arachnid. I surrender."

Shapiro, O'Leary, and a few troopers from the state police came out from inside one of the buildings. O'Leary was holding some kind of bulky device that looked like a jet-pack from an old B-movie.

"Otto Octavius," Shapiro said, "you are under arrest for about half a dozen crimes I really don't feel like listing right now. You have the right to remain silent."

As Shapiro read Dr. Octopus his rights, O'Leary, with the aid of the troopers, placed the device on his back. As soon as they did, Ock's metal arms went limp. Spider-Man knew that the neutralizer was a standard piece of NYPD equipment for taking in paranormal fugitives. In fact, the villian slipped into it with the ease of long practice—after all, this wasn't his first arrest.

"Do you understand these rights as I've read them to you?" Shapiro asked.

"I daresay better than you, Detective." Octavius was still smiling. "I also understand that this changes nothing in the long term."

A large NYPD truck had pulled up while he was being fitted for his new accessory. The troopers led him into it.

O'Leary grinned at Spider-Man. "Nice plan."

"Thanks." He had tracked Ock to the old USARC building the previous night, then called O'Leary and tried to sell the police on his crazy idea. Spider-Man had to be the one to lure Dr. Octopus out and into an open space where the sharpshooters could do their work. For one thing, the facility was a maze, one Octopus knew intimately, and if they tried to storm it, Doc Ock could fend them off for hours, with a virtual guarantee of causalties among the cops. For another, the facility was technically federal property. Getting a warrant for it would probably mean going through the FBI, which not only added to the paperwork, but also meant they'd have to share the bust with the feds, something Inspector Garcia was loath to do. It was hard enough for Shapiro to convince him to cooperate with the state police.

The parking lot was the ideal spot for the takedown, as it was an open space that gave everyone a clear shot.

Shapiro shook his head. "I still can't believe he just surrendered."

"I'm not at all surprised," Spider-Man said. "In fact, I was counting on it. Look, if he surrenders, he just goes to jail. Five'll get you ten he breaks out—God knows, he's done it enough times before. If he doesn't surrender, he gets shot. Maybe he lives, but he probably doesn't, and he's already been dead once. Would *you* want to repeat the experience?"

Snorting, Shapiro said, "Hell, I don't want to do it the once, thanks. You realize we don't have him on Triple X. I mean, he's got a dozen outstanding warrants, so it's no problem sticking him in Ryker's."

Spider-Man shrugged. "Arresting Trainer got the Triple X off the streets. Arresting Ock guarantees there won't be any more to replace it. No more gamma-heads, and probably no more gang war, since Ray-Ray's crew doesn't have it to deal anymore. Isn't that the important part?"

O'Leary sighed. "There'll probably still be some territorial crap, since the Ukrainians might wanna take their blocks back. But that's business as usual."

"Yeah," Spider-Man said, "and you get the credit for arresting Dr. Octopus."

Finally, Shapiro smiled. "That doesn't suck."

Offering his hand, Spider-Man said, "It was a pleasure working with you, Detective."

For a moment, Shapiro just looked at Spider-Man's proffered hand like it was diseased. Then, tentatively, he clasped it in a handshake. "Thanks for the assist."

Looking at O'Leary, Spider-Man said, "You too, Detective."

Grinning, she said, "The pleasure was all mine. And remember what I told you."

Spider-Man nodded, figuring that O'Leary's notions about hero/cop cooperation wouldn't go over well with Shapiro, which was why she was vague. "See you around," he said as he shot a web-line out to one of the buildings and swung away toward home.

I'm going to sleep for a week. . . .

EPILOGUE

Hector Diaz stared at the ceiling, waiting for the doctor to show up with his personal stuff and tell him he could finally go the hell home. His mom had crappy insurance, so he couldn't do any of the physical therapy that the doc said he was supposed to do without paying extra for it, and they didn't have extra to pay.

So he was just going home. *About damn time.*

Someone knocked on the door. He looked over to see some white lady wearing a suit. She wasn't wearing a lab coat or nothing, so she probably wasn't a doctor.

"Are you Hector Diaz? My name's Betty Brant; I work for the *Daily Bugle*."

Hector blinked in surprise. He knew that name from somewhere—that was it, that article he read on the bus. *What the hell's a reporter doin' talkin' to me?*

Then he figured it out. "I ain't talkin' to you, lady."

"You sure?" She smiled. "Lots of people like to see their name in the paper."

"Bitch, you stupid or somethin'? My name go in the paper, I catch another bullet, and this won't just be my shoulder, you feel me?"

The Brant lady sat down on the guest chair. "It's just—well, we have a mutual friend. Peter Parker."

Figures. "Mr. Parker ain't no friend. He a teacher."

"He sees it differently, I guess. Anyhow, he said I might be able to get you to comment on something."

Hector rolled over so his back was to the reporter. *Where's that damn doctor?* "I ain't sayin' nothin'."

"You sure? See, I have some information here. In the last two days, thirteen people died from radiation poisoning because they took Triple X. Fifty more have been diagnosed, and some of them may die of it, too. Ten more people have died from other complications—including a schoolmate of yours named Javier Velasquez, who suffered a fatal heart attack last night. At least seven people have died of gunshot wounds because of the turf war between Ray-Ray and the Ukrainians, plus people like you who were wounded. And I guess I wanted to know what you had to say about that."

Hector rolled back over. "Ray-Ray's dead. We got us a new crew chief now, bitch. And we'll be payin' those Ukrainians *back*. Now get your ass out my room!"

She stood up, and she wasn't smiling no more. "You know, Peter said you were a good kid—and that you were a smart kid. Too smart to get caught up in all this. But if Ray-Ray's old crew is 'we' to you now, then obviously Peter was wrong. You're just another slinger who's too stupid to realize that he's gonna die before he's old enough to vote."

Turning around, she left the room.

Hector rolled back over. Blowback had already done told him that they'd be getting back at them Russians—and that Hector had a place in the crew if he wanted it. "Ray-Ray was always talkin' you up, yo," Blowback had said. "And we needs us some good soldiers."

But, even though he told the reporter bitch that he

was hooked up with them, the truth was, Hector hadn't said yes.

Yet.

He stared out the window. *Where that damn doctor at?*

Eileen Velasquez hated the fact that she had to break her word.

At Carlos and Manuel's funeral on a long-ago cloudy Saturday morning, she swore that she would never again bury one of her children. Now, thanks to that terrible drug, she was doing it again. She heard on the news that Dr. Octopus created the drug, which meant that yet another one of those super-powered people were destroying Eileen's family.

"And so we commend this poor young soul to heaven, where he now resides with our Lord Jesus Christ after being taken from us too young."

No, she thought as the priest told all his lies about where Javier was now, *it's not because of the drug. The drug just gave him a road to take to hell, but if it wasn't that, Javier would've found something else. And that's my fault.*

"We take solace in knowing that Javier is in a better place now."

She looked through her veil at the faces of those who sat in the chairs or stood around the grave that already had two members of her family and awaited the third in the closed coffin hovering over the big hole in the ground. (Although the heart attack that killed Javier left his body in perfectly fine shape, Eileen insisted on a closed coffin for the wake so she wouldn't have to look at her son's face in death.) Her sister came, along with her daughter Rosanna, as did Carlos's brother and mother, the latter bawling her eyes out at the death of her grandson. Somehow, she found tears that Eileen couldn't, so disgusted was she with herself.

A few of Javier's friends were there, and Eileen was ashamed to realize that she didn't know any of their names. She had never paid close enough attention to what Javier was doing to even be aware of them.

Also present were the dean of students from Midtown High School—earlier, before the burial started, she conveyed the alleged regrets of Principal Harrington, who supposedly had another engagement—as well as Peter Parker and his wife. The science teacher's presence did not surprise Eileen. He was a good man, and she hoped that his other students appreciated him more than Javier did.

Then she looked down to her right at Jorge. The boy looked sullen and angry and fidgety, like he wanted to go home.

"In the name of the Father, and of the Son, and of the Holy Spirit, amen."

Eileen crossed herself as the priest spoke, and said, "Amen."

"Please rise."

As she and the others stood up, she finally let go of the vain hope that Orlando would come. She had left messages on his cell phone saying when the funeral was, and when she'd called his dorm hall phone, his roommate said he had gone off-campus for a few days.

But he didn't turn up. *And why should he? He didn't care any more about Javier than—*

She didn't let herself finish the thought.

After they lowered Javier's body into the ground and the proceeding broke up, Eileen stood about twenty feet from the grave, holding Jorge's hand. Several people came over to offer their condolences. Well, the adults did—the kids went off on their own, and the dean from Midtown High did likewise.

When Parker and his wife came over, he clasped her free hand in both of his and said sincerely, "I'm really sorry I couldn't have done more for Javier, Ms. Velasquez."

"You have nothing to be sorry for, Mr. Parker. You did everything you could. More than most. And I'll always be grateful to you for that." She even managed to give him a small smile through the veil.

Indicating the tall redhead next to him, Parker said, "This is my wife, Mary Jane Watson."

Parker's wife's smile could have lit up a Christmas tree. "Peter's said a lot of nice things about you, Ms. Velasquez—I wish we could've met under better circumstances. I'm sorry for your loss."

Bending over to look at Jorge, Parker said, "You must be Jorge."

Jorge nodded.

"I'm Mr. Parker—I was one of Javier's teachers. Maybe when you go to high school, I'll be your teacher too."

"I'd like that," Eileen said.

" 'M not."

Looking down sharply at her son, Eileen said, "What are you saying, Jorge?"

" 'M gonna die too, right?"

Eileen felt her chest tighten. "Oh God, no, baby, that's not gonna happen." She got down on one knee and let go of Jorge's hand so she could put both her hands on his shoulders. Looking him straight in the eye, she said, "I'm not gonna lose you too, Jorge. I won't let it happen. We're both gonna make it, you hear me?"

Jorge didn't say anything. Eileen supposed that was better than his denying it.

Soon enough, they walked out of the cemetery. Carlos's mother was still crying, and was being comforted by her remaining son. Eileen's sister was driving them all back to her house in Flushing so the family could gather, for which Eileen was grateful. She even invited the Parkers, but they politely declined, saying they'd promised to take Parker's aunt out for lunch.

After getting into the passenger seat of her sister's car, Eileen removed her cell phone from her purse and turned it on. As soon as she got a signal, the phone beeped to indicate voice mail. As her sister started the slow drive through the winding roads of the cemetery, she listened to the voice mail message.

"Hey, Ma, it's Orlando. Look, I'm—I'm sorry about Javier. He wasn't that bad of a kid—and even if he was, y'know, he deserved better than that. I tried to get some time off to come up, but my boss said he'd fire me if I didn't make my hours, and I can't really lose this job, y'know? So, uh, look—I'm sorry, okay? I'll try to call you later, Ma. Bye."

Eileen found herself playing the message a second time, simply refusing to believe that this was really Orlando.

But it was. Maybe he didn't make it up here, but he did make the effort—and he was considerate enough to call and say he'd call again later.

It wasn't much, but Eileen clung to the sound of her oldest son's voice like it was a life preserver.

Maybe there's a chance for this family after all. . . .

•   •   •

It was a solemn Peter Parker who entered his aunt's house, his wife at his side. Both were dressed formally, and in black, having just returned from Javier Velasquez's funeral.

It was only their first funeral of the weekend. Tomorrow was Valerie McManus's. She'd died of radiation poisoning. Tonight was opening night of *The Z-Axis,* after two good preview performances, and Mary Jane told Peter that Dmitri had agreed—after much bitching and moaning—to dedicate the show to Valerie's memory.

For now, though, they were visiting Aunt May, who had been discharged from the hospital the previous night . . . and who was very lucky to be alive.

As soon as Peter walked in, a spring entered his step almost involuntarily as a familiar—and beloved—aroma caressed his nostrils.

She made wheat cakes. God, I love this woman.

By the time he reached the kitchen doorway, rational thought took over. He saw his aunt standing over the stove, wearing the KISS THE COOK apron he and Mary Jane had gotten her for her birthday, and fixed her with a stern gaze. "Aunt May, *what* are you doing? We were gonna take you *out* to eat."

"Don't be ridiculous. Now take a seat, both of you. These will be ready any second."

In a more gentle tone than Peter had used, Mary Jane said, "May, you really shouldn't be straining yourself like this—you just got out of the hospital."

As she turned her head, Peter saw a familiar twinkle in his aunt's eye. It was the one she got whenever she was about to lecture Peter or Uncle Ben. "When you get to be my age, getting up in the morning is straining yourself. Either you let it ruin what's left of your life, or you get used to it and do what you want."

Chuckling, Mary Jane said to Peter, "And people wonder where you get your stubborn streak."

"Oh, I don't wonder it at all." Peter loosened his tie and entered the kitchen. "Guess we should give in to the inevitable."

"Looks like, yeah."

Aunt May flipped over the wheat cakes, and then turned all the way around. "Now let me get a look at both of you." She shook her head. "My, but you look snappy. What a pity it took such an awful occasion to get you to look so nice."

"Yeah." Peter sat down at the kitchen table. "I'm glad we went. Javier wasn't a bad kid—well, okay, he *was* a bad kid, but still. I just wish I could've done more for him. Maybe if I'd had a chance . . ."

Mary Jane put her hand on his. "Tiger, don't start this *again*. You can't help everyone."

Aunt May slid the wheat cakes off the skillet and onto a serving plate. "But it's good that you try. Such a pity that Otto did what he did."

Shaking his head, Peter said, "I never did get what you saw in him."

"The same thing you saw in that boy," Aunt May said, the twinkle back in her eye. "Who knows? If Otto had had a teacher in high school who cared as much about him as you did about that boy, he might have become a productive member of society instead of the horrible man he turned into."

Peter thought back on what he knew about Ock before the accident. *What would he have been like if he had started out as a good person? Would having the power the arms gave him still have turned him bad?*

Then Peter thought about Hector. He had steered Betty to him, in the hopes that maybe he'd listen to her, since he'd shut Peter out ever since getting shot. However, based on the message Betty had left, she wasn't holding out any hope for him.

He speared his wheat cakes with a fork. "Maybe you're right, Aunt May. And maybe I *can't* help everyone, but I'm gonna try to help as many as I can." He popped the wheat cake into his mouth, and it proceeded to deliciously melt and explode all at the same time. For a brief moment, Peter was a teenager again, being fussed over by Aunt May and Uncle Ben.

"That's my boy. Oh, and did you get to see that press conference the other day?"

Nodding as he swallowed, Peter then said, "Yup. Shapiro didn't tell me he'd invited a camera crew along to Ock's capture—they were probably hiding behind one of the parked cars."

Predictably, a press conference had been held at the 24th Precinct announcing the arrests of both Trainer and Ock, which included Inspector Garcia's showing off the huge stash of Triple X they took from Trainer's house, while the commissioner sang the praises of Shapiro and the task force. New York 1, a local cable news station, also had footage of Ock's capture at the industrial park. Peter wasn't sure why a dinky cable station got that exclusive, nor was he entirely happy that the fourth estate had been invited to the takedown, but he wasn't about to argue with the good press, especially when the commissioner also thanked Spider-Man for his assistance—while a nearly apoplectic Shapiro looked on.

"I bet Jonah swallowed his cigar over that one," Peter added.

"Good," Aunt May said. "He's been riding you for far too long, and it's long past time you got proper credit for what you've done."

Laughing, Peter said, "Thanks, Aunt May."

The twinkle came back. "And what's so funny, young man?"

"It wasn't all that long ago that you were talking about 'that awful Spider-Man.'"

"It also wasn't all that long ago that I thought Otto was worth marrying. But we all learn as we grow older, even when we're already old."

Turning to Mary Jane, Peter said, "Hey, speaking of proper credit, I never gave you yours."

"Me? What'd I do?" Mary Jane asked through a mouthful of wheat cakes.

"You were the one who talked Greg into talking to Shapiro. That's what got them the warrant for Trainer. That was a pretty big part of the whole thing."

Mary Jane patted her husband on the shoulder. "You can take all the credit, Tiger. I'll stick with acting."

Aunt May smiled. "I don't suppose there's the possibility of a seat at tonight's opening performance?"

Reaching behind her, Mary Jane unslung her purse from the back of the kitchen chair and removed an envelope from it. "Ask and ye shall receive. Two tickets, one for you and one for Aunt Anna."

Looking disappointed as she took the envelope, Aunt May asked, "Won't you be joining us, Peter?"

Peter shook his head. "Saturday nights are always bad out there, and there's still a turf war going on. And even though the Triple X is out of circulation, there's still plenty of it on the streets, which means more gamma-heads. I want to do what I can to keep the body count to a minimum. Besides," he added with a grin, "MJ could only get two freebies, and it's much better for two good-looking young single ladies to have a night on the town."

"Oh, Peter." Aunt May chuckled as she set the envelope aside. "Eat your wheat cakes."

"Yes, ma'am."

The sun shone brightly on West 100th Street, casting its warm glow on Una O'Leary's pale face. Wheeler and Fry had joined her for a quick pizza lunch, and they were on their way back from Sal & Carmine's on Broadway. All that was left for the Triple X Task Force was paperwork, which they'd been doing for two days straight—hence the need for a pizza break.

"Dr. Octopus. *Damn.*" Wheeler was shaking his head.

O'Leary looked up at Fry. "Has he said *anything* else for the last two days?"

Fry shook his head.

"You realize what this *means?*" Wheeler asked. "Press conferences, big drug busts, and Dr. Goddamn Octopus."

And you were definitely right about the web-head, Una. I don't care what Shapiro and Shanahan say, he was definitely in the right."

"Wait a minute," Fry said, "you're admitting that you were wrong about something? I gotta write this down, mark this day on my calendar."

"Hey, I can admit when I screw up," Wheeler said defensively.

"You can't prove that with any evidence that'll stand up in court, Detective," O'Leary said with a cheeky grin.

"Fine, bust my chops all you want. Doesn't matter, 'cause I'm in too good a mood. You *know* we're all gonna get promoted for this."

"Except Shanahan," Fry said. "This close to his thirty, they ain't gonna waste the pension."

O'Leary nodded. "And don't be so sure about the rest of us. I bet Garcia takes all the credit—and maybe Shapiro, especially after he got the bust on TV." She smiled at that, remembering that Shapiro owed a favor from almost a year back to Rosita Sanchez, a New York 1 News TV reporter, which he repaid by giving her exclusive footage of the Octopus bust, footage that would be shown—with the NY1 logo in the corner—on every other news outlet in the world for at least a week or two, and which now meant the station owed the precinct a favor, which was always useful.

Wheeler was still grinning. "Best of all, we got lots of OT, which means I can put more to the fund."

Rolling her eyes, O'Leary said, "You're never gonna get that bike, Ty. You're gonna get distracted by some pretty little thing and spend all your motorcycle fund on her. I guarantee it."

As the arrived at the front door of the Two-Four, Wheeler said, "I'm telling you, that Harley will be *mine*."

"Yeah, yeah."

Sergeant Larsen intercepted them as soon as they entered. "I'm still waitin' for twenty-four-hour reports from all three of you."

"We *know*, Sarge," O'Leary said. "We'll do it right after the arrest paperwork, the CSU paperwork, the paperwork from the state cops, and the paperwork requesting permission to burn all paperwork."

"Very funny." Larsen turned around and headed to the

men's room. "Oh yeah, you got some flowers from your boyfriend. It's on your desk."

O'Leary blinked. "I don't have a boyfriend."

"Coulda fooled me," he said as he went through the door.

Fry looked down at her. "Didn't you and Mike break up?"

"Twice." O'Leary went through the door that led up to the detective squad room.

"There's only one person it could be from," Wheeler said. "I mean, c'mon, she's been mooning over him the whole case."

"What are you *talking* about, Ty?" O'Leary asked with a murderous look at Wheeler as they started up the stairs.

"C'mon, Una, don't be so coy. Man of mystery, super-strong, agile—he's probably *great* in bed. You gonna get all kinky and make him keep the mask on?"

"You're gonna have a hard time riding that Harley after I break both your legs," she said as she entered the room.

Whoops and whistles sounded throughout the squad room as they came in. At the sight of her desk, O'Leary saw why: two dozen roses sat in a vase right next to her keyboard.

"So," Carter asked, a big grin on his face, "you two set a date yet?"

Petrocelli said, "Or is this a forbidden affair?"

"The love that dare not speak its name—or spin its web," Wheeler said, his grin matching Carter's.

Barron, the only other woman in the detective squad, walked up to her, put a friendly hand on her shoulder, and said, "Ignore them, Una. They're pigs. In fact, they'd have to improve to be as good as pigs."

"Which raises the question," Wheeler said, "of what's better, pigs or spiders?"

Deciding to take Barron's advice and ignore them, O'Leary instead walked over to her desk. The flowers were beautiful, and smelled fantastic, making the squad room—which always felt to O'Leary like it was one step removed from a locker room—a much more pleasant environment.

There was a note attached. THANKS FOR STICKING UP FOR ME. ALL THE BEST, FROM YOUR FRIENDLY NEIGHBOR- HOOD SPIDER-MAN. Also attached was a cell phone, which O'Leary realized was Ursitti's.

"So, is it gonna be a big church ceremony, or you gonna elope in the spider-cave?"

That was Shapiro, standing behind her. He did not look especially amused.

"Look, Jerry, he sent me flowers. It was probably be- cause I actually treated him like a person instead of—"

"A vigilante? A masked scumbag who works outside the law?"

"How 'bout a person who helped you get Triple X off the streets, got you on TV as the guy who nailed Dr. Oc- topus, gave you a way to repay Sanchez in spades, and made the task force and the precinct look good to the bosses? Not to mention everything he did with the gamma-heads."

"We didn't need him."

"For all of it? Maybe not. But we wouldn't have got- ten Octavius without him, and we'd have a lot more bodies without him."

Shapiro just stared at her for a second or two, then walked off without a word.

Guess I won't be inviting him to the wedding, she thought with a chuckle.

The jokes wouldn't be stopping for at least a week, but she didn't care. For years, she had been insisting that the NYPD would be better off working *with* the costumes instead of independently of them. This case had proved her right, finally.

Maybe some good will come out of it. . . .

Otto Octavius waited for his lawyer to arrive.

He sat alone in the huge vistors' room at Ryker's Island Penitentiary. Normally, up to two dozen prisoners could speak to visitors here, separated by special glass designed by Reed Richards of the Fantastic Four— proof not only against bullets, but most forms of direct energy. Today, however, Octavius had the place to himself, with all other visitations postponed until his was completed.

Surveillance cameras recorded every activity—though no sound, as the conversations that went on here were constitutionally protected. Three guards wearing specially designed armor stood at both the visitors' door and the door Octavius used to enter, supplementing the facility's guards. Those guards, as well as the ones in his cell block, which he had to himself, would remain for the duration of Octavius's stay. As far as the justice system was concerned, that span would be determined at Octavius's arraignment the following morning.

As far as Octavius was concerned, the span would be considerably shorter than that.

The door opened, and a tall, thin man with dark hair and small wire frame glasses held up by a large nose entered. This was Alan Schechter, Octavius's attorney. The Armani suit he wore had been purchased with the exorbitant fees that he had extracted from Octavius over the years.

Setting his briefcase down, Schechter took a seat opposite Octavius and picked up the phone that would allow him to converse with one hand. With the other, he opened the briefcase and removed a PDA.

"The guards out there are ridiculous." Schechter said. "And I understand they've got you isolated?"

Octavius, who had picked up his own phone, nodded. "I have the entire cell block to myself, yes."

"Tomorrow, I'll file a motion—this is cruel and unusual punishment. Without your arms—"

"Where are they?" Octavius asked a bit too eagerly. But he was always concerned when lesser minds had access to his arms.

"Right now they're in a federal facility." Using the wand for his PDA, he called up some information. "A warehouse in Elizabeth, New Jersey. I got a court order to keep them locked away there until your trial."

Octavius nodded. That could not have been an easy thing to accomplish—scientists were always eager to poke and prod at Octavius's work—and he found himself reminded as to how Schechter could justify taking so much of Octavius's money.

"In any case, I'll go to Judge Hernandez tomorrow and get them to move you—"

"Do not concern yourself. It is only fitting that they take such extraordinary precautions. I consider it a sign of respect that I so rarely get from law enforcement. Besides, the prattling of the other inmates annoys me."

Schechter nodded, and again used the wand on his PDA. "Fine. Anything else you need?"

"I find arraignments to be tedious. Anything you might do to delay this one until next week would be appreciated."

"Hm." Schechter tapped his cheek with the wand, then smiled and made a note on his PDA. "I've got a friend in the U.S. Attorney's Office. You were on government property when Spider-Man attacked you, and a lot of your outstanding warrants are federal. I should be able to get her to file a motion to have the case moved to Washington. It'll take at least a week to straighten it out."

Octavius smiled. "Excellent. By then, it will no longer matter. I will be gone from this place."

Schechter winced. "Will you *please* not tell me things like that? Lawyer-client privilege is one thing, but I'd just as soon you *didn't* make incriminating statements in my presence."

Scowling, Octavius said, "You work for me, Schechter, a job for which you are very well compensated. Do not presume to lecture me on what I can and cannot say."

"Fine, fine." Schechter made a few more notes, and then carried on about other legal minutiae that Octavius found tedious to deal with—which was another reason he paid Schechter so well.

The secondary aspects of his plan had gone imperfectly. In retrospect, he should not have entrusted that to Carolyn. Though she had great enthusiasm, she lacked subtlety. And by targeting Hunt, Haight, May Parker, and the others, he'd provided a signpost to allow the police and the arachnid to suspect him.

But his capture and incarceration were of little conse-
quence. The designer drug had already served its true
purpose: of providing him with sufficient income to at
last bring his latest plan to fruition.

Soon enough, the world would tremble at his feet. . . .

Spider-Man swung out over the Bridgeview Houses,
heading homeward after a long night. He had stopped a
group of Ray-Ray's old crew, now run by a guy called
"Blowback," before they were about to go shoot things,
and the cops apparently got a tip on one of the Ukrainians' stash houses, so there was no turf war tonight. He'd
encountered a few more gamma-heads, including a couple who were menacing some theatregoers on 45th Street
and a bunch of college kids stomping through the Clois-
ters.

Just one more thing to take care of.

Swinging around the Houses for a few minutes, he finally found what he was looking for. Lowering himself
on a web-line, he hung over a tree above the bench on
which his quarry sat.

"Hi there, Albert."

The junkie looked up in surprise. "No-face! The hell
you want, boy?"

Reaching into a compartment of his belt, Spider-Man
pulled out a crisp five-dollar bill. "Just wanted to pay up
my debt. You said five bucks was the going rate for the
intel you gave me, right?"

"Uh—yeah, I guess. Don't remember—just remember that you ain't got no face."

Spider-Man hesitated. Albert would probably just
spend this money on more drugs. *Although, based on how
slurred his voice is, he's probably already high. Maybe I'll get*

lucky and he'll get some food. And if not—at least I can't say I didn't try.

He handed Albert the bill. Albert stared at it for a second. "You should keep it. Buy y'self a face."

"I'll be fine. But you look like you could use a bowl of soup."

"Guess I *am* a little hungry." Albert snatched the bill. "Thanks, No-Face Man."

"You're welcome."

With that, Spider-Man climbed up his web-line to the tree, shot out another line, and swung toward home and his wife and his bed for a good—and, he thought, well-earned—night's sleep.

Acknowledgments

Primary thanks go to my enthusiastic, encouraging, and excitable editor, Ed Schlesinger, who has been an absolute joy to work with; my effervescent agent, Lucienne Diver; and the ever-encouraging publisher Scott Shannon.

Secondary thanks to Stan Lee and Steve Ditko, without whom we wouldn't have Spider-Man, and to the dear departed *Electric Company* children's show, which introduced me as a kid in the 1970s to Spidey.

Tertiary thanks to various Spidey scribes who've written the character in both comics and prose form in the years since Stan and Steve's day, and to whom I also owe a huge debt: Pierce Askegren, Samm Barnes, Brian Michael Bendis, Kurt Busiek, John Byrne, Adam-Troy Castro, Chris Claremont, Gerry Conway, Peter David, Tom DeFalco, J.M. DeMatteis, Todd Dezago, Diane Duane, Eric Fein, Danny Fingeroth, Craig Shaw Gardner, Glenn Greenberg, Paul Grist, Paul Jenkins, Terry Kavanagh, Howard Mackie, Bill Mantlo, David Michelinie, Mark Millar, Fabian Nicieza, Denny O'Neil, Jim Owsley (aka Christopher Priest), Dean Wesley Smith, Roger Stern, J. Michael Straczynski, Brian K. Vaughan, John Vornholt, Zeb Wells, and dozens of others that I know I neglected to mention by name. I would also be remiss if I didn't thank my collaborators on two previous pieces of Spidey prose: John Gregory Betancourt (my cohort on "An Evening in the Bronx with Venom") and José R. Nieto (my partner in crime on *Venom's Wrath*).

Village Playhouse Central is very loosely based on the Manhattan Theatre Source in Greenwich Village. Like VPC, MTS has musicians playing in the lobby before showtime—I know, because I've been one of those musicians several times. Thanks to all the good people there who've treated me well. Trust me, any negative aspects of VPC were for dramatic purposes and in no way reflect on the fine folks at MTS.

Thanks also to Ian Wakefield, Bruno Maglione, Ruwan Jayatilleke, and all the other fine folks at Marvel; the New York Police Department's most excellent and informative website (http://www.nyc.gov/html/nypd/home.html); SpiderFan.org, the best online resource of info about this novel's hero; the Elitist Bastards, just on general principles; Magnum Comics in the Bronx, which had back issues when I rather desperately needed them; and Tom Brevoort and Kurt Busiek, for some timely research assistance.

The usual gangs of idiots: the Geek Patrol, the Malibu folks, the Forebearance, CITH, CGAG, all the people at Riverdale Kenshikai, and the folks on various online bulletin boards, e-mail lists, and LiveJournal, who all keep me going to some degree or other. Also them that live with me, both human and feline, who do likewise.

Finally, a big thank you to some folks I worked with in the past, who deserve a moment of due respect in print: Keith Aiken, Jeff Albrecht, Nathan Archer, Pierce Askegren, Michael Asprion, Terry Austin, Dick Ayers, Mark Bagley, Robin Wayne Bailey, Steve Behling, Julie Bell, eluki bes shahar, John Gregory Betancourt, Dennis Brabham, Ginjer Buchanan, Mark Buckingham, Jim Burns, John Buscema, Kurt Busiek, Steven Butler, Richard Lee Byers, Dennis Calero, Adam-Troy Castro,

Joey Cavalieri, Joe Chiodo, Manny Clark, Dave Cockrum, Nancy A. Collins, Richard Corben, Greg Cox, Roger Cruz, Peter David, James Dawson, Tom DeFalco, Tom De Haven, Thomas Deja, Dave DeVries, Sharman DiVono, Colleen Doran, Max Douglas, John S. Drew, Diane Duane, Jo Duffy, Tammy Lynne Dunn, Emily Epstein, Vince Evans, Steve Fastner, Eric Fein, Danny Fingeroth, Sholly Fisch, Ron Frenz, Michael Jan Friedman, James W. Fry III, Alex Gadd, John Garcia, Craig Shaw Gardner, Gabriel Gecko, Christopher Golden, Glenn Greenberg, Ken Grobe, Tom Grummett, Bob Hall, Ed Hannigan, Tony Harris, Glenn Hauman, Doug Hazlewood, Jennifer Heddle, C.J. Henderson, Jason Henderson, Greg and Tim Hildebrandt, Nancy Holder, Bob Ingersoll, Tony Isabella, Bruce Jensen, Joe Jusko, K.A. Kindya, Scott Koblish, Dori Koogler, Ray Lago, Michelle LaMarca, Andy Lane, Bob Larkin, Katherine Lawrence, Stan Lee, Steve Leialoha, John Paul Leon, Rick Leonardi, Rebecca Levene, Clarice Levin, Steve Lightle, Ron Lim, Scott Lobdell, Steve Lyons, Eliot S! Maggin, Alexander Maleev, Leonardo Manco, Ashley McConnell, Bob McLeod, David Michelinie, Grant Miehm, Al Milgrom, Tom Morgan, Will Murray, Duane O. Myers, José R. Nieto, Ann Nocenti, Patrick Olliffe, John J. Ordover, Carol Page, George Pérez, Dan Persons, Byron Preiss, Ayesha Randolph, Bill Reinhold, Darick Robertson, Madeleine E. Robins, Steven A. Roman, John Romita Sr., Luis Royo, Paul Ryan, Jenn Saint-John, Joe St. Pierre, Robert Sheckley, Evan Skolnick, Louis Small Jr., Dave Smeds, Dean Wesley Smith, Steranko, Michael Stewart, Steve Rasnic Tem, Mike Thomas, Stan Timmons, Juda Tverski, Deborah Valcourt, Brian K. Vaughan, John Vornholt, Matt Wagner, Robert L. Washington III, Lawrence Watt-Evans, Len Wein, Richard C. White, Casey Winters, Chuck Wojtkiewicz, James A. Wolf, J. Steven York, Mike Zeck, Ann Tonsor Zeddies, Phil Zimelman, Dwight Jon Zimmerman, and Howard Zimmerman.

About the Author

Keith R.A. DeCandido is thrilled to be returning to writing the web-swinger, as his first published fiction, as well as his first novel sale, both starred Spider-Man: the short story "An Evening in the Bronx with Venom" (written with John Gregory Betancourt) in the 1994 anthology *The Ultimate Spider-Man*, and the novel *Venom's Wrath* (written with José R. Nieto) in 1998. On his own, he also wrote the 1997 story "Arms and the Man" for the *Untold Tales of Spider-Man* anthology, as well as stories in *The Ultimate Silver Surfer*, *The Ultimate Hulk*, and *X-Men Legends*. Outside the realm of Marvel prose, he has written novels, short fiction, eBooks, nonfiction books, and comic books in the universes of *Star Trek* (in all its incarnations, plus a few new ones), *Farscape, Gene Roddenberry's Andromeda, Buffy the Vampire Slayer, Resident Evil, Xena,* and more, with several visits to various best-seller lists along the way. His most recent work includes the original novel *Dragon Precinct,* a high-fantasy police procedural; *Articles of the Federation,* a look at the politics of the *Star Trek* universe; *Serenity,* the novelization of the Joss Whedon film; *Security,* part of the monthly *Star Trek: S.C.E.* series of eBooks; and the *Star Trek* short stories "*loDnI'pu' vavpu' je*" (*Tales from the Captain's Table*) and "Letting Go" (*Distant Shores*). A student of Kenshikai karate, Keith lives in New York City with his girlfriend and two loony cats, where he is working on an X-Men novel, among many other things. Find out more useless information about

Keith at his official website at www.DeCandido.net, read his absurd ramblings on LiveJournal under the not-particularly-clever user ID of "kradical," or send him an e-mail at keith@decandido.net and tell him *just* what you think of him.